THE BOY WHO GLOWED IN THE DARK

THE BOY
WHO GLOWED
IN THE
DARK

OREST STELMACH

THOMAS & MERCER

Text copyright © 2014 Orest Stelmach
All rights reserved.

Published by Thomas & Mercer, Seattle

www.apub.com

Amazon, the Amazon logo, and Thomas & Mercer are trademarks of Amazon.com, Inc., or its affiliates.

ISBN-13: 9781477822845
ISBN-10: 1477822844

Cover design by David Drummond, Salamander Hill Design

Library of Congress Control Number: 2013957008

Printed in the United States of America

For the children of Chornobyl

AUTHOR'S NOTE

Chernobyl and Odessa are located in Ukraine, but these popular English spellings are derived from the Russian language. The proper spellings for these cities based on the Ukrainian language are Chornobyl and Odesa. In this novel, I will continue to utilize the proper English spelling for all Ukrainian words. Thanks to all the fans of *The Boy From Reactor 4* who wrote me and suggested this change.

PROLOGUE

One week earlier

IF A MAN LIVED LONG ENOUGH, HE RISKED BECOMING WHAT HE once hated.

Luo stood at the edge of Park Slavi in Kyiv, the capital city of Ukraine, watching people rush to work. They looked miserable. City folks spent their lives chasing treasure in hopes of escaping that same city. Luo had never understood the obsession with treasure. Until now.

A slender man with a dark complexion appeared. He looked like the man in the picture Luo had bought from the guard at Chornobyl. They called him the scavenger because of his ability to extract value from the most unlikely places. He was a loner with a reputation for elusiveness and toughness.

Luo turned his knapsack to make the yellow peace sign visible. The scavenger's eyes went to the sticker and stopped. He studied Luo, glanced in each direction and approached. The scavenger's fence had arranged a code for the two men to use to confirm their identities.

"Two friends go hunting bear," the scavenger said in Russian. "One gets a rifle, the other a pair of skis. Which would you choose?"

"The skis," Luo said.

"You won't outrun the bear on your skis."

"I don't need to outrun the bear. I just need to outrun my friend."

The scavenger thrust his hand forward. "Hayder," he said.

Luo shook it. "Luoravetian."

Hayder frowned.

Luo knew his Russian sounded coarse to people outside Siberia. That made his unusual first name incomprehensible to some. "Luo," he said.

Hayder nodded. Better.

Luo started down one of two paths that wound into the forest.

Hayder took three steps and stopped. "Why are you leading me this way?" He craned his neck around the bend, but trees obscured his view.

"I'm not leading you anywhere." Luo motioned toward the people strolling around the park. "Just getting us some privacy."

"Is something going to happen to me if I follow you down that path?"

"Yeah. You're going to realize just how paranoid you are."

"Paranoia keeps the scavenger alive." Hayder pointed toward the second path, the one that followed an access road into the woods. "We go this way instead. And we stop at the edge where the people can still see us."

Luo slung his knapsack over his shoulder. It contained his weapons of choice. "Sounds good. How about you lead on, and I'll follow you."

They walked down the second path.

"What's the job?" Hayder said.

"Diamonds," Luo said.

"Diamonds?"

Luo noted the inflection in Hayder's voice. Speak of gold and you got a thief's attention. But promise him diamonds and he forgot his own name.

"Magadan diamonds," Luo said.

"Magadan." Hayder frowned. "Siberia? You're from Siberia?"

Luo nodded. "In the 1970s, an asteroid hit Russia between Krasnoyarsk and Yakutia. It left a meteorite crater about one hundred kilometers wide. Filled with diamonds."

"Asteroid? You're kidding me."

"It's called the Popigai Astroblem, and it's supposed to contain trillions of carats of diamonds. Enough to satisfy worldwide demand for the next three thousand years."

"Is this common knowledge?"

Luo ambled further down the path out of sight of the other visitors. Hayder was so focused on the diamonds he shuffled along to keep pace, seemingly oblivious to his own movement.

"It was a secret until the Russians declassified the documents in 2012," Luo said. "The mine is a start-up. They've taken some samples. I have a man on the inside." Luo stopped. He turned to face Hayder, positioning himself at the proper angle to ensure the scavenger kept his back to the access road. "But I need someone with special skills."

A light flickered in Hayder's eyes. "Why me?"

"I need a man who's comfortable negotiating an industrial site in the dead of night. Someone experienced in slipping in and out of tight places. Someone like the finest scavenger ever to prowl Chornobyl and its Zone of Exclusion." The Zone of Exclusion was the thirty-kilometer radius around Chornobyl's nuclear power plants. "The man who stripped more engines from radioactive vehicles, more steel from abandoned buildings, and more spare parts from shuttered nuclear facilities than anyone else."

Hayder remained expressionless for a moment. Then he nodded. "That would be me."

Luo sighed with relief. "Good. I needed you to confirm I had the right man."

Three men burst from behind a thicket of trees. They grabbed Hayder's arms and legs. One sealed the scavenger's mouth with tape. Another took the gun from his pocket.

A white van screamed down the access road. The rear doors opened. The men lifted Hayder and threw him in the back. Then they climbed inside after him. Luo followed and slammed the doors shut behind him. The driver took off.

The men tied Hayder's arms and legs to a chair.

Fifteen minutes later, the van pulled over in an empty field. The three men and the driver got out.

Luo sat on a bench opposite Hayder. Anger shone in the scavenger's eyes. He wasn't afraid. Luo was impressed.

"The fence said you were a prudent man," Luo said. "So I figured you'd insist on taking the other path. The one near the access road. Now, I'm going to remove the gag from your mouth so you can answer my questions. If you scream for help you'll only end up hurting yourself. Do we understand each other?"

Hayder nodded. Luo removed the tape from his mouth.

Hayder swore and worked his jaw loose. Then he glared at Luo. "Do we know each other? Have I done something to you?"

"No."

"Then what do you want?"

"The truth," Luo said.

"The truth about what?"

"Nadia Tesla."

"Who?"

"The woman you escorted into the Zone last year with your friend, the professor. The one who moonlights as a taxi driver."

Hayder's eyes widened. Recognition gave way to disgust. "The entitled American bitch? What about her? I don't even know her. It was in one day, out the next."

"What was her business in the Zone?"

"What about the diamonds?"

"Diamonds? What diamonds?"

Luo dropped a thick roll of hryvnia, the Ukrainian currency, on the table in front of Hayder. The scavenger stared at it. Still a chance for him to make a profit.

"What was Nadia Tesla's business in the Zone?" Luo said.

Hayder picked up the pace of his delivery. "She was meeting a relative. An uncle."

"How could she be meeting an uncle when no one lives in Chornobyl?"

"People live in Chornobyl. Not many, but they're there. Squatters. People who love their land and their homes. They return even though it's illegal."

"And her uncle was one of them?"

Hayder shrugged. "Maybe. There was some gossip in the Zone a week later."

"Gossip?"

"There's a café. The workers from the reactors go there. People hear things. They talk."

"And what did they say?"

"That an American woman had met with an old man. And that the old man is dead."

"Did Nadia say anything about a boy during the trip?"

"A boy?" Hayder frowned.

"Yes. A boy from Chornobyl."

"A boy from the Zone? No."

"Is it possible she was meeting a boy in the Zone that night? At her uncle's house?"

"I don't know. You should ask the babushka."

Luo's ears perked up. "What babushka?"

"The gossip was the American woman had met with a squatter. A sick old man who lived with a babushka that took care of him."

"Do you have a name?"

"No." Hayder eyed the money. "I wish I did." He frowned at Luo. "You know, if all you wanted was information, we could have done this over coffee."

"We both know that's a lie," Luo said. "You needed to know I'm serious."

Hayder paused, then nodded. "What now?"

"My men will release you. You're free to go. The money is yours. It's payment for your silence. But if I hear you asking questions about anything we discussed today, you won't be asking many more questions after that. Do we understand each other?"

"Yeah. We understand each other."

Luo summoned the men he'd hired and told them to release their prisoner. They were old army buddies. A military career had left him with friends all over the former Soviet Union. Most of them were more than willing to moonlight for a few extra bucks.

Luo's next lead was in Chornobyl. He actually had to go to the radioactive wasteland himself. Only idiot tourists went there. He dreaded the notion, but his pursuit of the treasure left him no choice. He was obsessed with it.

He had lived long enough to become what he once hated, but that wasn't what shocked him. The big surprise was that he couldn't have been happier about it. No other endeavor had ever fulfilled him so much. Nothing he had ever done had given him such joy.

CHAPTER 1

* * *

BOBBY'S FINGER HOVERED OVER HIS KEYBOARD. WITH ONE stroke he was about to cancel his Facebook account. Making his life public had exposed him. Increased the odds someone from his prior life would recognize him. He'd gone ahead and created an account anyway. He had fans. Female fans. Gorgeous female fans. From places like Detroit, Chicago, Montreal, and Toronto. Even Sweden and Holland. They watched his videos on YouTube and sent letters to Fordham. It was all so flattering. He couldn't refuse.

But now his conscience was nagging at him. He'd promised Nadia, his cousin and guardian, to stay away from social media. No one else could know about his past. No one.

He pressed the RETURN key and followed the proper procedure to confirm his account had been cancelled. Less than a minute later his smart phone buzzed. He checked the screen.

A text message. From Derek Mace, his best friend and personal bodyguard on the Fordham Prep hockey team.

Yo, Bobbyorr, you there?

The team had bestowed the nickname because he reminded them of the Bruins legend.

Bobby typed his answer. What's up, killer?

You're really out?

Yeah.

My mom heard you beat the rap.

She heard right.

You're out for good?

As long as I stay out of the penalty box.

Awesome!

Yeah.

How was jail?

Bobby remembered the claustrophobia, the trembling in the middle of the night, the beatings, and the ten days in the infirmary that followed.

It wasn't.

Wasn't what?

A place you ever want to visit. I have to go now.

Wait. We have to celebrate.

Thanks, but I'll pass.

I have your favorite snacks and refreshments. Crème soda and popcorn.

That was their code for beer and pot. Bobby remembered drinking and getting stoned with Derek, some of their other teammates, and a bunch of girls. That was before he was charged with the murder of an English businessman. After almost ending up in jail for the rest of his life, the thought of doing something so stupid was unimaginable. Honest to God, he thought, it was as though someone else had borrowed his brain.

On a diet. No more crème soda or popcorn for me. See you next week.

Bobby turned off his phone.

He shut down his other social media accounts and connected to his public e-mail account. He'd created it so he could isolate messages from strangers via social media.

Three messages leaped off the screen. They'd been sent intermittently during the last two weeks from the same sender. The subject line had been left empty in each case.

The sender's name was *GenesisII26486*. He recognized the numbers immediately. April 26, 1986. The date of the explosion at the Chornobyl nuclear power plant. More importantly, he recognized the phrase *Genesis II*. It stirred memories, tapped his heart, and left him stunned. The subject of the e-mail had been left blank, as though the author knew the sender's name alone was enough to capture his attention.

The sender was right. The only person who knew the meaning of *Genesis II* besides him was dead. The e-mail meant someone else knew the secrets of his past. The questions were who had discovered him and how had he obtained his information?

Bobby opened the e-mail.

There was no message, just a link to an attachment. Bobby clicked on the file. It took forever to load. A photo unfolded on the screen. He stared at it dumbfounded.

"Nadia!" he said.

She came running from her bedroom. He stood up and met her in the doorway. Relief washed over her face. It gave way to confusion.

Bobby stepped aside to let her in.

"Computer," he said in Ukrainian. He would have liked to have said something more but he was too shocked to form a complete sentence. Besides, nothing more needed to be said.

Nadia looked at the screen. Bobby stared over her shoulder.

It was a photo of a necklace and a locket in the palm of a boy's hand. It looked identical to the locket Bobby's father had given him in Ukraine. They'd learned three weeks and three days ago that Bobby's locket contained part of a precious formula. The other half of it was missing. There was no way to know if the second half of the formula even existed.

"Why did you take a picture of yourself holding the locket?" Nadia said.

"I didn't."

"Then who did?"

"No one."

"I'm confused."

"That's not my hand."

Nadia's eyes widened.

Bobby edged past her and slipped into his chair. "There's another locket."

"There's another boy," Nadia said. "When was this sent?"

"There are three e-mails. The last one was sent five days ago. I just opened it."

"Who sent it?"

"The sender's name was *GenesisII26486*."

"Does that mean anything to you?"

Nadia had proven her love. Bobby knew he could trust her. Still, for reasons beyond his comprehension, he couldn't admit he knew the meaning of the phrase. He desperately wanted to, but he couldn't stand the thought of talking about his past. He just couldn't.

"The last five numbers are the date of the Chornobyl explosion," Bobby said. "In Ukraine they put the day first, the month second. But *Genesis II*. No. That doesn't mean anything to me."

"Can you get any more information about where it was sent from?"

Bobby summoned the source information. Half a page of gibberish came up. Bobby pointed at the screen with his pen.

Sender> Okuma-asahi.net.

"This is where the message originated," he said.

"Asahi," Nadia said. "That sounds Japanese."

"Must be the local Internet provider."

Bobby searched. Asahi Net was, in fact, one of Japan's top broadband providers. While the sender's name had struck a familiar chord, the Japanese source baffled him.

"What about Okuma?" Nadia said.

Bobby searched again. A *Wikipedia* page offered five subjects named Okuma. Nadia and Bobby scanned the list. Bobby didn't look beyond the fourth entry. He knew Nadia was staring at the same entry without even bothering to look at her.

Okuma was the name of a Japanese town in the Futaba District. It was part of a larger district known throughout the world for all the wrong reasons. The second boy had sent the message from this location.

Fukushima.

"Are you thinking what I'm thinking?" Nadia said.

"Fukushima," Bobby said. "The only place other than Chornobyl to experience a level seven disaster on the International Nuclear Event Scale."

"You know anyone in Fukushima?"

"No."

"Tokyo?"

"No."

"What about Facebook friends? Or your other social media followers?"

"Nope. Hockey's not a big deal in Japan."

"Have you answered the message?"

"Not yet."

Part of Bobby wished he'd been honest with her. But the other part shut him down. He could always confess later.

"What should we do?" she said.

Bobby thought about her question for a moment. "Play the fox," he said.

Bobby knew his father, a notorious con artist, had given her the same advice when she'd met him in Chornobyl on his deathbed. *With foxes, we must play the fox.*

Nadia smiled. Not a blatant full-tooth smile like the hockey moms gave everyone when they came into the rink to pick up their kids. Just a subtle one to let him know she got it. She was cool that way, too. She knew how to hide her emotions, not make a big deal of things.

They debated what to write. Nadia advised him to be conservative and say as little as possible. Let the sender do the talking. Eventually he would reveal himself. But Bobby was his father's son. He had started to realize that during his stint in jail. The sender would be expecting a tame approach. The optimal course of action was to provoke him with the unexpected.

Bobby suggested they answer with a question. What are the stakes?

The answer was the fate of the free world. It was the line that had started it all more than a year ago, when a man whispered it in Nadia's ear before collapsing on a New York City street. If the full formula existed, it could affect the fate of the free world. A nuclear power with a cure for radiation would have an advantage over its enemies. If the second locket contained the rest of the formula, the boy who possessed it would understand the message.

Bobby sent his reply. Nadia went back to bed. Bobby set his computer to ping with the arrival of a new e-mail. He tried to sleep but couldn't.

The computer pinged three times over the course of three hours. The first two e-mails were spam. The third wasn't.

Bobby read the message, saw the light on under Nadia's door and called her. She hurried to his room in a robe and pajamas. She peered over his shoulder and read the response.

The fate of the free world depends on us.

A minute later, a second e-mail arrived with instructions.

Sunday. Tokyo. The mural at Shibuya train station. Noon. Meet in front. Just you and Nadia. My friend will find you.

Genesis II.

Bobby found information about a mural at Shibuya station on the Internet. It was called the *Myth of Tomorrow*. It was an abstract picture consisting of fourteen panels.

It depicted a human figure being hit by a nuclear bomb.

CHAPTER 2

NADIA TOLD BOBBY TO GET SOME SLEEP. HE'D JUST BEEN RE-
leased from jail that morning. She'd informed his teachers
at Fordham Prep that he would return to school next week. She
wanted him to rest and recuperate first. They'd agreed it was a
prudent idea, noting it was mid-April, and there was plenty of
time for him to catch up before June.

She lay awake in bed until 5:00 a.m. Questions swirled in her
head. She needed a shower, a cup of coffee, and a discussion with
Johnny Tanner. Johnny was her attorney and best friend. He
knew the truth about Bobby's true identity, that he was Nadia's
cousin from Ukraine and his real name was Adam Tesla. Johnny
had helped them escape the clutches of Russian mobsters when
Bobby had first arrived, and defended him successfully against
the recent murder charge.

Nadia left a message at 6:00 a.m. Johnny returned her call
half an hour later.

"What's this about life and death?" he said. His voice
sounded distant, as though he was on a car speaker.

"Are we alone? Is there anyone else in the car with you?"

"We're alone. And you're officially scaring me."

Nadia described the e-mail, its source, and its contents. Johnny usually played it cool, but he couldn't conceal the note of excitement in his voice.

"Do you believe it's genuine?" he said. "That there really is a second locket?"

"There are three possibilities. First, it's a hoax, there is no second locket, and the goal is to steal Bobby's locket."

"Toward what end? If there's no second locket, no completion of the formula, who would care about it?"

"Someone who knows the rest of the formula, thinks he knows how to get it, or believes the entire formula is on Bobby's locket. Second possibility, it's real but the sender's intentions are not noble."

"Meaning the goal is to steal Bobby's locket and have them both."

"Correct. Third possibility is the preferred outcome. There is a second locket and it's in the possession of a good boy."

"You're sure it's a boy and not an adult?"

"It's a small hand."

"Could be a woman," Johnny said. "Or a small man."

"Fair point. Duly noted."

"What do you make of the response to Bobby's e-mail?"

"This started a year ago when a stranger who said he knew my father whispered 'Fate of the free world' in my ear, suggesting it depended on me. Whoever sent the e-mail knows the potential importance of the formula in question. Odds are high he knows it's a countermeasure to radiation."

"Any idea why this is coming from Japan?"

"No. Bobby says he doesn't know any Japanese people. I believe him."

"It's eerie. Because of the nuclear disaster in Fukushima. I mean, it makes you wonder if there's a Japanese scientist with the other half of the formula, or something like that."

"I agree," Nadia said. "It's remarkable to get these e-mails from the only other place to experience a level seven nuclear disaster. But we have to stick to the facts and not let our imaginations run away from us. The invitation made reference to a friend. So we know there are at least two people involved. Possibly a boy and an adult. Possibly two adults."

'What about the timing of all this? Right when Bobby gets out of jail? Is that a bit of a coincidence?"

"Three e-mails were sent over two weeks. The last one five days ago, when things didn't look good for Bobby at all. Anyone who knew the particulars of the case at that point would have thought there was little chance Bobby would be released soon."

"Meaning whoever sent the e-mail didn't know what was happening in Bobby's life. Didn't know he was in jail."

"Agreed. If you have a second locket, and you know the kid that has the first one is in jail on murder charges, you don't send a message that assumes he's going to be there to read it. You worry about how to get him a message in jail."

"And the sender knows you exist. He used your name. If he thought Bobby was in jail, he would have found some way to get you the message instead of him."

"Especially given the stakes."

"The alleged stakes."

Nadia chuckled. "Right. The alleged stakes. Thank you, counselor."

"Sorry. Occupational habit. So what's your next move?"

"I'm not sure. I can't see Bobby going to Japan after everything he's been through in the last three weeks. Not on skimpy evidence. Not when this whole thing could turn out to be a hoax. And he needs to get back to school. He needs to return to normal life."

"I hear you. And you can't go either."

"Why do you say that?"

"You can't leave him alone. He was on meds in jail for the claustrophobia. He got beaten up. He had a rough ride. You say he needs to return to normal life? You need to be there."

Nadia wanted to argue but saw his point. The sound of traffic subsided as though Johnny had pulled into a garage.

"There's too much unknown for either of you to go," Johnny said.

"What do you suggest? We try to change the agenda and get them here? I doubt that's going to work—"

"I'm going," Johnny said.

"Oh, right. Sorry. You must have court. Will you have any time later this morning?"

"No. You don't understand. I'm going to Tokyo. Instead of you."

It was preposterous, but the offer soothed Nadia's soul. "Johnny, you're the nicest guy ever to pass the bar and the best friend a person could have, but there's no way you're going in my place."

"The only other person who could do this is your brother. But he just spent a week in Eastern Europe with you and he has a business to take care of. I'm your man."

Nadia already felt indebted to Johnny for all he'd done for Bobby and her. So much so she could never repay him. This would only increase her debt. "Johnny, this is way beyond the call of friendship."

"You mean as opposed to getting kidnapped and interrogated by Victor Bodnar, and listening to him murder two men while I sat chained to a chair in a meat locker?"

Victor Bodnar was one of the mobsters who had chased Nadia from New York to Eastern Europe and back in pursuit of the formula. After they returned to New York, he'd kidnapped Johnny to coerce information about Nadia and the locket. Johnny had stood up to him, and had seen to it that she'd never hear from the old man again.

"I see your point," Nadia said. "But that's all the more reason I can't let you do it."

"I was an exchange student in Tokyo during college for a year. Granted, it was a long time ago and I've forgotten all of the language I knew. But I still know how to say hello, bow properly, and act less like a *gaijin*."

"Gaijin?"

"A foreigner. An outsider who doesn't belong."

"What about your court cases? You're probably juggling several."

"Two. I'm wrapping up an immigration case this afternoon. And I can ask another associate to cover for me on the burglary. I've covered for her multiple times. She owes me."

Nadia protested. The more she did so, the more Johnny insisted he was going.

"Even if your associate covers for you," Nadia said, "what explanation will you give your boss for leaving in the middle of the week?"

"I'll tell him it's a family matter."

"Aw, Johnny. You're so sweet. But seriously. You can't lie to your boss."

"Maybe it's not a lie. I don't have any family. Which makes you guys the closest thing I got. Maybe that's saying too much. But that's what it is."

Johnny was counselor, confidante, and friend, but she had no romantic feelings for him. None whatsoever. He wore a ponytail, drove a muscle car, and loved the spotlight. Nadia preferred understated men. And yet his words struck deep in her heart and left a mark.

"You're too much, Johnny Tanner."

"Good. It's settled. Forward me the e-mails. Should we send a new e-mail and be up front that you're sending a delegate?"

Nadia pondered the question. "Yes. We should be honest."

"Good. The fewer lies, the better."

"My motto exactly."

"I'll get a phone that works in Japan. You should give them my number and get one from them. And try to get a description of this friend I'm supposed to meet with."

"They'll probably ask for the same."

"A six-foot-two, two-hundred-ten-pound gaijin with a pony-tail is probably going to stand out in Tokyo."

"Nice image. Thanks for that. I'll arrange for the hotel and plane ticket, pay for your expenses."

"Including the hostess at the Turkish bathhouse?"

"How quickly they fall off their pedestals."

"It was inevitable." A car door slammed shut. "The guy on the pedestal has nowhere to go but down."

CHAPTER 3

JOHNNY LANDED AT TOKYO'S NARITA AIRPORT AT 9:05 P.M. ON Saturday. He took the Narita Express to central Tokyo and caught a taxi to the Hotel Century Southern Tower in the Shibuya district. After checking into his room, he called Nadia to let her know he'd arrived, ate some sushi, and went to sleep.

On Sunday he enjoyed a breakfast of steamed rice, grilled fish, rolled omelet, seaweed, and pickled vegetables. Afterwards he spent the morning reacquainting himself with the city. Shibuya was the western hub of Central Tokyo. Young people partied in Shibuya. Older people tended to avoid this part of town. The roads were not as pristine, the storefronts not as elegant as in other parts of the city. Cheap restaurants, karaoke bars, and nightclubs crammed the streets. It was Johnny's kind of place.

He'd studied at Tokyo's Sophia University eighteen years ago as an exchange student from Seton Hall. His return was no different than his first visit. The crowds, noises, and smells overwhelmed his senses. The sheer mass of humanity moving along sidewalks and climbing onto subways made New York City seem small. The cacophony of sounds hurt his eardrums. Buses, cars, and trains. The ring of a thousand pinball machines hitting their targets simultaneously in Japan's popular pachinko parlors. It was urban chaos and Johnny loved it.

The smell of fish mixed with exhaust to form a uniquely Tokyo scent. This smell, in turn, stirred memories. The stress of nightly language memorization. The rock star status that resulted from him being tall, young, and American. Cute college girls dying to practice their English with him at all hours of the night. And that little guy in pink tights who pressed his thigh against Johnny's leg on a crowded subway bench. Eighteen years ago the experience had nauseated him. Now it made him laugh.

He visited the Shibuya train station twice. First in the morning, as soon as he left the hotel at 7:30 a.m. Genesis II had picked the perfect location to put them both at ease. On a weekday, two and a half million people used the station each day. Even on a Sunday morning, it was so crowded there was simply no way to create a trap. There were literally hundreds of witnesses walking by the mural every minute. The only people who weren't moving were the cops watching the turnstiles and a gaunt man loitering by the side door of the main entrance. He was disheveled with flecks of gray in his shoulder-length hair, a lost look in his eyes, and a begging bowl in his hand. A homeless man was an embarrassment to himself and the community. Hence, everyone pretended he wasn't there to save face.

Johnny returned to the station a second time at 11:45, fifteen minutes before the meet. He stood in the corner against the wall opposite the mural and waited. He tried to study the faces of the people walking by but there were too many of them. The exercise left him dizzy.

"Mr. Johnny Tanner?" A young man's voice, Japanese accent, high-pitched.

Johnny turned. A boy had snuck up to his side. Carrot-colored hair with black roots covered his ears. He was dressed in a black t-shirt and leather jacket with designer jeans. He looked like a Japanese punk rock version of Bobby.

"Yeah. I'm Johnny Tanner. Who are you?"

"May I see identification, please?"

"Excuse me?"

"Your passport. To see your passport." The boy blushed and bowed. "Please."

Johnny looked around. No one was paying attention to them. He turned back. The kid stood with a stiff posture, hands thrust in his pants. He seemed too nervous to be a professional operator of any kind. Johnny pulled out his passport, opened to his picture, and extended his hand so the boy could see it.

The boy's eyes widened. He studied the name, the photo, and Johnny. Tension eased from his face. He exhaled audibly—a uniquely Japanese expression of relief and gratitude—bowed again, and followed it up verbally. "Thank you, sir. Thank you very much."

Johnny returned the bow. It was an instinctive thing. He didn't bend his waist or dip his head as low as the boy did. He was acknowledging, not deferring.

"What's your name?" Johnny said.

The boy didn't answer. Instead he pointed to the mural. "You have seen painting?"

"Yes. I have seen the painting."

"Taro Okamoto. Very famous Japanese painter. Painting is called *Myth of Tomorrow*."

"I'm more focused on today. For instance, you know my name, but I don't know yours."

"We must worry more about tomorrow and less about today."

Great. Another philosopher. Like Victor Bodnar. He was always saying stuff like that. "Who are you? What's your name?"

The boy smiled. "Answers. Yes. Outside." He extended his arm toward the exit to the front of the station. "This way, please."

"We don't need to go outside. We can stay here. You have something you want me to take a look at?"

The boy ignored Johnny. Instead he widened his smile. "To follow, please."

He turned his back and headed toward the exit.

21

Johnny let the boy lead the way. The kid had made a point of emphasizing the mural. The mural had a nuclear theme. That wasn't by accident, Johnny thought. It had to be a reference to the formula.

The boy walked through the double door outside the station. Johnny followed.

A rowdy bunch of teenagers cut in front of him. They were hurrying into the station as though they were late for a train. They joked and jostled, elbowing the other pedestrians out of the way. Johnny peered over their heads. Saw the boy. A man wheeled a vending machine forward and obscured his view. Johnny pushed the last teen out of his way. The man with the vending machine moved further forward.

The boy was gone.

Johnny searched the perimeter of the station. He tried to hurry—even run—but it was impossible to take more than three steps without bumping into someone. A fleeting sense of desperation gripped him. Had someone lifted the boy? He'd confirmed Johnny's identity. Why would he have vanished of his own accord?

What a disaster. He couldn't have scripted it any worse unless the kid had been harmed. Which was not entirely out of the question, Johnny thought.

He returned to the front of the station. Commuters rushed past him in each direction. Johnny stood facing the front door. He studied the same exit the boy had used to leave the building. Looked around one more time.

Nothing.

His only course of action was to wait or return to the hotel. Then he saw that the homeless-looking man was staring at him. He widened his eyes slightly as though he was praying Johnny, the gaijin, would come over to help him. None of his own countrymen cared.

Johnny didn't know the proper etiquette in Japan. He'd never seen a single homeless person during his previous stay in Tokyo.

If he gave the old man a few yen, people might think he was encouraging the man to live in the street. But ignoring him felt even worse.

Johnny walked over and gave the man a five-hundred-yen note. The man's eyes widened with glee. He took the bill and nodded. Then he hugged Johnny. A bow would have been customary. The hug was so unexpected, Johnny found himself patting the beggar on the back out of sheer instinct.

The beggar's whisper sounded soft and steady in Johnny's ear. "Where are you staying?"

The man's English was impeccable. Johnny tried to pull back to look at the man's face but he hung on tight. Refused to let Johnny move.

"Which hotel?"

Johnny hesitated, then let his instincts take over. "Hotel Century Southern Tower," he said.

"I will call you."

"Who are you?"

"Be careful. We can't assume we're alone."

"What does that mean? You're being followed?"

The man let go of Johnny and walked away. He slipped his bowl into his jacket pocket, righted his posture, and accelerated his pace.

Then he entered the station and vanished among the crowd.

CHAPTER 4

———— ❄ ————

Luo enjoyed the tour of Chornobyl village and Pripyat on Sunday morning more than he expected. Pripyat was the name of the town that had been built within the village for the benefit of the nuclear power plant workers. It had been abandoned since 1986. Visiting the nuclear ghost town had become a cult experience. Prior to his tour, Luo couldn't understand the appeal. After seeing the damaged reactor and walking around Pripyat, however, he had a better sense of the attraction.

Chornobyl offered an eerie glimpse of what Earth looked like without humans. The tourist could decide if it was a glimpse into the past or the future. Either way, it was a desolate vision shrouded in mystery but punctuated with hope and possibility. It was the latter observation that surprised Luo the most. He had expected to experience a sense of loss and discomfort. He certainly felt those sensations, especially at the memorial statue to the firefighters who perished from radiation sickness. But he was also left with a sense of rebirth under way. The Zone of Exclusion was thick with vegetation. A variety of wild animals, many formerly extinct, roamed the land.

After the tour was over, the grumpy guide left. Luo stood by the gate to the power plant with a Ukrainian cop. The inspector looked like a boxer gone to pot. He studied Luo's dark complexion, leather skin, and small eyes. Luo knew the look. Some Russians looked down on people who didn't resemble the image in their mirror. Evidently some Ukrainians shared the same affliction.

"Where are you from?" the inspector said.

Luo smiled. "It doesn't really matter, does it?"

The inspector spat on the ground. "You must know someone important if I was forced to get out of bed and meet you here on a Sunday morning."

"Now there's something that does really matter." Luo's former commander, a retired general, had gotten him access to the Zone.

The inspector raised his eyebrows. "Black Berets?"

The Black Berets were Russian special forces. They dealt with domestic counter-terrorism, riot control, and special situations. Some of those situations were rumored to have occurred in foreign countries. Luo knew firsthand the rumors were true.

He stared at the inspector but didn't say a word.

The inspector nodded. "I can always tell. Chechnya?"

Luo stiffened. The mere mention of the place raised his blood pressure.

"First war or second?" the inspector said.

"Like I told you."

The inspector frowned. "Told me what?"

"It doesn't matter." Luo looked the inspector in the eyes again. "Tell me about the fire in the village."

"One of the abandoned homes burned down. About a kilometer and a half away. The fire trucks from the power plant put it out."

"When was this?"

"Five days ago."

"You investigated?"

The inspector lit a cigarette. "Everything burned to the ground. There was no sign of human life. As there shouldn't be. It's prohibited for anyone to live in the Zone of Exclusion."

"If there are no people, how did the fire start?"

"I didn't say there are no people. I said there are no people living here. There are workers in the power plant. And the occasional trespasser can't be ruled out. For the record, the fire was started by causes unknown."

"Off the record?"

"Off the record, there may be squatters. Old people who came back home."

"And the house that burned down?"

"It was obvious someone had been living there. There was a freshly tilled garden beside the ashes. Someone was getting the land ready to plant a garden. And the outhouse."

"What about it?"

"It had been used recently. And I don't think it was the wild boars. Do you?"

"Did you find any human remains?" Luo said.

"No. But we found shell casings. From a rifle, a shotgun, and a handgun."

"Not your garden variety vegetable-growing tools. What did you make of that?"

"I didn't make anything of that. Because there's nothing to make. Who knows when the bullets were fired and for what reasons? There've been poachers, scavengers, and thieves roaming the Zone for decades. Anyone could have fired those bullets."

"Including the person who was living there?"

"Highly unlikely."

"Why?"

"It was a babushka."

The same babushka the scavenger, Hayder, had mentioned. She'd taken care of Nadia Tesla's uncle and stayed in the house after he died.

"You're certain?" Luo said.

"Her name is Oksana Hauk. It was carved into the bottom of some cookware that survived the fire. My men and I went door to door through the area. We found her living with an old couple half a kilometer away."

Luo pulled a roll of bills from his pocket. "I need to talk to her immediately."

The inspector licked his lips. "Off the record?"

"What record? I'm not even here."

The inspector drove them through the woods to a ramshackle home. He knocked on the door and identified himself as a policeman. No one answered. He turned the doorknob and went inside. A minute later he emerged covering his nose with his sleeve. He coughed and waved for Luo to come over.

"Looks like someone else was looking for the same information you are," the inspector said. "And he got here first."

They went into the house. The stench of rotten flesh hit Luo right away but he was used to it. Two babushkas and an old man lay dead on the floor. They'd been executed professionally. Single bullet to the head. The scene confirmed to Luo that he was on the right track and added a new wrinkle.

Someone else was looking for the treasure, too.

CHAPTER 5

J OHNNY WAITED IN HIS HOTEL ROOM ALL DAY FOR THE MAN from the train station to call. He ordered chicken yakitori and a bowl of buckwheat soup for dinner. He passed on the Japanese beer and washed his dinner down with bottled water and green tea instead. It was a major sacrifice. The Japanese drank beer with everything. Anyone could buy it in vending machines on street corners all over Tokyo. There was a reason they drank it with their cuisine. It was delicious. But under the circumstances, Johnny didn't want even a drop of alcohol impeding his judgment or slowing him down.

He fell asleep watching a Japanese game show featuring housewives in pink miniskirts battling each other in a singing competition for a free hot tub. When the phone jarred him awake, the clock said 11:27 p.m.

"I'm in the bar," a man said.

Johnny recognized the voice. It was the beggar from the train station.

He hung up before Johnny could reply.

Johnny got dressed and went to the bar. Most of the tables were occupied by businessmen in dark suits and ties. Shibuya may have been the playground for the young, but the businesses were owned and operated by grown men.

A young singer with an exaggerated hourglass figure and peroxide hair sang an Adele tune onstage. She was more bosom than voice, but that seemed to suit the audience just fine. It suited Johnny well, too. There was talent and then there was talent. She was accompanied by a band. A sign on an easel at the entrance to the bar said the band's name was Melbourne. Australian talent, Johnny thought. He'd never gotten down under that way. But now, with Nadia in the picture, he wasn't even tempted.

Johnny found the man at a table for two in the back. A candle provided just enough lighting for Johnny to recognize him. He wore a gray plaid sports jacket over a black dress shirt. He'd washed his hair and shaved. He looked ten years younger. Still, even the candlelight couldn't hide the creases in his face. They spoke of hardship and suffering and commanded Johnny's respect.

An adorable waitress with a pageboy hairdo appeared. The man ordered Suntory whiskey on ice. Johnny didn't want to dull his senses with alcohol but he had no choice. Men in Japan were expected to drink and drink heavily when in the company of other men. He ordered a Sapporo beer. He'd been craving one since dinner.

"I am Nakamura," the man said, after the waitress left.

In Japan, men called each other by their last names. "I'm Johnny Tanner."

"I know."

"Why are you here?"

"You know why I'm here. Nadia Tesla, and her cousin, Adam, received e-mails from my friend. I'm here on his behalf, just as you are here on their behalf."

"What is your friend's name?"

Nakamura thought about the question. "Let's just call my friend *Genesis II*."

"What do you do for a living?"

"I work with an organization called Global Medical Corps."

"You're a doctor?"

"Yes."

29

"What kind?"

"The impoverished kind. Global Medical Corps goes where they are needed. We were on the ground in Fukushima within forty-eight hours of the earthquake and tsunami on March 11, 2011, providing medical assistance, setting up temporary housing, delivering key household items. And of course, providing medical support. There were 59,000 evacuees. Some are still living in makeshift shelters."

"That was a real tragedy. I'm sorry for your country's troubles." Johnny bowed his head slightly and let a few seconds pass out of respect. "Where did you learn to speak English so well?"

Nakamura paused as though remembering something, and then smiled. "I was an exchange student for a year in high school. Oshkosh, Wisconsin. Cheese country. I lived on a farm. I liked it so much I went to college at the University of Wisconsin. In Madison. Much of our work has been done in countries where English is the common language so I've been able to keep it up."

"Who was the kid at the train station? The one that met me at the mural?"

"A college student. A volunteer."

"Volunteer?"

"The Corps relies on volunteers. Students from all over the world take semesters off to work with us, give back to the community."

"So he's not Genesis II?"

"No. He is not Genesis II. It was just a precaution. To make sure you were who you said you were."

"Why the precaution?"

"Genesis II has confided in me as a friend. He believes he has something of extreme value. Something that could change the world. He has led a troubled life, and as a result is not a trusting person. He sometimes suffers from anxiety and delusion. He is constantly fearful."

"At the train station, you said we can't assume we're alone."

"I have no reason to believe I'm being followed, but Genesis II said to expect the unexpected. He said that you should do the same. I trust him, and believe in him and the power of the treasure he possesses."

"Tell me what you know about the treasure. I need to be convinced this is all real."

Nakamura started to answer and stopped. Two men in slick suits walked by their table. One of them glanced alternately at Nakamura and Johnny. The men seated themselves at a table closer to the stage. Johnny spied bulges under their jackets. He was reminded of what his teachers had told him during his first day as an exchange student. The further from the center of Tokyo, the greater the influence of the *Yakuza*, the Japanese organized crime syndicates.

"That was a very American question," Nakamura said.

"What do you mean, American question?"

"Blunt, direct, inappropriate. I could ask you the same. What do you know about the treasure? But that would be rude, and a waste of time. Because you would merely deflect the question and we would engage in a battle of wits until our drinks arrived."

"You've got the wrong man, friend. I don't deflect questions. Ask anything you want. You might not like the answer, but I won't waste your time." Johnny kept his voice down and maintained a calm expression on his face. He wanted his demeanor to contrast with his words to lend them even more power. "That's me being very American, as opposed to the Japanese, who'll wait twenty years to publicly own up to a mistake and then commit suicide. Is that your idea of appropriate behavior?"

Nakamura appeared stunned.

"Oh, have I got your attention? Are we done bullshitting each other here?"

Nakamura stared at him.

Johnny said, "In the e-mail, Genesis II used the phrase, 'Fate of the free world depends on us.' What did he mean by that?"

"You know what the treasure is, so you know what he meant by that." Nakamura smiled. "See? The battle of wits begins despite your assurances to the contrary. Who will reveal himself first?"

"I'm not the one wearing the kimono. You can see right through me and I wouldn't have it any other way. What made him choose those exact words?"

"Genesis II said those words would have meaning to Nadia and Adam Tesla. And that given you were their representative, they would have meaning to you. Was he right?"

Johnny shrugged. "Maybe. Maybe not."

"Says the man without the kimono."

Johnny smiled.

The waitress arrived with their drinks and two bowls of salty Japanese crackers and nuts.

"I have to ask you another question," Johnny said. "It's going to sound blunt, direct, and inappropriate."

"No kidding," Nakamura said.

"Who is Genesis II?" Johnny didn't expect Nakamura to answer the question or unintentionally reveal a clue, but he knew Nadia would be disappointed if he didn't ask.

Nakamura looked away. "I expected more from you. But you are such an American, aren't you?"

"Yes, and proud of it. Does Genesis II know Adam?"

Johnny studied Nakamura's reaction for a tell of some kind. He got nothing. Instead, Nakamura continued looking stone-faced at the stage.

"How did you and Genesis II meet?"

Nakamura sipped his whiskey. "I've given you enough information for you to answer that question yourself."

Johnny remembered their earlier conversation. "You're a doctor. You're working in Fukushima. You must have met Genesis II in Fukushima. Genesis II is a survivor of the earthquake, tsunami, or the nuclear disaster."

Nakamura's eyebrows furrowed a smidge. It was just enough of a physical reaction to tell Johnny he was wrong.

"No," Johnny said. "He's not a victim. He's a volunteer."

Nakamura lifted his chin.

"Hot dog. Score one for the boy from Jersey."

They sipped their drinks some more. A moment of silence passed between them. Johnny's victory proved momentary. He still needed proof the locket existed and contained a formula, and he was no closer to that than when he arrived.

"So you know who I am," Johnny said. "I know who you are. I travelled here to meet you. You're calling the shots, but I may or may not play along. What do you suggest we do now?"

Nakamura slid a flash drive memory stick across the table to Johnny.

"What's this?" Johnny said.

"A token of good faith. When you see it on a computer monitor, you'll understand."

"Understand what?"

"That the second half of the formula exists."

Johnny's heart thumped. "After I take a look at it, I'd like to meet with Genesis II."

Nakamura straightened the lapels of his jacket. "I'm sure you would. But that's not going to happen. He will only meet with the boy. He will only meet with Adam. Adam must come to Fukushima. He must come immediately. And he must bring the locket."

Nakamura stood up, knocked back the rest of his whiskey, and left.

Johnny went to the business center to use one of the computers. He slipped the flash drive into the USB port. It contained a single file. The file was called "Genesis II."

The file consisted of two strings of chemical symbols. Each string contained four hexagons and a chemical formula. It could have been gibberish or proof the second half of the formula existed. There was only one way to find out.

Johnny rushed to his room to call Nadia.

CHAPTER 6

N ADIA SAT OPPOSITE DR. ERIC SANDSTROM IN HIS OFFICE AT Columbia University on Monday afternoon. He was a professor emeritus, a respected radiobiologist who taught one class a week to keep his mind active at age eighty-five.

"This is interesting," he said, after studying the symbols Johnny had e-mailed from Tokyo.

"What is?" Nadia said.

"It's a modified version of Five-Androstenediol, just like the one you showed me three weeks ago. Except it contains an additional enhancement. The formula you showed me before had a partial description of two new proteins. This one further describes those two proteins but doesn't fully define them."

"Meaning some symbols are still missing."

"Yes."

"Can you draw any conclusions from what you do see, Professor?"

He removed his glasses, sprayed a lens cleaner on them, and began wiping them with a soft tissue. "Five-Androstenediol is a direct metabolite of a steroid produced by the human adrenal cortex. That steroid is called DHEA. The Armed Forces Radiobiology Research Institute discovered Five-AED, as it's called, in 2007. They performed clinical trials using primates with the pharmaceutical company Hollis-Eden. Their initial results were excellent. Close to 70 percent more monkeys treated with Five-AED survived acute radiation syndrome than those that were not treated."

"I remember being told about that," Nadia said. Karel, the zoologist in Chornobyl, had explained Five-AED to her. "I never quite understood why the research project was dropped a short time later when the trials were so successful."

"No formal explanation was given," Sandstrom said. "But it's a major leap to treating humans from treating monkeys. The scuttlebutt in the scientific community was that the production of white blood cells and platelets was insufficient. White blood cells are essential to life. Platelets promote blood clotting. To increase production of platelets and white blood cells, an additional protein or proteins needed to be introduced to the formula."

"Thus creating a modified version of Five-AED."

"Precisely."

"And could the symbols you're looking at be part of these missing proteins? Could they be part of the solution?"

Sandstrom put his glasses on and studied the paper again. "They might be. On the other hand, they might not be. Regardless of how promising the formula looks—and it does look interesting to me—you would simply never know until clinical trials were conducted. No one could answer that question for you by simply looking at chemical data."

"Why do you say the partial formula looks interesting?"

"For the simple reason that it appears to be relevant—incomplete but consistent with the formula that you brought in a week ago. And given you have come here twice, I've inferred you've gotten them from two different sources. All of which leads me to believe the results of a prior experiment—perhaps in a different country—are being recovered piece by piece." His eyes widened. "Am I right?"

Nadia had been afraid of confiding in anyone—even a stately old professor—but what choice had she had? She needed to trust a scientist to understand the formula.

"Can you at least tell me the scientific source of your discovery?" Sandstrom said.

Nadia hated to say no, but she had no choice. She remained mute.

Sandstrom nodded with understanding. "Can you tell me the country of origin?" When Nadia didn't answer, he leaned forward in his seat. "The former Soviet Union, perhaps? There was an old recluse there. A genius there by the name of Arkady Shatan."

Nadia lost her breath for a moment. Arkady Shatan was the name of the Russian scientist who'd conducted experiments in the Zone and supposedly given the formula to Bobby's father, her uncle Damian. Like Damian, however, Arkady was dead, leaving the partial formula Bobby had been given a mystery.

"It's best for both of us if I don't elaborate any further," Nadia said. "I have to ask you to trust me, Professor. And in turn, I have to put my trust in you, sir."

"You have it, my dear."

"Have you spoken to anyone about my previous visit? About the partial formula you've seen before today?"

He didn't hesitate. "Absolutely not. To what benefit? You asked me to keep our discussions confidential. And I have done so. Besides, at my age, if I told anyone about what you'd shown me, they would assume I was suffering fantasies. It was in my best interest not to discuss your discoveries with anyone."

"Good. Let's keep it that way."

"Do you understand the medical implications of such a formula? If the risk of radioactive contamination were mitigated, it would open up an entire new world of medical treatments. Millions of lives would be prolonged and saved."

"Yes," Nadia said. "But there may also be military implications, if one country were to get a hold of the formula and keep it from others."

Sandstrom frowned. "That could not be allowed to happen.

If you disseminated the formula to the world at large that risk would be eliminated. Surely that is your plan, is it not?"

"Yes," Nadia said, honestly. "That may be a bit trickier than it sounds, but that's the plan."

Before that plan could even be contemplated, another one would have to be carried out. Nadia and Bobby would have to travel to a country where they didn't speak the language or know anyone. Nadia wished there were an alternative solution, but there wasn't one.

The stakes were too high.

They had to go to Japan.

CHAPTER 7

———————❄———————

BOBBY RAN HIS HAND ALONG THE SLEEK BLACK SUITCASE Nadia had just bought him. It was one of those Swiss Army designs, with a neat aluminum handle that popped out with the press of a button. Nadia said it was made for the young business traveler. It looked like something James Bond would stick in the boot of his Aston Martin after a night of gambling. The Swiss sure knew how to make cool things. Bobby imagined closing the trunk of his own sports car . . .

Come on, focus, man. Focus.

He wheeled the suitcase to the corner of his room and left it there like a piece of modern furniture he could admire. Then he pulled his old duffel bag out from his closet and began to pack.

From the moment he read the e-mail his thoughts had been consumed with Eva. Bobby had grown up living with his father's friend, a disgraced former hockey player. The man became Bobby's guardian, hockey instructor, and personal tormentor. Bobby simply referred to him as the Coach. Bobby had thought Eva was the Coach's daughter, but he later learned she was his niece.

As a fifth grader, he'd looked up to her. She was only a year older, but that year seemed like ten in grade school. Eva didn't want anything to do with him. They walked to school together, but once they got close she made him wait so she wasn't seen entering the playground with him. They never talked about anything personal. They only discussed who was going to do what chores around the house.

When Eva started secondary school, things got worse. She started wearing purple lipstick and makeup, and dressing in black from head to toe. Bobby turned fourteen and started to dream about kissing those lips. He became tongue-tied in her presence. On the rare occasion she looked at him across the dinner table and asked him a question—such as to please pass the butter—his heart would start beating so fast he feared his chest would explode. But she wanted even less to do with him.

Bobby was known as the freak in school, with his shorn ears and introverted personality. Everyone knew he suffered from radiation syndrome. No one wanted to touch him for fear of getting infected. This was a superstition, carried over from the days following the reactor's explosion. But superstitions died hard. Radiation syndrome sufferers were shunned by society. Not even his teachers wanted to come near him.

The secret he and Eva shared was that she suffered from the same disease. Initially, Eva didn't have a physical handicap like Bobby. She was able to keep her condition a secret. Eventually she had to have surgery on her thyroid, however, and the other kids in school noticed the scar at the base of her neck. Her friends stopped talking to her. She became a freak, too, the female equivalent of Bobby. A month after Eva's illness was exposed, she started walking into school with Bobby by her side. No longer did he have to wait until she was out of sight so that her friends didn't see them together. She didn't have any friends left to worry about except for Bobby.

On the last Friday of each month, the Coach would pick them up in his car after school and drive them sixty miles to the Division of Nervous Pathologies in Kyiv. The radiation in their bodies was measured and recorded in their dosimetric passports. Then they received physical exams. Most patients went home after the checkup was completed. But not Bobby and Eva.

Instead, the Coach drove them to the office of a retired radio-biologist named Arkady Shatan. Dr. Arkady, as Eva and Bobby called him, injected them with a special serum. Dr. Arkady insisted that if the serum stayed in their bloodstreams long enough, it would counteract the radiation in their bodies and cure them of their illness. In fact, not only would the serum cure them, Dr. Arkady said it would make them stronger than the average person. The Coach and the doctor swore Eva and Bobby to keep their injections a secret.

If the treatments brought them closer, the side effects made them inseparable. They shared nightmares, anxiety, and occasional hallucinations. Dr. Arkady said the effects would fade over time. He was right. They faded but never disappeared completely. Attacks came randomly, and still persecuted Bobby, as they had in jail two weeks ago.

Throughout this ordeal, the Coach had his own problems, and Eva and Bobby suffered accordingly. He drank and gambled his pension away. Sometimes toward the end of the month they wouldn't have enough money left to buy food. Eva and Bobby became scavengers, scrounging what they could. Stealing radio-active car parts from the Zone of Exclusion was their specialty. They were strong, lean, and agile, and could slip in and out of vehicle graveyards with ease.

Then one night, life changed forever. They were scavenging in the Zone when a group of hunters stumbled upon them. It wasn't unusual to find a poacher roaming Chornobyl in search of game for a local restaurant, but these were different kinds of hunters. Their prey was human. Criminals on the lam often hid in the Zone, and these hunters must have thought they were doing society a favor and enjoying a hobby at the same time. Scavengers were by definition criminals, too.

Bobby saved Eva and accidentally killed one of the hunters by pushing her into the radioactive cooling pond. Eva suffered a severe injury to her leg, and died of a staph infection at the hospital. Bobby was so heartbroken he had trouble getting out of bed for the next six months.

As he wedged a roll of toilet paper into his duffel bag, Bobby wondered who else knew the phrase *Genesis II*. Dr. Arkady had died two years ago. There were two possibilities. First, Dr. Arkady's personal assistant might have heard it. Her name was Ksenia Melnik. She was a sweet woman. Bobby had liked her. And she had a son, Denys, a few years older than Bobby. He was a jerk. Bobby had liked him less.

Could Dr. Arkady have given Ksenia Melnik the second half of the formula? Could the e-mail have come from Denys? Why would Dr. Arkady divide the formula in two? Because he was an eccentric old man, Bobby thought. Or, for some more logical reason that wasn't clear yet. There was a method to the madness of brilliant old men. There was still another possibility.

There could have been another patient. Another boy.

The problem with both those possibilities was they didn't explain why the e-mail came from Fukushima. He couldn't shake the explanation he and Nadia had imagined. That there was a second scientist in Japan, conducting the same experiments as Dr. Arkady, the two of them in constant correspondence until Dr. Arkady's death. The timeline of events suggested the two scientists would have begun their collaboration before the Fukushima accident took place, but that didn't make it less likely. Japanese fears of nuclear disaster ran deep. Bobby knew this from school. They were rooted in Japan's World War II experiences in two cities—Hiroshima and Nagasaki.

"What are you doing?" Nadia appeared in his doorway holding the handle to an older suitcase on wheels.

"I'm done." Bobby zipped the duffel bag, slung it on his back, and let the strap fall across his chest.

"That's not what I mean. Why are you taking that ratty bag when I bought you a beautiful piece of luggage?"

Bobby didn't want to tell her the truth. He didn't want to scare her. "Because it's so beautiful. I don't want to scuff it up. I'd rather look at it for a while and then use it once the novelty wears off."

Nadia flashed a smile. "Oh sure. That makes sense." She sealed her lips tight. "Unpack. I bought it so you could use it, not look at it. Let's go."

"I'm not taking the suitcase. Please. Let's not argue over this."

"Why? You can't seriously be concerned you're going to nick it."

Bobby had already lied to her about *Genesis II*. He didn't want to lie to her again. He took a deep breath and exhaled. "It'll be hard to run with a suitcase."

"What?"

"It's easier to run with the bag."

"Run? What are you talking about? Who's going to be running?"

"We are."

Nadia frowned. Suspicion spread across her face. "Why do you say that?"

"If the formula is real, someone else probably wants it. And if someone else wants it, we're going to have to run. Just like we had to run from Ukraine."

"We're going to Japan. Not Ukraine."

"Doesn't matter where we're going. The formula's the thing. Right?"

"If it's real."

"Yeah. Right. If it's real."

She narrowed her eyes. "Do you know something I don't know?"

Bobby shook his head. "No."

Bobby kept a straight face but he could feel her eyes penetrate him. They'd only known each other for a year but they'd endured the trip to New York from Chornobyl and his murder charge. Nadia could read Bobby better than his teammates' parents could read their kids.

"You were excited when you first got home from jail," Nadia said, "talking to me like normal. But ever since the e-mail came you've clammed up. And now you're packing as though you're going to need to run."

Bobby tried to hold her eyes but couldn't. His father had been a master con artist. Bobby was discovering he was his father's son, capable of concocting plots and lying to anyone necessary to extricate himself from a dangerous situation. But he couldn't stand lying to Nadia. He owed her his life.

"You do know something," Nadia said. "Don't you?"

Bobby saw the knowing look in her eyes. On the one hand he didn't want to discuss the treatments with her, relive the horrors he'd shared with Eva. On the other hand, he longed for her to push him a little more so he'd tell her the truth.

Nadia walked up to him and put her hands on his shoulders. He'd told her never to touch him when she'd done the same thing at the Kyiv train station. But now he didn't mind it so much. In fact, although he wouldn't have admitted it to anyone, he found it comforting.

"All we have is each other," she said. "If you know something it has to be related to the e-mail." Bobby could see her mind working furiously. She was so smart. "The name. *Genesis II*. You recognized it. It means something to you. Doesn't it?"

Bobby nodded before he could decide whether he wanted to or not. He held his breath, waiting for her to yell at him, but she didn't.

Instead, she patted his shoulder. "That's okay. I'm sure you had your reasons. The important thing now is we're getting on a plane in two and a half hours to go to Tokyo. I need to know if we're in danger. If Johnny's in danger. Who or what is *Genesis II*?"

Bobby told Nadia about Dr. Arkady, Eva, and the treatments.

"*Genesis II* was what Dr. Arkady called us," Bobby said. "Eva and me. He said we would be a fresh start for mankind. The person with the second locket, who signed the e-mail, the one Nakamura is calling *Genesis II*, has to be someone who knows about us. Who knows about our treatments."

Bobby told Nadia about Ksenia Melnik, Dr. Arkady's assistant, and her son, Denys.

"Why didn't you tell me this right away?"

Bobby felt himself blushing. "The treatments. We promised Dr. Arkady to keep them confidential. I didn't want anyone to know. I had some kind of injections. I don't even know what they were." He didn't mention the side effects. They weren't relevant to their trip and the mere thought of them made him nervous. And he didn't need to be nervous before a fourteen-hour flight.

"And that's it?" Nadia said. "There's nothing else. No other reason why you think . . ." She eyed his duffel bag. "We're going to have to run."

Bobby shook his head. "That's it. Someone knows about the formula. There's going to be competition for the formula. We're going to have to run."

Nadia smiled. "Japan is one of the safest countries in the world. Tokyo is one of the most crowded cities in the world. We'll be okay. But you can take your duffel bag if it makes you most comfortable."

Bobby nodded at her suitcase. "You should switch to a bag like mine. There's still time."

Nadia laughed. "Thanks but I'll be okay."

Her cell phone rang. She answered it, thanked the person on the other end, and hung up.

"Our car's here," she said. She turned and grabbed her suitcase. "Let's go to Tokyo."

They took the elevator to the ground floor. The doors opened. Two men stood in front of the front desk speaking to the doorman. One was lean with gray hair. He wore an expensive blue suit and tie. The other was bald with cinderblock shoulders. He also wore a fancy suit. It was black with narrow white stripes, and stretched taut against the giant's frame, looked like designer prison wear.

Bobby studied the older man. Sunken cheeks and square jaw. Distinctly Slavic features. They were Russian or Ukrainian mobsters. Bobby had seen enough of them during his childhood in Ukraine to know the look.

"*Chorty*," Bobby said.

Nadia frowned. "What?"

Chorty was the Ukrainian word for *devils*. The front desk was twenty feet away and the men were standing sideways. They were in the middle of an animated conversation with the doorman and weren't paying attention to the elevator. Bobby grabbed Nadia by the lapel of her coat.

"They're here for us," Bobby said.

"Who's here for us?" Nadia's voice trailed off as her eyes went to the men. Bobby could see the recognition in her eyes. Two Slavic-looking mafia types at her apartment building. It was too much of a coincidence.

"Freight elevator," Bobby said.

They slipped out of the elevator and hurried down the corridor to the side entrance. Nadia said hello to the doorman who accepted deliveries and stormed past him out the side door. Bobby followed. She took a hard right onto the sidewalk on Eighty-First Street. They hurried to the end of the block. Took a left turn onto First Avenue and hustled forward another half block. Ducked into an alcove in front of a giant day care center for dogs.

Nadia pulled out her cell phone and called the car service. "I had to drop my dog off at the day care center," she said to the operator. "Would you please tell the driver I'm sorry for the inconvenience and ask him to pick me up a couple of blocks away?" She proceeded to give directions to their current location.

Bobby peered around a wall at the sidewalk behind them to see if anyone had been following them. He didn't see anyone suspicious.

"There may be more men," Bobby said. "In a car. Watching our car."

"That would not be a good thing. Even worse would be if they figure out we're going to Tokyo."

"Don't worry," Bobby said. "I packed for misdirection."

Nadia frowned.

A black Lincoln Town Car pulled up. The name Tesla was handwritten on a sign in the front windshield.

"That's a slight giveaway," Bobby said.

Nadia swore under her breath. "You think?"

The driver stored their luggage in the trunk. He took the sign down from the windshield and tossed it in the passenger seat beside him.

"What terminal at JFK?" he said.

"Terminal one," Nadia said. "Did the doorman from my building come out to see who you were picking up?"

"Yeah."

"Did he ask what terminal?"

"No. One of the other guys did."

"What other guys?"

"There were two guys in suits with him. They looked like security. The way they asked, I thought they were coming with us in a backup car. For a minute there, I thought you were a congressman or something."

"Why, do I look untrustworthy?" Nadia said.

She glanced at Bobby and nodded. Now she believed him, Bobby thought.

The driver pulled up to a red light. "You seem a little out of breath. You guys okay?"

"Yeah," Bobby said. "We're okay."

"Yeah," Nadia said. She glanced at Bobby again. "We had to run."

CHAPTER 8

———————— ❄ ————————

L UO DROVE TO A HEALTH CLINIC THIRTY MILES NORTH OF Kyiv on Monday morning. The Division of Nervous Patholo-gies was located on a campus consisting of four multistoried buildings that resembled concrete slabs. It was an abomination only man could have conjured, and a Soviet man at that. The campus was surrounded by a gorgeous forest, a pleasant contrast that reminded Luo of home.

Luo met with an administrator in a stark office with metal furniture.

"There were four medical classifications for Chornobyl vic-tims," the administrator said. "Sufferers, evacuees, cleanup workers, and nuclear plant workers. Our job was to formulate diagnostics, create medical classifications, and prescribe treatments."

"Did you find any records for a boy named Tesla?"

The administrator reached for a manila folder. "I did. There were twenty-eight people named Tesla. Fifteen of them males."

"How many would be in their late teens today? Between six-teen and eighteen."

"Three. Two were from Kyiv. One was from Korosten. I remember the one from Korosten. His name was Adam. Incred-ible case."

"Why incredible?"

"He was a stage II sufferer. Physical deformity at the ears. Thyroid problem. Not as bad as the girl."

"Girl? What girl?"

"Adam came for dosimeter updates and treatments with a girl. They lived with the girl's uncle. What was her name? It began with a vowel. Anna. No. Irina. No. Eva. Yes. That's it. Eva."

"Tell me about them."

"They both had the benefit of being *serednjaky.*"

Luo frowned.

"*Serednjak* is the Ukrainian word for middle-of-the-road, as in a wheat field. They say it's best not to be the tallest or the shortest blade of wheat but somewhere in the middle. That way when the combine passes over you, you're sure to be cut. The blade may mangle the tall wheat and miss the short one, but it's sure to cut the one of average height. And so it was here, at the Division of Nervous Pathologies."

"How so?"

"The short wheat—those who were not sick enough—might not have gotten any treatment. The tall wheat—those who were very sick—might have been too fragile to survive the treatment. The serednjak had the best chance for survival."

"And to your knowledge they survived?"

"Both of them were stage II sufferers since birth. Their mothers lived in Pripyat in 1986 when the disasters occurred. And they were born in the area. Their symptoms worsened as they aged, which is typical. When the prognosis for Eva's thyroid condition became grim, she had the requisite surgery. She was fifteen or so at the time. Which would have made Adam fourteen." The administrator stared into space as though recalling an extraordinary event. "And then it started happening."

"What started happening?"

"The radiation in their bodies began to gradually recede."

"What? It went away?"

"Yes. We asked questions but found nothing in their diets or lifestyles that could explain their steady improvement." The administrator checked his manila folder. "The last record I have of the boy visiting is approximately two years ago. Nothing since."

"Do you have an address? A next of kin?"

The administrator gave Luo their home address in Korosten. "Eva passed away two years ago. Had an accident that required hospitalization. Died from an infection. Girl overcomes one illness only to succumb to another. What a tragedy."

"She's happier in the spirit world, I am sure," Luo said.

The administrator frowned. "What spirit world?"

"The one beneath the earth."

The administrator looked like he'd swallowed something bitter. "Where did you say you were from?"

"North of Moscow. Anyone else mentioned in the file?"

"An emergency contact by the name of K. Melnik. There's an address in Kyiv. Might be a physician. Or a family friend. I don't know. I never interacted with this person, and there is no record of him in my notes."

Luo thanked the administrator and went back to his car. He placed a series of calls to Korosten and learned that Eva's uncle had been a Soviet hockey player before being convicted of manslaughter. He drank and gambled his pension away. He also died seven months ago.

That left one lead, the mysterious K. Melnik noted as an emergency contact for Adam. Luo drove to Kyiv. K. Melnik lived in an elegant old four-story apartment building overlooking the River Dnipro.

A police car was parked at the curb in front of the building. The front door was open, and two uniformed policemen stood chatting near the stairs.

Luo walked by the policemen into the foyer and studied the names by the buzzers and apartment numbers. A person named

Ksenia Melnik lived in apartment 4B. Luo wasn't surprised the contact was a woman. Unlike the administrator, he'd made no assumptions about the person or her relationship to the boy. He'd learned during his tours in Chechnya not to make assumptions about any civilian.

He pressed the buzzer to Ksenia Melnik's apartment. No one answered.

One of the cops appeared beside him. "You know this person?" He looked suspicious and angry, like most Ukrainian cops.

"I'm a friend of a friend. He asked me to stop by and say hello to her."

"Tell your friend that won't be possible."

"Why not?"

"Because Ksenia Melnik is dead. Robbery—homicide. Last night."

"How did she die?"

"A bullet to the head."

Just like the squatters in Chornobyl. "Anyone in the neighborhood see anything?"

"No, but her son was hiding in the closet the whole time. He says he didn't see their faces. Said he hid in the closet like a coward and let them kill his mother."

"Is he home right now?" Luo said.

"Yeah. The detectives are with him upstairs right now."

"I'd like to extend my condolences when they're done."

The cop frowned. "I thought you didn't know her."

"I didn't. But my friend does. And he'll never forgive me if I don't pay my respects on his behalf."

CHAPTER 9

NADIA WONDERED IF SOMEONE WAS WAITING FOR THEM AT the airport. The trip to JFK took a little over an hour. The driver dropped them off at the departure area for terminal one. The curbside was jammed with vehicles. Shuttle buses, limos, and cars pulled up and then moved on. "Do you see our friends anywhere?" Nadia said.

"No," Bobby said. "But they know we're here. If there's just two of them, they're behind us. But if there's another team, they're already here. Waiting for us. The good news is they don't know where we're going yet. Because if they knew, they wouldn't have asked the driver what airport and what terminal."

"You are my nephew, aren't you?"

"Actually, I'm your cousin."

Bobby was right, but Nadia loved to tease him otherwise. "So disrespectful. Haven't you been through this with your aunt before?"

They checked in, proceeded through security and passport control, and emerged at the corridor leading to the gates.

"There they are," Bobby said. "Up ahead. On the left. Near the golf store. In suits. Sipping coffee, pretending they're having a conversation."

Nadia glanced their way. Two more rugged-looking Slavs seeming just a little out of place. They glanced at Nadia.

"They saw me looking at them," Nadia said.

"That's okay," Bobby said. "They know who we are. We know who they are. Now they know we know who they are. What do they say in America?" He switched to English. "Level playing field."

"Our gate is up ahead." Nadia checked her watch. "The flight leaves in fifty minutes. We have time until the final boarding call. Keep walking past the gate. Pretend we're taking a different flight."

They walked by the Slavs and continued past gate five. Out of the corner of her eyes she could see the destination posted on the board.

Tokyo.

Bobby followed her past their gate. The corridor ended a hundred yards ahead. Nadia saw the sign for gates nine, ten, and eleven at the far wall.

"We have to pick one of these gates," Nadia said. "We'll sit down and pretend it's our flight. They'll come over to take a look. Their goal will be to see where we're flying so they can communicate that to their boss. The question is how can we make them believe we're actually boarding a different flight so they don't know we're going to Tokyo."

Bobby considered the question for a few seconds. "I can do that."

"What? How?"

"Yeah," Bobby said, staring into space. "I can definitely get rid of them." He turned to Nadia. "You're always telling me I have to trust you. The question now is, do you trust me?"

"It's not a matter of trust. It's a matter of concern. What do you have in mind?"

"We need to find another flight. The one we want them to think we're taking."

They ambled past gates seven and eight. Nadia checked the gate on the left.

"Seoul," she said.

"Beijing on the other side," Bobby said.

They passed restrooms and a coffee shop and arrived at the final trio of gates.

"Grand Cayman Islands," Nadia said.

"Cool," Bobby said. "They'll assume we're going on vacation. That might make sense."

More logical than Seoul or Beijing, Nadia thought. Then she saw the destination at gate ten. "Forget the Caymans. Look."

Bobby glanced at the departure board. Lufthansa Airlines flight 8840 to Frankfurt.

"Frankfurt to Kyiv is a common route," Nadia said. "They'll assume we're headed to Ukraine."

"It would be the logical deduction."

"Nice."

Bobby led the way to an empty cluster of chairs at gate ten. Nadia checked her surroundings. A family of five with two screaming children, a middle-aged couple with bronzed skin, a pair of honeymooners with their eyes on each other.

The same two Slavs were seated at gate nine behind them. One was reading a paper, the other tapping his mobile phone.

"They're behind us," Nadia said.

"I'm sure they are," Bobby said.

She checked the departure board. "The Lufthansa flight boards in less than fifteen minutes."

Bobby took a deep breath. "That should be enough time." He slung his bag over his shoulder.

"Wait." Nadia wanted to throttle him. She reminded herself to keep her voice down. "You want to share your plan with your aunt?"

"No."

"Why not?"

"You might try to stop me, and we don't have any other options." He smiled sweetly. "Don't be scared, Auntie. I prepared for this scenario."

"How?"

"I told you. I packed for misdirection."

CHAPTER 10

———————— ❄ ————————

B OBBY REHEARSED HIS PLAN AS HE APPROACHED THE REST-
room entrance.

"Hey." A young man in a New York Rangers hockey jersey
stepped forward. "You're that hockey player from Fordham. The
one that beat Gaborik in that race in Harlem. Your name is
Bobby . . ." His voice trailed off as he tried to remember Bobby's
last name.

"Sorry, man. You must have me confused with someone else."

The man's jaw dropped. He looked as though he wanted to
say something else but wasn't prepared for Bobby's answer.

Bobby bolted into the restroom, found an empty stall, and
locked himself inside. He tried not to slip on the floor, which was
wet and disgusting. The hook on the back of the stall door had
been ripped off. Just like Ukraine. He wiped the toilet seat with a
handkerchief and rested his bag on top of it. He was wearing
jeans, a button-down shirt, the navy sports jacket Nadia had
bought him in Alaska, and black loafers. He hated those clothes.
Nadia said they made him look respectable but they felt stiff and
wrong on him. They made him look like someone he wasn't, an
entitled prep school kid with rich parents. That made them perfect for misdirection.

He swapped the sports jacket for a forest-green fleece with a high collar and exchanged the loafers for his hiking boots. He put on a black cap with flaps that covered his ears. Ran his hand along the back and stuffed his long black hair under the cap. Lifted the collar to cover his neck. Donned a pair of wire-rimmed reading glasses. Zipped his bag shut and left it on the toilet seat.

Then he jumped up, grasped the top of the door with both hands, and vaulted into the air. He lifted one leg over the door to straddle it, swung the other one over, and jumped down to the ground.

Most of the other men stood at urinals with their backs to Bobby. One man was washing his hands at a sink. He stared at Bobby's reflection in the mirror. Another traveler stopped in his tracks. Bobby sauntered past them toward the exit. The man at the sink turned his attention to his hands. The one who'd just walked in headed for an empty urinal.

This was New York. It was an airport. People did strange things all the time. Maybe the door to the stall was locked because the toilet was out of order. Maybe Bobby needed to go so badly he'd jumped the wall to use it. No one cared. Everyone had an agenda. No one wanted any trouble.

Bobby paused behind the line of men using the hand dryers. One man finished and started to leave. Another one did the same. Instead of stepping up to use one of the machines, Bobby lowered his head and followed the two men outside.

The man in the Rangers uniform stood to his left as he exited the restroom. Bobby circled to the right of the other two men, looked down, and powered past them. He marched back down the corridor away from the high-numbered gates toward security. He stopped near a cluster of pay phones in a center aisle and slid into one of the cubicles. Glanced back toward the restroom.

The man in the Rangers uniform was still standing near the door waiting for Bobby to come back out. A moment later, a young woman in a similar jersey emerged from the women's room. They fell into conversation and walked away.

Bobby headed back toward the waiting area. He hugged the right wall to remain hidden from view. He spotted the Slavs. One was still seated behind Nadia. The other had moved across the corridor so he could keep an eye on the men's room. He clearly hadn't recognized Bobby when he'd come out.

Bobby ducked under the rope and walked up to a pair of agents at gate nine. One of them smiled and chatted with a customer, while the other banged away at her keyboard. Bobby chose the latter. She had an air of authority about her.

"This station is closed," the agent said. "Would you wait in line behind the others, please?"

Bobby kept his head low so she couldn't see his eyes below the bill of his cap. "Help," he said.

"Yes. The agent to my left can help you."

"No." Bobby lowered his voice to a desperate whisper. "I mean, *help.*"

"Excuse me?"

"I just saw a man pull two guns from under the seat of the pay phones. They were taped to the bottom."

"Could you repeat that please?"

"There are two of them. They said something about taking care of business. They're here near the gate. They're near the gate, do you hear me?"

"Where are these men? And could you look up as you speak to me, please?"

Bobby described the Slavs and their precise location. "I think they're going to kill someone."

The agent hesitated. Bobby couldn't see her face but he could sense she was evaluating the risks of taking action or doing nothing. She picked up the phone, dialed three numbers, and turned her body away from Bobby and the other passengers. She whispered something, listened, and hung up. Then she put the phone down.

"You wait right here," she said.

She turned and bustled toward a man in a suit and tie standing near the gate to the airplane.

Bobby took his phone out of his pocket and dropped it on the floor. He fell to his knees to pick it up. He scooped the phone up, kept his body bent, and ducked out of sight behind a group of passengers. Followed them back toward the restroom.

An unmarked door burst open along the wall. Two uniformed policemen emerged. One held a two-way radio close to his mouth. The other held his hand on the gun in his holster. They hustled toward gate nine.

Bobby marched past them into the men's room.

A businessman with a briefcase was trying to open the stall Bobby had locked from the inside. Then a toilet flushed, a man stepped out of an adjacent stall, and the businessman took his place.

Bobby hoisted himself to the top of the door and climbed into the stall. His bag was sitting on the toilet seat exactly where he'd left it. He took off his cap, let his hair fall to his shoulders, and changed back into his original clothes. When he was done, he pulled out his cell phone and called Nadia.

"Where are you?" she said.

"Men's room."

"I thought so. I saw you go in but I didn't see you come out."

"Good."

"Good?"

"Yeah, good."

"I'm confused. All hell's broken loose here. First a couple of cops showed up. Then six guys in suits joined them. Had to be TSA or Homeland Security or something like that. They broke into two teams of four and guess what they did?"

"Arrested the two guys?"

"They took them away. I'm guessing someone managed to accuse them of a crime of some sorts and they were hauled away for questioning. Is this your handiwork?"

"Nah. I'm just a constipated kid stuck in the bathroom."

"You want to tell me how you managed that?"

"Later."

"Two more Port Authority cops showed up at gate nine. They talked to an agent—a large woman, looked like she was in charge. Then they went around the waiting areas—with the agent—as though they were looking for someone."

Bobby looked down at his bag. His green fleece protruded from a gap in his duffel bag. He stuffed it inside and zipped the bag shut.

"They're looking for someone who doesn't exist." He checked his watch. "Our flight is boarding. Meet you on the plane."

The two Port Authority cops and the agent from gate nine were searching for him in the corridor, shops, and waiting areas.

None of them even noticed the well-dressed young man that walked by them. He looked like an entitled rich kid from Manhattan, not like a con artist's son from Chornobyl.

CHAPTER 11

NADIA CALLED SIMEON SIMEONOVICH FROM THE PLANE. HE wasn't available so she left a message with his assistant that she would be on a plane for thirteen hours and she would call back.

The Russian oligarch had recently retained Nadia's services as a forensic security analyst to scrub the books of a Ukrainian energy company he wanted to buy. Nadia had travelled to Kyiv on his behalf and met with the company. She'd also investigated Bobby's past during the same trip, and discovered the backstory behind his arrest for murder in New York. That information had helped Johnny win the case.

Simeonovich was forty-two years old, divorced with two young children, and dating a twenty-seven-year-old Russian socialite. Still, they weren't married and Simmy, as his friends called him, was one of the world's most eligible bachelors. He was the opposite of what Nadia had expected—understated and humble. He'd helped Nadia and her brother get out of Ukraine when they'd feared for their lives. Simmy had expressed interest in seeing Nadia again in New York. They'd shared instant chemistry.

Nadia called him again an hour later. She was put on hold for less than ten seconds.

"Where are you?" Simmy said.

"Not sure. Somewhere over Canada?"

"Where are you headed?"

"I'm afraid I have to postpone our dinner plans for Friday night. There's a risk I won't be back home in time and I don't want to cancel at the last minute."

"That's very thoughtful of you. I appreciate the call. It leaves me with a bit of a problem, though."

"I know. You said you were looking at a new company. You need an analyst. If you can wait twenty-four hours, I'll know more about my immediate availability. I still might be back in New York by Friday. If not, I'd be happy to recommend someone else."

"Whoever it is you have in mind, that person won't do."

"How can you be so sure?"

"What are the odds this person will pick up a menu and know better than I do what I want for dinner?"

Nadia always started out the conversation with business, and secretly hoped he'd twist it into flirtation. "You never know," she said. "Someone else might do an even better job than I did in Lviv. Imagine the implications if that person were a man."

"The implications would be that I'd leave the restaurant hungry."

"Why's that?"

"Because I'd be asking for the check right away and getting out of there as fast as I could."

"That's understandable. We all react to temptation in our own individual ways."

"How dare you . . ." He laughed. "You are so insolent sometimes. Nobody else talks to me like that. If you were working for me on an assignment right now, I would fire you for that."

"That would be unhealthy."

"Why?"

"Because there'd be no one to order dinner for you and you might starve."

"I hate when that happens."

"What? When you starve?"

"No. When I don't have the quickest wit in the room."

"Shall I dumb it down for you?"

"On the contrary. But I'll tell you what you can do for me."

"What's that?"

"Tell me where you're going."

A wave of disappointment washed over her. If only the repartee could have gone on indefinitely. But it couldn't, and now he'd guided the conversation back to where he'd started. Her location. She was tempted to tell him. No, she realized. She wanted to tell him. She'd called to make sure he knew she might not make dinner on Friday. But she'd had a subconscious motive, too. She wanted him to know where she was. Simmy had offices all over the world, including a small one in Tokyo. Nadia had no one to rely on other than Johnny. A motivated billionaire could provide a safety net. The kind only global power and unlimited resources could buy.

Then an image of her father flashed before her, warning her that a Ukrainian should never trust a Russian.

"I'd like to tell you," Nadia said. "But I can't."

"Can't? Or won't?" Simmy hesitated. "Still can't trust the Russian, can you?"

Nadia started to protest.

"That's okay. The oligarch doesn't get love unless he's giving his money away. Then the people adore him. Now. Let's see. You're somewhere over Canada and you're flying for at least thirteen hours."

"That's assuming I told your assistant the truth. I could have made up the amount of time I was going to be in the air just to confuse you."

"No. That wouldn't be your style. You're an honest person. Non-stop to Russia is only nine hours. Europe is even shorter. India is a bit longer . . ."

"Sometimes the fog is so heavy over San Francisco, it takes twice as long to get there."

"Very funny. Africa is about right, but what personal business could you possibly have there? The Middle East is also the right distance. That's a possibility. And then there's Asia. Japan, Hong Kong, China."

"I've always wanted to go on safari."

"I'm intrigued. You know I love a good mystery."

"I'm pleased you're pleased."

"I have offices in Beijing, Tokyo, and Dubai. Granted, they are small offices. Mostly consisting of two men, one local, one of mine. But my men are capable. They speak the local languages. If I can be of any assistance, you have my cell phone."

His words carried an ominous foreboding. The last time Simmy had offered her his assistance, she'd ended up being chased by killers through the Priest's Grotto, an underground network of gypsum caves in western Ukraine.

"I'm sure I won't need any help, but it's incredibly kind of you to offer."

Nadia meant what she said, except for the first part.

She wasn't sure of anything at all.

CHAPTER 12

———— ❄ ————

Luo waited outside the Kryzhynka skating rink in the Olympic National Sports Complex in central Kyiv. The sun shone on a brisk Tuesday morning. A wind whipped Luo's face. It was April in Kyiv, the equivalent of summer in Siberia. Normally such weather didn't faze him in the least. This morning, however, he couldn't get warm for some reason. Every time he tried to find a spot in the sun, some students from the Kyiv Sports Institute would gather to chat and cast a shadow on him.

He'd spoken to the detectives investigating the murder of Ksenia Melnik, the woman listed as Adam Tesla's emergency contact. After contributing a thousand hryvnia to their retirement funds, the detectives confirmed it was a robbery-homicide. Ksenia Melnik's son had hidden in the closet and placed an emergency call to the police from his cell phone. But the perpetrators escaped before the cops arrived, taking the woman's cash, sterling silver tea set, and rare book collection.

After speaking with the detectives, Luo tried to meet with the dead woman's son but he refused to let him into the apartment. Said he didn't care to meet with any old friends of his mother. Told him to go away or he'd open the door and give him a beating he'd never forget. Luo had a mind to teach the boy some manners, but restrained himself. His sole purpose in life was never far from his mind.

The treasure. Nothing mattered except finding the treasure.

A rowdy group of six young men burst out of the Sports Complex. They carried equipment bags and hockey sticks. Luo recognized Ksenia Melnik's son, Denys, from his picture on the Western Ukrainian Amateur Hockey League website. He was an eighteen-year-old defenseman for the Hockey Club Express. The season had ended in March. The website said that he lived with his mother in Kyiv.

Not anymore.

Luo walked up to the gang and blocked their path. Hockey was popular in Siberia and Luo had played as a teen. There were even two professional teams now. When he was growing up, the Russian version was a cerebral game with an emphasis on skills and tactics. But the North American style had influenced Russian play, and now there was a violent edge to the game.

As a result, Luo wasn't surprised to see the young men's faces tighten when he obstructed their path. Two of them closed their fists. Luo hadn't even stated his business and yet they'd already revealed themselves. Physically strong, mentally weak.

He handed Denys a business card. "I'm Luo Davidov," he said. He'd made up the last name yesterday at the printer's shop. "I'm a scout with Donbas-2."

Donbas-2 was a professional hockey team from Eastern Ukraine. They were the reigning champions of the Ukrainian Professional Hockey League, and a gateway to the national team, which competed in international events. Every amateur dreamed of playing for Donbas-2.

Denys took the card and stared at it as though it were a notification of a large inheritance.

"May I speak with you in private?" Luo said.

"Sure," Denys said. He glanced at his friends with a mixture of shock and expectation. This was the moment he'd been waiting for his entire life, he seemed to be saying.

Luo led the way onto the sidewalk and around the corner toward the parking lot behind the stadium. They sat down on two empty soda crates near the rear entrance.

"We've been tracking your progress," Luo said.

"You have?" Denys said.

"Yes. Just last week I was talking to Wayne Gretzky about you." Gretzky, widely considered to be the best hockey player ever, was of Ukrainian descent.

"*The* Wayne Gretzky?"

"What? There's more than one?"

"No, I mean, I . . ."

Luo pretended to listen as he pulled his boomerang out of his knapsack. It was different from the version he'd used to herd reindeer as a child. The wings were made of steel and honed to a sharp edge.

He slammed the sharp edge across Denys's left boot, aiming for the line where the toes met the foot.

A thunk was followed by the sound of metal on metal.

Denys screamed.

Luo pulled the boomerang out of his boot. "Steel toe?"

Denys stood up. Fury and fear crossed his face. "What the hell?"

Luo pointed the boomerang. "Sit down or I'll kill you as you stand."

"Who are you?"

"I'm the guy you wouldn't talk to yesterday. I'm the guy you're going to talk to today."

Denys pretended to seethe some more to prove he wasn't intimidated. But he was. He knew better than to run or raise his hand to Luo.

He sat down instead. "Talk about what?"

"Tell me in your own words what happened last night."

Denys repeated the story he'd told the police.

"I've heard all that. Now I need to hear what you didn't tell the police."

"I told the police everything."

Luo lifted an old coffee cup from the ground with his left hand. He sliced it in half with a flick of his wrist.

"I doubt it," Luo said. "The police can't be trusted. They just want the case to go away. There was no reason for you to be honest with them. But there are reasons for you to be honest with me. Don't you think?"

Melnik's eyes remained on the boomerang. "There were two of them."

"How did they get in?"

"I don't know. I was lying in bed listening to music on my headphones. Next thing I knew I heard a scream. I got up and looked out the door and saw two guys with guns. Maybe they conned her into opening the door by saying it was an emergency. Maybe she needed to take out the garbage and they were waiting outside."

"What did they look like?"

"They looked like businessmen. Except one of the men had a ring on his finger. It was gold with a black jewel in the center. In the form of the letter *Z*."

The ring didn't sound familiar. "Did this ring mean something to you?"

"Yeah. My mother once showed me a book with a picture of seven men. Actually, it was six men and a woman. All wearing the same ring. She said if a man with that ring ever approached me I was to avoid him at all costs."

"What book?"

"It was a rare book on hunting. It was in the shelves with the others. They took them. The men who killed my mother."

"Did your mother say how she came to know about these people?"

"No. I just assumed they were powerful men. The type of men who could do whatever they wanted. The kind of men you hear about but don't talk about. At least not out loud."

"What did you hear them say to your mother?"

Melnik appeared surprised. "How did you know I heard something?"

Luo had no idea if Melnik had heard anything. In his experience, leading questions were the most productive way to uncover secrets. Many people were too anxious or nervous to realize the questions were a trap.

"You just told me," Luo said.

Melnik picked up a pebble. "They asked her about one of Dr. Arkady's patients."

"What patient?"

"A kid. A couple of years younger than me. His name was Adam Tesla."

It was the name Luo had longed to hear. "What did they ask?"

"I didn't hear. I ducked into my closet and called the police."

"Did you know Adam Tesla?"

"I knew who he was. We weren't friends or anything like that. I used to see him at Dr. Arkady's office."

"Why was he visiting the doctor?"

"He was getting treated for acute radiation syndrome. Him and the girl."

"Girl?" Luo's pulse picked up. "What girl?"

"Her name was Eva. I don't remember her last name. She died. Then Dr. Arkady passed away, too. I never saw Adam Tesla again."

"What else do you know about this Eva?"

Denys tossed the pebble and shrugged. "Nothing."

"Did you hear your mother say anything?"

Denys took a deep breath. He pulled his shoulders back. A

locket revealed its shape from beneath the fabric of his shirt. It was hanging from a necklace around his neck.

"Japan," he said.

Luo frowned. "Come again?"

"'Japan.' I heard my mother say, 'You'll find what you're looking for in Fukushima, Japan,' and then they killed her." Denys stared at Luo with a blank look. "Happiest moment of my life."

CHAPTER 13

———— ❄ ————

JOHNNY LED NADIA AND BOBBY ALONG THE STREETS OF Shibuya toward a low-key shabu-shabu restaurant, where customers cooked their own dinners on a skillet at the table. They'd left New York on Tuesday and arrived in Tokyo Wednesday afternoon. Johnny's jet lag had vanished from the moment he'd laid eyes on Nadia. His gut told him she was in more danger than either of them knew, but at least the three of them were together.

Nadia and Johnny walked close together so their conversation couldn't be overheard. They let Bobby get a few steps ahead of them so they could keep an eye on him. He gaped and gawked at the people and the neon lights.

"We were followed from my apartment to the airport," Nadia said. She told him how Bobby duped airport security into taking the men into custody.

Johnny wasn't surprised by the kid's balls or skills. The backstory to his murder accusation had established he was no ordinary seventeen-year-old. "Who were they?"

"Don't know," Nadia said. "They looked straight out of central casting for Russian or Uke mafia types. Right off the streets of Moscow or Kyiv. But when things look one way, they're often another."

"Yeah, but in this case, given Bobby's from Ukraine and you guys spent all that time there, odds are high they are what they look like. Which leaves only one question."

"Who do they work for?"

"Exactly."

Nadia shook her head. "You got me."

"Could it be someone who knows about the formula?"

Nadia thought about the question. "Johnny, at this point, it could be anyone. Bobby and I had the same conversation about the source of the e-mail, the person who called himself Genesis II. We shouldn't make any assumptions. When we assume, we create a bias that can prevent us from seeing the truth."

Johnny chuckled. "You sound like a lawyer."

"Heaven forbid."

They walked quietly for ten more minutes until they arrived at the restaurant. It was packed and noisy. Johnny looked around for suspicious characters, especially Caucasians, but didn't see any. If locals were following them, he wouldn't know it.

Nadia's phone rang while they were perusing the pictures on the menu. She lowered her voice and turned away. It was a quick exchange but enough to put a healthy glow on her face.

"How's your Russian sweetheart?" Johnny said.

Nadia fired a quick glance at Bobby. She frowned at Johnny as though he'd embarrassed her. "He's my client, not my sweetheart, sweetheart."

"What did he want?"

"Nothing."

"Nothing?"

"It's a game. It's silly. He's trying to figure out where I am. And how did you know it was him on the phone?"

"You were blushing. You know, the way a woman does when she's talking to any old client."

Nadia blushed some more. Johnny savored the victory until he realized he was losing the war. She didn't blush like that in his presence, and he didn't play silly games. He was too busy solving her problems and trying to keep her and Bobby alive.

They ordered plates of beef and exotic Japanese vegetables. Johnny's phone rang while they were waiting for their food. He recognized the voice from the bar.

"Are they with you?" Nakamura said.

"Yes," Johnny said.

"Let me talk to her."

Johnny handed his phone to Nadia. "He wants to talk to you."

Nadia leaned in close to Johnny so they both could listen without using the speakerphone. "Hello?" she said.

"Is your cousin with you?" Nakamura said.

Nadia took her time answering. "Maybe."

"Ask him what Dr. Arkady used to give him when he was done with treatments."

Nadia glanced at Johnny. Johnny shrugged and nodded. Nadia repeated the question to Bobby.

"Marzipan," Bobby said.

Nadia repeated his answer into the phone.

"You brought the locket?" Nakamura said.

Johnny glanced at Bobby. The locket was in its original place, hanging on a necklace around his neck, hidden beneath his turtleneck. Nadia had told Johnny that they'd photocopied the engravings and left copies at home and in a sealed envelope with the professor from Columbia. She'd given him instructions to disseminate the contents of the envelope to the scientific press if she and Bobby suffered fatal accidents during their trip or disappeared. If the second locket did contain the rest of the formula, she wanted the world to know about it.

"Yes," Nadia said. "We brought the locket. Are you going to bring yours?"

"Put Mr. Johnny Tanner back on the phone."

Johnny leaned in. "I'm here."

"Tomorrow. Ten-thirty a.m. There's a hot springs resort called

Higashiyama Onsen. It's in a town called Aizuwakamatsu. It's a three-hour train ride from Tokyo. Three and a half hours by bus. There's a café near the lobby. Tell the maître d' you're waiting for me. He'll get me."

"Why do we need to go there? Why can't we just stay in Tokyo?"

"Because I am not in Tokyo anymore."

"Why did you leave Tokyo?"

"Because I'm a working man," Nakamura said. "The nuclear reactors in Fukushima prefecture are located in Okuma and Futaba. Okuma and Futaba are at the epicenter of the twenty-kilometer Zone of Exclusion. Radiation levels are severe. No humans are allowed in the Zone. They are ghost towns. Aizuwakamatsu contains the largest settlement of refugees from Okuma. That is why I will be there. And that is where Genesis II will be."

CHAPTER 14

NADIA STARED OUT THE WINDOW OF THE AIZU LOOP BUS.
Water gathered steam down a river and plunged over rocks.
It pooled in a basin and rolled slowly along flat terrain. Then it
fell in shining twenty-foot-long sheets to another tier. The process repeated itself along four successive drops to the bottom of
the waterfall. From there fury turned to foam that gradually
merged into a gentle stream.

She'd left the hotel with Bobby and Johnny at 7:30 a.m. on
Thursday morning. They'd taken a bullet train along the Tohoku-
Shinkansen line from Tokyo to Koriyama Station and transferred
to a regular one along the Banetsu-sai line. The trip to Aizuwaka-
matsu took a little more than three hours. The Aizu loop bus took
an additional fifteen minutes. It dropped them off at Ryokan
Higashino at 10:55 a.m.

An air of tranquility engulfed Nadia when she stepped off
the bus. Nakamura was a genius. He'd chosen a perfect location
for the meet. A hot springs resort. A place of reflection and con-
templation that would defuse tension.

A *ryokan* was a traditional Japanese inn, Nadia learned. This
one looked tired and run down. Some of the wood shingles needed
repair. A woman in a blue kimono with a red sash across her mid-
section greeted the three of them in an entrance area. Johnny said

a few words in Japanese that ended with "Nakamura-san." The woman bowed and said something to Johnny, who returned the bow and smiled.

They took their shoes off and followed the woman down a maze of corridors to a steel door. The woman opened the door, bowed, and stepped aside. Nadia followed Johnny and Bobby into another corridor with rooms on each side and another door at the end. A second woman in a kimono placed three small canvas bags on the floor.

She slammed the door shut behind them. Darkness enveloped them.

Nadia rushed forward and tried to open it. The doorknob didn't budge. She tried with both hands. Nothing.

"Locked," she said.

Johnny tried to open it but couldn't. "You've got to be kidding me."

"Our shoes," Bobby said. He pulled his hiking boots from one of the canvas bags. The other two bags contained Nadia's and Johnny's shoes.

An engine rumbled nearby. Tires rolled toward the door at the end of the corridor. Brakes screeched.

Metal slid against metal. It was the sound of a sliding door opening. Another metallic sound came from the door. A key slipping into a hole. A deadbolt snapped open. A second key slid into place.

The door swung open into the interior of a truck. It was hugging the back of the building.

A slender Japanese man stood inside the truck. Stacks of linen were piled high behind him. Three large gray rucksacks rested beside the linen. The interior smelled of fresh produce. Leaves spilled from the cracks of a crate.

"I am Nakamura," he said, bowing in front of them.

Nadia recognized the name Nakamura, but the man looked far older than the one Johnny had described.

"Please get in truck," he said. "We must go quickly."

Johnny said, "Who are you exactly?"

"Nakamura Hiroshi."

"You're not the Hiroshi Nakamura I know," Johnny said. "But you do look like him . . ."

"I am his father, the owner of this hotel, and we are late. To truck, please. My son is waiting for you. Every minute is most important."

They climbed into the truck and sat down on a bench nailed to the floor along the driver's side of the van's interior. Nakamura climbed through the cabin into the driver's seat and took off. He never opened the door. He never stepped outside.

He shifted into gear and drove onto an access road behind the inn.

"Where are we going?" Nadia said.

"To meet my son."

"Why couldn't he meet us himself?" Johnny said.

"It was not convenient."

"Why not?" Nadia said.

Nakamura thought about this for a moment. "You will understand when you see him."

He followed the same path the bus had taken in reverse, and then merged onto a thoroughfare headed east.

"How long have you owned the inn?" Nadia said.

"I bought the inn and moved to Higashiyama Onsen last year. Before that I lived with my wife in Minamisoma. You know Minamisoma?"

"No," Johnny said. "What prefecture?"

"Fukushima prefecture. You remember the three-eleven earthquake and tsunami?"

"Three-eleven?" Nadia said.

"The Great East Japan Earthquake," Nakamura said. "We call it the three-eleven earthquake. It happened on three—eleven—eleven. March 11, 2011."

"We remember," Johnny said.

"Who can forget the pictures," Nadia said.

"Those pictures do not tell the entire story. To understand the three-eleven earthquake, you must first understand the Ring of Fire."

"Ring of Fire?" Nadia said.

"Yes. Japan has been the battlefield for a world war for centuries and it has been slowly losing the battle. The three-eleven earthquake. It was inevitable."

"What world war?" Johnny said.

"The one being fought beneath the sea."

Johnny and Nadia exchanged concerned glances. Perhaps the elder Nakamura was not entirely in control of his mental faculties.

"What war beneath the sea?" Nadia said.

"The war between the Pacific and Atlantic oceans. The surface of Earth is made of crust. The crust is made of plates. They are constantly destroyed and created by underwater volcanoes caused by heat from radioactive decay of Earth. The underwater volcanoes around the Atlantic Ocean do battle with the Pacific Ocean. One ocean get larger, other ocean get smaller. The Atlantic Ocean is making plates of crust faster than Pacific Ocean. Atlantic Ocean is winning. Pacific Ocean is gradually shrinking. In three hundred million years, there will be no more Pacific Ocean. It will be a mountain.

"Worst of volcanoes run down the center of Japan—like a human being's spine, yes? It cause earthquakes and tsunamis more and more dangerous over time. That is why geologists call Japan the Ring of Fire. The three-eleven earthquake. It was inevitable. Because of the Ring of Fire."

Johnny said, "What did you do for a living before you bought the inn, Nakamura-san?"

"I was a physics professor," he said. "But geology. It makes me very fascinated. On the day of the great earthquake, one of the plates under Japan snapped upward. It caused the Japanese island of Honshu to move eight feet closer to America, and four hundred kilometers of the coastline of Japan to drop two feet. This caused a magnitude nine earthquake. It lasted for six minutes and released six hundred million times more energy than the bomb that fell on Hiroshima. Two days later volcanoes exploded on Japanese island of Kyushu and in Antarctica. And planet Earth started rotating almost one second faster."

"Where were you when the earthquake hit?" Johnny said.

"I was in Tokyo lecturing at a university. Japan has an advanced warning system for earthquake. That system gave us one minute warning. At first everyone thought it was just another earthquake. The students carry cell phones. They were communicating with each other on the social media. On Twitter. Before the earthquake, I did not know what Twitter was. Now everyone in Japan knows Twitter. The twitters started getting more frantic. A student shared a picture of his parents' house collapsing. Another showed a woman hugging the ground for support. Then it hit us. Computers started to slide off desks. Skyscrapers started swaying like rocking chairs. The next six minutes felt like six hours. The only way we could tell when the earthquake stopped was when the ceiling fan stopped swaying."

"How did everyone get home?" Bobby said.

"People walked. Elevators, trains, buses, and cars. They all stopped. Tens of thousands of people walked home. There was no traffic. They walked in streets. They walked calmly. There was no running. There was no panic. From the first moment there was Japanese solidarity. An unspoken understanding that we would get through this together. Only when we got home did we realize exactly what was happening to our country. Roads cracked and disappeared under the Earth. Cars and houses were thrown like toys."

"How long until the tsunami started?" Johnny said.

"Within an hour, a tsunami washed away Sendai Airport along the eastern coastline. Cars and planes were swept away. A camera from a helicopter caught a picture of a driver trying to steer his vehicle away from the wave. He was swallowed whole. The waves were black. Black like night. Entire towns were washed away. I was in my hotel room in Tokyo, just sitting and trembling. Finally I got the message from wife that she had arrived at her cousin's house in the mountains."

"Ah," Nadia said. "Your wife wasn't travelling with you."

Nakamura appeared pensive in the rearview mirror. "'I am safe,' she said. 'I have made it to higher ground.' I can remember the relief. I can remember sending my son a note that his mother was safe."

Nadia was about to say thank goodness, but stopped herself. Nakamura's words spoke of a happy ending, but there his tone was too somber.

"It turned out I spoke too quickly," Nakamura said. "High ground was not high enough. No one had ever imagined a tsunami of this force. No one ever imagined waves thirty-nine meters high."

Nadia had used the metric system so much during her two trips to Eastern Europe she could do the numbers in her head. "A hundred thirty feet," she said.

"And so the *salary men* in Tokyo who thought their wives would be safe in the mountains discovered that they were the safer ones," Nakamura said. "The skyscrapers were built to survive an earthquake, but the mountain was not tall enough to withstand the tsunami."

"We're very sorry for your loss," Nadia said.

Nakamura merged into the right lane to exit.

"Life is suffering," he said.

"*Ganbaro*, Nakamura-san," Johnny said, "*So desne*?"

Nakamura's eyes lit up with appreciation. "Yes," he said, with a quick bow to the rearview mirror. "*Ganbarimashou*."

Johnny glanced alternately at Nadia and Bobby. "It's a special phrase in the Japanese language," he said. "It means stay strong, stand tall. Keep fighting."

"Kyoto operates on a different electric grid than Tokyo," Nakamura said. "The people in Kyoto were much less affected than in other parts of Japan. Still, they conserved electricity to donate to relief efforts. There was wind, snow, and rain in Kyoto after the earthquake, but there were no cherry blossoms that year. People smiled less. But they woke up from complacency. Adversity reminded us how to be strong as a nation. The aftershocks only strengthened our resolve."

"Aftershocks?" Bobby said.

"More earthquakes," Nakamura said. "Two measuring 7.7 and 7.9 within a month. Eighteen hundred more measuring 4.0 or higher within a year."

"Almost two thousand earthquakes?" Bobby said.

"Yes," Nakamura said. They drove quietly for half an hour until Nakamura spoke again.

"There are three gray satchels beside linen," he said. "You will find personal protective equipment inside. Please put them on."

They opened the bags. Each one contained white overalls, shoes, rubber gloves, plastic goggles, and a respirator.

A bolt of anxiety wracked Nadia. "Hazmat suits?"

"Yes. Radiation suits."

"Why do we need radiation suits?" Johnny said.

"My son can explain. We will be meeting him soon. Please to prepare. You do not need to put breathing equipment on yet. My son will show you how."

They put their suits on.

Ten minutes later Nakamura turned into an empty gas stand, drove past the pumps, and accelerated around to the back. A small parking lot backed up to a wooded lot. Two jalopies sat rusting in the lot beside a garbage Dumpster. A crisp white van sat idling beside the old cars. Japanese lettering covered the side of the van. Beneath it was the English translation. Global Medical Corps.

A younger man resembling Nakamura sat behind the driver's seat.

"That's him," Johnny said.

The younger Nakamura opened the door and emerged before his father could back into the space beside his van. The elder Nakamura directed them toward the rear door, which would keep them hidden from the front of the gas stand. The younger Nakamura opened the rear door and introduced himself to Nadia and Bobby.

"Into the back of my van," he said. "Quickly, please."

"Where are you taking us?" Nadia said. She held her purse in one hand, a respirator in the other. She knew the answer to the question. Given the equipment they'd been asked to wear, there was little doubt about where they were going. Still, the question had to be asked.

"To meet with Genesis II," Nakamura said.

"Where is the meeting?" Johnny said.

"In a place that guarantees us total privacy and safety. In the No-Go Zone."

Nadia remembered the blown reactor, radioactive red forest, and ghost town of Pripyat.

"In the Zone of Exclusion."

CHAPTER 15

———— ❄ ————

THE THOUGHT OF ENTERING ANOTHER ZONE OF EXCLU-
sion—another radioactive ghost town—might have made
someone with Bobby's experiences anxious. To Bobby's own surprise, it didn't. From the moment the old man had told them where
they were going, a strange fascination gripped him. How would the
two radioactive ghost towns compare? Would he see signs that reminded him of Chornobyl, or would it be completely different? The
more he thought about it, the more he couldn't wait to get there.

The old man left in his truck. Nadia, Johnny, and Bobby followed Dr. Nakamura into the back of the van. He closed the door
and handed out shortwave radios with earpieces. They were very
cool, something the KGB would have used in the old days when
they were tailing suspected spies. Then the doctor showed them
how to wear their respirators. Technology had improved. They
made the old rubber gas masks Bobby had found piled high in an
abandoned Chornobyl classroom look like alien body parts.
Vented cups and mouthpieces fit snugly over his nose and mouth.
At first they felt a little claustrophobic, but adrenaline washed
away the sensation.

Once they were comfortable with the respirators, Dr. Nakamura told them to take them off for the next leg of the trip. Nadia
sat in the front in the passenger seat. Johnny and Bobby sat in the

second row of seats. Dr. Nakamura guided the van back onto the main road and headed further east toward the coast of Japan.

"We have a half-hour drive to the checkpoint at the Exclusion Zone. I'm sorry I couldn't pick you up myself but I had to get this van. And I couldn't have you show up at the Global Medical building. That's why I had to ask my father for a favor. I had to have him drive you out here. We had you go out the back door at the inn straight into the truck just in case someone was following you. Per Genesis II's request."

"I presume the checkpoint is guarded," Nadia said.

"Yes."

"Will the guards ask us for ID?" Johnny said.

"They know me, and I usually have someone with me. There's a slight risk because there are three of you this time, but I don't think it will be a problem."

"I could pose as a journalist if that would help," Nadia said. "I've done it twice before with good success."

"No," Dr. Nakamura said. "That would not help. That would not help at all."

"You make it sound like it might actually put us at risk."

"It would accomplish the opposite of what you are hoping. It would make you extremely unpopular and draw immediate attention to you."

Nadia appeared shocked. "Why?"

"Because the earthquake and tsunami changed perceptions of foreign media forever. The only reliable sources of information were social media. Facebook. Twitter. Elder generations who didn't know what the words meant grew to rely on them for timely, accurate, and objective updates. The foreign press was all about headlines. It made the disaster sound worse than it actually was. It painted a hopeless situation. Made it sound as though the apocalypse was arriving. Japan was already communing and rebuilding while the rest of the world was still watching a train wreck."

"Good to know," Nadia said. "My primary alter ego is worthless in Japan."

"If they ask, I'll tell them you're volunteers. If they see your faces they might ask questions because the volunteers are mostly college students. So when we are two minutes away, I will ask you to put your breathing equipment back on. It will hide your faces. The guards won't ask you to take it off. They don't know who's been exposed to radiation. They don't want any contact with you. So we should be okay."

"I don't understand something," Bobby said.

Nakamura raised his eyebrows and tilted his ear toward the back seat.

"If there are no people in the Zone of Exclusion, why would anyone need a doctor? How could anyone need treatment or medical supplies, when there's no one to treat?"

"Officially," Dr. Nakamura said, "there are no people living in the Zone of Exclusion. But unofficially . . ."

Just like Chornobyl, Bobby thought. "There are squatters."

Dr. Nakamura frowned. "Squatters?"

"People who've come back to live in their homes even though they're not supposed to," Bobby said.

"Yes. The woman we are visiting today does not have long to live. She insisted she wants to spend her final days in her own home. The government allowed her to go back, but kept it quiet so they did not set a bad example for other people who are not seriously ill and simply want to return. I help take care of the woman."

"You and who else?" Nadia said.

"Another doctor alternates days with me. And there are a few volunteers who take turns staying with her overnight. Last night, it was a certain volunteer you want to meet."

Soon they would know if there was a complete formula. Soon Bobby's curiosity would be satisfied regarding the second boy's identity. Was he Japanese, Ukrainian, or something entirely different?

They stopped at a gas stand along the way to use the restrooms. Two minutes before arriving at the checkpoint, they put on their respirators. A series of red and white cones appeared on the road ahead. Six men dressed in black coats and pants milled around a mobile home. One of them marched into the middle of the street and lowered a red flag. It contained three Japanese characters. The word "Stop" was written in English below them.

The guard walked around toward the driver's side. He scanned the car's interior. The other guards stopped chatting. They stood by the mobile home and watched. Bobby was surprised they weren't carrying rifles. In Ukraine, the guards at the Zone carried rifles. But these guards wore black coats that fell between their hips and knees. Bobby guessed they had weapons concealed beneath them. Maybe that was the Japanese way. In Ukraine, everything was in your face. Success, failure, honor, corruption. Even guns. From what he'd read in his guidebook on the plane, the Japanese liked to keep a civil face, and keep their emotions hidden beneath the surface. Apparently they liked to keep their guns hidden as well.

A truck rolled up to the checkpoint from the opposite side. It was headed out of the Zone. The driver and his passenger wore blue hazmat suits. The guard took one look at it and waved it through.

Dr. Nakamura rolled down his window. He exchanged some rapid-fire dialogue with the guard. There was some nodding, smiling, and pleasant-sounding conversation. It was clear by their exchange the guard and Dr. Nakamura knew each other.

The guard glanced in the back of the van. He gave Johnny, Nadia, and Bobby a quick once-over and let them through. They drove past the other guards along the main road. A cityscape awaited them ahead.

"Welcome to the city of Okuda," Dr. Nakamura said. "Welcome to the Zone of Exclusion."

The words fascinated Bobby. He'd never imagined they'd be spoken anywhere but in Pripyat. But now here he was, in another

Zone. Another nuclear ghost town. It was as remarkable to him that human beings had allowed such an accident to happen. Didn't anyone pay attention to what happened in Chornobyl? Didn't people understand that what could go wrong with nuclear power would eventually go wrong, no matter how small the odds?

No, he thought. And they still didn't. Not even after Fukushima. No one wanted to understand. People were lazy. They didn't like to change. It cost too much money and effort.

They approached the town. The road resembled a hastily constructed jigsaw puzzle. Appliances lay scattered along a patch of land. Bobby couldn't count all the rice cookers. They must have been washed away by the wave. Refrigerators, televisions, and microwave ovens. He had once scavenged the junkyards of Chornobyl for anything that could be sold on the black market. The refrigerators would have motors. Some of the microwaves might still work. Plenty to scavenge here. Plenty of money for the making.

They drove into town. Empty shops, homes, and restaurants packed block after block. Some had been reduced to rubble. Many were partially damaged, with blown-out windows and caved-in roofs. Others stood untouched and abandoned. Electric wires ran along the side of the street, still in place high along poles. Traffic lights blinked yellow at intersections.

The scene mesmerized Bobby. The town dwarfed Pripyat, made it look like a college campus that had been overtaken by the wilderness. This was a twenty-first-century city turned ghost town. Pripyat was so overgrown one didn't expect to see humans. Here one held his breath expecting someone to step out of a door any minute. But no one did. To Bobby, Okuda cast an eerier spell than Pripyat. It was a modern town in a wealthy country, which made its emptiness all the more stark and remarkable.

They came across eight folding chairs lined up in the middle of the street. One of the chairs had been kicked over. The rest looked as though they were waiting for their owners to come out of the nearby coffee shop with cups of green tea. Dr. Nakamura drove onto the sidewalk to pass them. The chairs had been left by people who'd waited until the last second, Bobby thought. People who didn't want to leave their properties regardless of the risks, and were forced to evacuate by the government. There had been plenty of those in Chornobyl, too.

And then there were the animals. Cats sat in windows by themselves, or prowled the alleys in groups. A dog dug through a garbage can. A pair of cows stood at an intersection beneath a red traffic light. They looked lost and hopeless. They refused to move until Dr. Nakamura sounded his horn. Two blocks further up the road, a horse ran around the corner and disappeared.

They turned right. A sign said they were headed toward the Fukushima Daiichi Nuclear Power Plant.

"The power plant was built too close to the sea," Dr. Nakamura said. "The tsunami flooded the generators that provide the power to the pumps. The pumps that sent cooling waters to the reactors. When the pumps failed, the only thing that would have prevented the reactors from melting down was seawater. But the government hesitated because the seawater would ruin the reactors, which were very expensive to build. By the time they changed their minds and flooded the reactors with seawater, three reactors had full meltdown."

"Government men," Bobby said. "Never trust government men."

"I wouldn't have said this before the nuclear disaster," Dr. Nakamura said. "But you may be right. The situation in Fukushima today is far worse than the outside world knows. In a few minutes, I will show you. Once you have seen with your eyes, all will be clear. Then we will meet with Genesis II."

CHAPTER 16

NADIA CRANED HER NECK AS NAKAMURA STOPPED ALONG an elevated road above the Fukushima Daiichi Nuclear Power Plant. It looked like an industrial city unto itself. It was divided into two sections. The part furthest inland stood on higher ground. It consisted of several office buildings. A football-field-sized parking lot contained twenty to thirty cars.

The area beyond the office buildings stretched for half a mile to the sea. Cranes, communication towers, and water tanks stood on the horizon. A web of dirt roads surrounded them. Six rectangular buildings stood amidst the cranes. Four of the buildings looked like they'd been stripped to their metal studs.

"Are those the reactors?" Nadia said.

"Yes." Nakamura pulled out binoculars and handed them to her. "Reactors one, two, and three were the ones that experienced full meltdown. The Fukushima reactors released eighty-five times the amount of cesium as the reactor in Chornobyl. But it is our reactor four that is the main concern today."

Nakamura told her to count four rectangular buildings from the left.

Nadia looked through the binoculars. "I see a half-melted pile of iron in the shape of what used to be a building." She shifted her focus to the sides of the reactor. "With some sort of support beams on the sides."

"The support columns were added later to keep the building intact," Nakamura said. "It's the iron you see in the middle of the building that's the problem."

"Why?" Nadia said.

"That iron consists of one thousand, five hundred and thirty-two spent nuclear fuel rods. They are surrounded by cooling waters thirty meters above the ground. You just can't see the water from here."

Nadia stared at the exposed, radioactive rods. "How can that be? They're uncovered. Open to the air."

"Yes," Nakamura said. "They're just sitting there. Waiting for disaster to strike again."

Nadia couldn't believe her eyes. Even the Soviet Union knew better. They'd dumped a gazillion tons of sand over the reactor and then built a metal tomb around it. Granted, the tomb was less than robust and it was falling apart now and in the process of being replaced, but at least they'd followed a path of common sense.

Bobby asked her for the binoculars and took a look himself. "No sarcophagus," he said. He, too, sounded incredulous. "Why is there no sarcophagus?"

"The response of the people of Japan to the earthquake, tsunami, and nuclear disaster has been strength and solidarity. The response of the government to the cleanup and nuclear risk has been weakness and cronyism. Cleanup efforts have been given to large Japanese corporations that have no experience with nuclear matters. Small companies and foreign companies were encouraged to make proposals. None were accepted.

"On July 22, 2013, more than two years after the disaster, the government finally confirmed what local fisherman had been saying all along. The plant was leaking radioactive water into the Pacific Ocean since the tsunami. It took all that time for the government to admit that TEPCO—Tokyo Electric Power—was still lying about plant conditions. The Prime Minister ordered the government to step in. A month later, seven hundred metric tons leaked out of a storage tank and they stepped in to secure that, too.

"If the building crumbles for any reason, if it is weaker than the government says, if there is another earthquake of a magnitude seven or higher, the water would pour out, the fuel rods would burn, and you would have an oxygen-eating fire that could not be put out with water. That would lead to the kind of contamination science has never contemplated. It could make Japan uninhabitable, and with the oceans and wind, lead to global disaster."

"The kind the Western press predicted," Nadia said.

"This time," Nakamura said, "they would be right. Emergency workers would not be able to get close to the fire. Robots would melt. There would be no immediate solution to putting out the fire. Radiation would leak into the air and sea and could not be stopped."

"Why don't they move the rods to someplace safe?" Bobby said.

"They cannot dislodge the individual rods. It is too dangerous. The only way to move them is to move the entire fuel rod canister."

Bobby's voice picked up urgency. "Then why don't they do it?"

"It would take a crane that can lift one hundred tons. The only crane that could do that was destroyed in the disaster. This is the truth. These are the stakes. This is what Genesis II wanted you to understand. This is how important the formula may soon be to Japan. To the entire world. We must not let personal agendas get in the way of the greater good."

Nadia remembered the original e-mail from Genesis II, and the phrase that sounded so familiar. "Fate of the free world," she said.

"Yes," Nakamura said. "If reactor number four collapses, the fate of Japan and the world will depend on this formula."

Fate of the free world now had two meanings. Initially it suggested that if the wrong people got their hands on it, they could use it to gain an upper hand in a nuclear confrontation. Now it also referred to the imminent risk of an epic nuclear catastrophe in Japan, one that could destroy the world. With each passing moment, the formula's importance was growing, just as surely as the people who came in contact with it were dying.

"Chornobyl and Fukushima," Nakamura said. "Fukushima and Chornobyl. They are forever linked in history as the only level seven nuclear disasters the world has known. In Chornobyl, it was reactor number four that melted down and caused the first international catastrophe. In Fukushima, it is reactor four that poses the threat of becoming the first global catastrophe. You think this is a meaningless coincidence? The number four is the unluckiest number in Japanese culture."

"It's pronounced *shi*," Johnny said.

Nakamura nodded somberly.

"So?" Nadia said.

"*Shi*," Johnny said, "is also the Japanese word for death."

CHAPTER 17

T HE NEIGHBORHOOD REMINDED NADIA OF HARTFORD. THE owners believed in paint, power washing, and curb appeal. The neatly groomed front yards beckoned for a child and a golden lab. But there was no living thing in sight.

Nakamura parked in front of a yellow ranch-style house. The shades were pulled. Johnny and Bobby carried boxes of food and supplies. Nakamura rang the doorbell. When no one answered, Nakamura opened the door and they went inside. He didn't bother using a key. There was no need for door locks in a ghost town.

They took off their shoes in the foyer and followed Nakamura past a small living room and kitchen into a bedroom. A gray-haired woman lay propped up on pillows on a bed. She smiled at Nadia, Johnny, and Bobby. Said something in Japanese. Nakamura told them to come closer. Although she sounded weak, the woman seemed cheerful.

Nakamura introduced them in Japanese, and translated in English. The woman's name was Yamamoto. Johnny bowed and said a few words in Japanese to her. The woman beamed. She replied in rapid-fire Japanese. Johnny seemed to understand what she said and answered, but got lost in the further exchange. Still, his attempts only increased the cheerfulness of her disposition, and the strangeness of the situation.

Nakamura asked the old woman a question. It started with a word that sounded like *yoshi*. After the woman answered, Nakamura smiled and nodded.

"Genesis II is in the house next door," Nakamura said. "Mrs. Yamamoto owns both properties. Her husband was an airline executive and bought it as an investment many years ago. Mrs. Yamamoto uses it for storage. She accumulated many things during the years she travelled around the world with her husband. She asked Yoshi to go there to retrieve some photo albums for her."

Johnny leaned into Nadia's ear. "Did you hear?"

"Yes."

"Genesis II's name is Yoshi. He's Japanese."

Thoughts swirled around Nadia's head. Chornobyl and Fukushima. Fukushima and Chornobyl. As Nakamura had said, they were forever linked. And now, for reasons she couldn't fathom yet, it appeared the formula shared a similar link. A boy from Ukraine, another from Japan. If that were true, it might confirm her theory that scientists from both countries had worked together to develop a radiation countermeasure. But that was just her own pet theory, she reminded herself. She had no evidence to back it up, and there were countless other explanations.

Nakamura studied the vials of prescription medicine on the nightstand beside a pitcher of water. A remote control with a red button rested beside the phone. It looked like a panic button a patient pressed if she needed immediate assistance. The other nightstand contained a collection of framed photos.

Johnny was studying one of the photos. It showed a pair of young teens holding surfboards, a wave preparing to crash on the shore behind them. When Nakamura finished his conversation with Mrs. Yamamoto, she turned to Johnny and said something.

Johnny smiled. He glanced at Nakamura uncertainly. "Did I hear the word for brother?"

"That is Mrs. Yamamoto and her brother. When they were children. Their grandparents were killed in the American bombing of

Nagasaki in 1945. The nuclear disaster in Fukushima has brought back painful memories for the older generation. At least two hundred thousand people were killed in Hiroshima and Nagasaki from the explosions themselves. Sixty percent of the victims burned to death. Can you picture that? They burned to death. The long-term effects of radiation syndrome followed. Some of the emotional healing that took place is now coming unraveled. There is an unspoken fear that Japan may experience such suffering again."

Johnny studied the picture again. Looked for something positive to say. "Please tell her she and her brother look like good athletes."

Nakamura told her. He listened to her answers and translated. "Her brother was her inspiration until his death last year. He was one of the Fukushima Fifty."

Nadia remembered the newscasts during the nuclear disaster. Fifty TEPCO employees volunteered to stay at the power plant to stop the leakage and prevent further disaster.

"We heard about these great men in America," Johnny said. "I'm sure they did the entire world a great service. We all owe them a debt."

Nakamura translated, and Mrs. Yamamato nodded her appreciation.

"He died from shame," Nakamura said. "The Fukushima Fifty were among the men who stood by as the reactors melted down. They were not prepared for what happened. Some people consider them heroes, but others believe they're to blame for the disaster. When the disaster was finally stopped, credit went to the Prime Minister. It is a very Japanese thing. To let credit rise to the top, and blame fall to the bottom. When the press took photos of the Fukushima Fifty, Yamamoto-san was one of the men who turned his back to the cameras. Out of shame. He died because he wouldn't leave his apartment to go to the pharmacy to get his heart medication. In the end, it was not his illness but his shame that killed him."

Someone screamed.

The sound came from outside the house. It was far enough away to sound muted, but loud enough that its meaning was unmistakable. Someone was in trouble.

Genesis II was in trouble, Nadia thought.

Nakamura and Johnny rushed toward the front door.

A second scream. This one was muffled, as though one person had silenced another.

Nakamura and Johnny burst out of the house. Nadia caught the screen door before it hit her in the face. She flung it open and stepped outside.

A young man struggled to free himself from two burly men. The young man had his back to Nadia. He had short black hair, long legs, and narrow hips.

It was the boy. It was Yoshi. It was Genesis II.

The beefy men wore leather jackets. They looked like the duo that had followed Bobby and her to the airport. The Slavs. They'd found Bobby and her in New York. Now they'd found Genesis II in Fukushima.

A large truck rumbled backward down the street. It stopped. The rear door rolled up. A third man reached out with his hands. The other two men lifted Genesis II off the ground. The third man grasped him by the lapels of his shirt and jacket. The men shouted at each other in Russian over the din of the truck's idling engine. The two men holding Genesis II had their backs to the house. The third man didn't look up until it was too late.

Nakamura lowered his shoulder and rammed one of the men in the chest. The man groaned. Released his grip of Genesis II and doubled over.

The second man on the ground held onto Genesis II. He turned.

Johnny drove his fist into the man's jaw. The man toppled backward against the truck. Johnny reached for Genesis II, but the third man in the truck pulled him up into the cabin and out of Johnny's outstretched hands.

Bobby started toward the truck. Nadia grabbed his arm and stopped him. Shoved him to the ground and sent him rolling on the lawn.

Nakamura put his hands on the bed of the truck to lift himself up. Johnny did the same on the other side. Nakamura had his back to the man he'd hit. He didn't see that the man was recovering and pulling something out from beneath his coat.

"Hiroshi, watch out!" Nadia said.

The man behind Nakamura pulled him to the ground and drove a knife through his throat. Blood spurted. The Russian pulled the knife out, twisted the doctor around, and plunged it into his heart. Nakamura slumped to the asphalt.

The third man stomped on Johnny's hand to prevent him from vaulting into the truck. The killer pulled the knife out of Nakamura's chest. Johnny must have sensed the danger. He dropped down to the ground and faced him.

Nadia ran down the stairs and ripped a boulder out of the stone wall. Sprinted toward the man with the knife. Johnny had removed his belt to defend himself. Nadia would sneak up behind the man with the knife and pummel him in the head—

Something caught her eye on the left in her peripheral vision.

A fourth man was sprinting around from the back of the house. Who was he? He must have been there all along, covering the back entrance. Knife in his right hand. Overhand grip.

Nadia threw the boulder at him. It bounced off his chest.

He closed in with shocking speed. Running was useless.

He would be upon her in seconds.

CHAPTER 18

J OHNNY GRIPPED THE ENDS OF HIS BELT IN EACH HAND. He made circles with his wrists, gathered the leather around them, and pulled the belt tight.

The man with the knife assumed a fighting stance. Legs bent, left foot in front of the right. He held the knife in his fist, blade down. He moved his hands in a circular motion, bobbed and weaved on the balls of his feet. His movements were precise. His eyes shone with intensity and confidence. He was trained. Experienced. Ex-military, Johnny thought.

Johnny had grown up a street fighter in Newark. A street fighter always had a chance. Especially when there were no guns involved. And if the Russians had guns he'd already be dead. But they weren't on home turf. And they hadn't been in town long enough to get them.

The man threw a left jab. Johnny deflected it with his left arm. The man circled and jabbed two more times. Johnny pushed his arm aside.

The man lunged with the knife.

Johnny stepped back. The knife came up short of his heart. A stab of fear energized his countermove. He brought the belt under the man's wrist. Pulled up. The man resisted but Johnny gritted his teeth and pulled harder. He told himself he was stronger than the other guy. *All those years in the gym.* When the man groaned and stood his ground, Johnny commanded himself to insist he was stronger—

The man's knife hand rose. Johnny kicked him in the balls.

The man groaned and doubled over. They'd both been holding their breath. Johnny gasped for air as he reared his foot back and aimed at the man's head.

The man blocked the kick with his free arm. Exploded to his feet. Pulled his knife hand back and grabbed the belt with his free hand, both with the same motion. Thrust the blade toward Johnny's chest.

Johnny shifted to the right and pulled back.

The blade came straight at him. And then stopped. The man had run out of reach. Johnny swung his left forearm and deflected the man's knife hand away. He kicked with his left foot. Connected with the man's stomach. The man recoiled but regained his footing immediately. *The bastard simply would not go down.* Johnny prepared to deflect another thrust of the knife—

The second man barreled into Johnny. Tackled him to the ground. Johnny crashed to the asphalt. The fall knocked the wind out of him. Pain shot through the back of his head. He tried to move but the man was too heavy. For the first time, a touch of panic gripped him. He immediately told himself to relax, and that mere thought freed his mind. Johnny wrapped the belt around the man's neck and pulled as hard as he could. The man thrust his fingers toward Johnny's eyes.

Johnny smashed his forehead into the man's nose. Pulled the noose tight, wrapped his legs around the man's ankles, and rolled hard to the left.

Johnny's torso flipped to the top. They reversed positions. A surge of hope. He was on top. He had the advantage— The first man. Where was the first man?

A sense of dread seized him. He knew he was about to be killed even before he felt the weight of the first man on his back, the fist crashing down the back of his neck. The force of the blow left him barely conscious. It twisted his neck to the right, just enough for him to see the knife being raised above his head.

At the same time, his hands went slack. The second man, beneath him, coughed and spit in his face. Johnny felt his airways constrained. He realized the second man was now choking him from below.

A kaleidoscope of memories flashed through his mind. They ended with Nadia, laughing at something he'd said, eyes sparkling and lips open. God how he loved those eyes. She was speaking but he couldn't hear any words, all he knew was that she was happy and carefree, the way he longed for her to be.

Except she wasn't happy or carefree. She was about to be killed, too.

A burst of adrenaline awakened him. He tried to breathe but couldn't. A knife was about to plunge into his back. Nadia was going to die, too.

A split second left.

Do something.

CHAPTER 19

———————— ❄ ————————

BOBBY WATCHED THE FIRST MAN PLUNGE THE KNIFE through Nakamura's neck. He stuck it in one side, and a third of the blade came out the other. The killing mesmerized Bobby. It shouldn't have. He'd killed two people himself, in self-defense, so he shouldn't have been shocked. But he was. He'd never seen a knife thrust through a man's throat. It was so grotesque he couldn't stop thinking about it. His mind replayed the scene as the doctor's body fell limp on the road—

Johnny was in trouble. He'd fought off his man but now the man with the knife was coming for him. And the man he'd fought off would soon recover. There would be two of them. Two on one.

Johnny had saved him from a life in prison.

Help him.

Bobby started toward the truck. Someone shoved him to the ground. He turned. It was Nadia. She picked up a boulder and raced to help Johnny—

A fourth man came flying from around the house. Clearly the athlete of the four. If you send a man to watch the back of the house, make sure he's the one who can run, just in case he has to chase someone.

Bobby jumped to his feet. In the time it took him to rise, the fourth man blew past him. Nadia threw her boulder. It hit him in the chest and slowed him down but just for an instant. He raised his knife in the air.

Bobby raced toward her, knowing he was too late, fearing that he would only get himself killed, too, certain that he couldn't live with himself unless he did everything possible to save her.

A whistling sound. Like a hockey puck flying past his left ear on open ice, only louder. A light gust of wind ruffled the hairs on the nape of his neck.

An object hit the fourth man in the neck. His head fell off his body. His legs collapsed beneath his headless torso. A black object fell to the ground beside the body. It looked like the wing from a toy airplane.

Bobby glanced behind them to see where the object had come from, who had launched it, and how. He saw nothing and no one.

He pivoted toward the truck. The man with the knife was about to jump on top of Johnny.

Bobby exploded, summoning all the power in his hips to catapult himself forward. The man with the knife jumped on Johnny. Slammed his fist into Johnny's neck. He raised his knife hand in the air—

Bobby was twenty strides away. He wouldn't make it in time.

Another whistling sound. This time he heard it in his right ear. A black blur flew through the air. It twisted and turned and sailed across the lawn toward the man with the knife. It severed his arm and landed in the side of his head.

The severed arm and the knife in its grip fell to the ground. The man went limp on top of Johnny.

Bobby raced to Johnny. Bobby reared back and kicked the man in the head repeatedly until he lost consciousness. Then he hauled him off Johnny's back. Up close he could see the object buried in his head. It was a boomerang, its wings sharpened to a razor's edge.

Bobby pulled Johnny off the unconscious man beneath him. Johnny coughed and gagged.

"Are you okay?" Bobby said.

He stammered and nodded.

An engine rumbled to life. Exhaust billowed in their faces.

Nadia arrived breathless. "Shit."

A whine was followed by a grinding noise. The truck slipped into gear. The engine wailed.

Two dead men. One unconscious. Johnny struggling to regain his breath.

The truck rolled forward. Genesis II was on board. Bobby had caught a glimpse of him from behind while the third man—the driver—pulled him off the street into the truck. There was nothing familiar about this Yoshi at all. He was just some Japanese kid, who quite possibly had the key to the formula that would change the world, and someday save it from the people who inhabited it.

Bobby watched the truck pull way. There was nothing he could do to stop it. Nothing he could do to save Genesis II.

A face appeared in the window of the back door. It stayed there for one second, just long enough for the eyes to lock onto Bobby's and for the image to register in his brain.

The truck gathered speed and started to pull away.

Bobby stood staring at the empty window trying to understand what he'd just seen. It made no sense, but one thing was certain.

He could not let that truck get away.

CHAPTER 20

———————— ❄ ————————

L UO STOOD NEAR A HOUSE THIRTY METERS AWAY FROM THE action. He'd thrown the boomerangs as soon as he'd rounded the corner and had seen what was happening. He was rushing to help the woman and the man overcome the other Russian men but the scene unfolding before him caused him to stop in his tracks.

The boy was chasing the truck.

What was he thinking? The truck was picking up steam but the vehicle's engine didn't have much torque. Just like the Japanese cars Luo had driven in Moscow. They were powered by smaller engines that took time to build speed from a standstill. This shortcoming was only magnified in a heavy truck.

The boy covered ten meters to the truck's bumper in two heartbeats. A narrow metal frame protruded from the bottom of the truck. It was the length of the bumper. A tow-hitch was attached to it, the kind a utility truck might use to attach a generator for emergency repair.

Five strides away from the bumper and on the verge of collision, the boy didn't slow down. Instead, much to Luo's amazement, he accelerated as though he'd been catapulted from a slingshot. He slid under the truck and grasped the metal frame. Luo looked for his feet under the truck but couldn't see them. That meant he'd either found a foothold or was using his stomach muscles to hold his legs in the air. The odds of finding a foothold so quickly seemed low, which suggested the kid was staying alive by performing a gymnastics maneuver. It was among the boldest and most athletic maneuvers Luo had ever witnessed. But no matter how strong he was, the kid would have to find a foothold soon. If he didn't, he'd fall onto the road and have to pray one of the wheels didn't roll over his legs.

The boy was the key to the treasure.

Luo sprinted around the back of the house to a parallel street.

He'd flown to Tokyo as soon as he'd finished talking to Denys Melnik. His hotel had arranged for a translator. The latter placed some phone calls to Tokyo hotels on his behalf and discovered that Nadia Tesla and Bobby Kungenook had reservations at the Century Southern Tower in Shibuya. Luo was not surprised. It was just a matter of time until they, too, discovered that answers awaited in Fukushima. Just like Luo, and the men who'd killed Ksenia Melnik. That's what a treasure did. It lured people.

He'd followed Nadia and the boy on the train to Aizuwaka-matsu. His Siberian facial features and Black Beret tradecraft had helped him blend in and avoid detection. He'd stolen a car from the parking lot beside the inn and caught up to the old man's truck on the highway. When the Global Medical Corps van pulled into the gate to the Zone of Exclusion, Luo drove on. He passed a barricaded entrance via a side street and wove his way through a lightly wooded forest to get inside the Zone. Eventually he spotted the van half a kilometer away. By the time he'd circled to park on the side street, a second truck had arrived and the fight had begun.

Now he would need to do the same in reverse. Luo climbed behind the wheel of the car he'd stolen, shifted into drive, and took off. This time he would not be following civilians and medical personnel. This time he would be following the boy.

And this time he had no idea where he was going.

CHAPTER 21

NADIA WATCHED THE TRUCK DISAPPEAR WITH BOBBY BE-neath it.

Johnny looked ashen and disheveled. The remaining Russian lay unconscious beside him. "Where's Bobby?"

"Gone." Nadia ran to Nakamura's body. "Get in the van. I'll get the keys. They must be on him. Quick. We have to follow."

"Follow what?"

"The truck. He's on it. Or under it, to be more precise." She cringed at the sight of Nakamura's limp body. He'd been a doctor and healer until he came in contact with the formula. Now he was dead. She suppressed her discomfort with the task at hand, held her breath, and fished the keys to the truck out of his pants. "I'll explain in the van."

"Your bag," Johnny said. "It's in the house."

Her wallet and passport were in the bag. "Shit."

She raced into the house, down the hallways, and into the bedroom.

The old woman's brow creased as soon as she saw Nadia. She unloaded a barrage of questions in Japanese. Nadia saw the panic button in her hand, the phone beside her. Good, Nadia thought. Her doctor was dead and the volunteer was gone. If she became ill, she could get help. By the time they arrived, Nadia and Johnny would be gone.

Nadia grabbed her bag and ran out the door. The phone rang behind her. The shrill ring gave way to the burble of the van's engine. Johnny sat in the driver's seat. Nadia raced to the passenger seat and climbed inside. Johnny took off.

"Left turn at the first intersection," she said.

"Same way we came here."

"That's where he went."

"It was a TEPCO truck," Johnny said. "I saw the lettering on the side. He could get out the main exit if he has a hazmat suit. The guards didn't seem to be paying much attention to the folks that were leaving the Zone."

"Did those guys look like the type who would finesse an entry or exit?"

Johnny turned left. The tires squealed. "No. You're right. They came in off the grid."

Johnny pressed the throttle. They zipped through the residential area, passing home after home without sign of life. Johnny slowed down through the first two intersections, fearing another car would appear at the worst possible place at the fatal moment in time. When he reached the third intersection, however, he crossed it at full speed.

"I just can't figure out why Bobby would do something so reckless," Nadia said.

"Genesis II is on that truck, right? What did Nakamura say his name was? Yoshi?"

"Yeah. But Bobby's no fool. He has his father's instincts. He understands danger. He measures probabilities before he acts. He weighs pros and cons. He calculates a risk-adjusted reward for any action he takes. It's all subconscious. It's instinctive. But that's how his brain works. You saw that in him when you got him off for murder, didn't you?"

"Not sure his brain is working right."

"What's the probability he can hang onto that truck the entire trip?" Nadia said.

"What was the probability he could latch onto it in the first place?"

"And if he does hang on, what's the probability the driver or one of his buddies at the destination sees him and kills him?"

"Is this Nadia staying positive?"

"Bobby knows that. But he still did what he did. What does that tell you?"

Johnny considered the question. "He must know something we don't."

"Impossible. He didn't tell me what *Genesis II* meant initially. He just didn't want to get into it. But his guilty conscience caught up with him before we left for the airport. He told me everything."

"You're sure he wasn't playing you?"

"Positive," Nadia said.

"You said it yourself. The kid's a natural con artist."

"No. Not that morning. He was emotional. He wasn't acting. I'd stake my life on it. He told me everything that was in his heart."

"Then if he does know something we don't know, it can mean only one thing."

"He learned something between the time we left the apartment and he ran after the truck."

"Maybe from those Russians at the airport," Johnny said.

"He didn't talk to them."

"Maybe he met someone at the hotel."

"He wasn't out of my sight long enough."

They drove toward the center of town. Nadia kept her head on a swivel but didn't see any trucks or signs of human life.

"There's another thing we need to talk about," Johnny said.

Nadia imagined the driver capturing Bobby. This time there would be no angel there to save him.

"The boomerangs," Nadia said.

"Who threw them?"

"No idea. An angel."

"You see anybody?"

"Nope," Nadia said.

They drove another mile until they came upon the intersection to the main road in town. A bilingual sign instructed them to turn left for the exit from the Exclusion Zone. Johnny stopped at the intersection.

"We can drive around if you want," he said. "But the odds are high this guy is out of the Zone by now. These guys were organized. They had a plan."

Despair gripped Nadia. She'd found Bobby in a radioactive wasteland in Ukraine, and now she'd lost him in a similar one in Japan.

"Our best bet is to get back to the hotel and wait for a phone call. He's got his own cell, right?"

"Yes."

They put their hazmat suits back on. Their respirators cloaked their faces. Five blocks away from the open stretch of road that led to the exit from the Zone of Exclusion, Johnny pulled into a side street and parked beside a post office. He picked a spot that gave them a distant vantage point of the guardhouse. They waited until a vehicle arrived on the opposite side of the guardhouse, looking to gain entrance to the Zone. In this case, two enormous dump trunks arrived with three pickup trucks in tow.

Johnny wasted no time. He drove to the gate. The guard was engrossed in a conversation with the dump truck driver and waved them through. The hazmat gear prevented him from seeing Nakamura wasn't at the wheel.

When she'd first arrived, Nadia had noted the similarities and differences between Chornobyl and Fukushima. Nature had reasserted its control over the former, while man was still wrestling with the residual risks of the latter. Both seemed casualties of unlikely events—the mismanagement of a crumbling Soviet empire and a natural disaster of unlikely magnitude. Now that she was leaving, Nadia noted another unfortunate similarity. She was leaving Fukushima as she'd left Chornobyl. In search of a boy who could change the world.

Except now there were two of them.

CHAPTER 22

JOHNNY DROVE FOR THREE HOURS. AS SOON AS THEY ENTERED Tokyo city limits, he got off the highway. He parked the car on the street near a warehouse. The sidewalks were empty except for the stray passerby. Nadia found an all-purpose cleaner and some paper towels in a box in the back. They used it to wipe down the surfaces they might have touched. Then they left the truck, found the subway, and went back to their hotel in Shibuya.

During the trip, Nadia asked Johnny if he thought she should call Bobby's mobile phone. Nadia was the most logical thinker he knew. When she asked his opinion, it usually meant she didn't like the conclusion she'd reached. Johnny loved those moments. They were the most intimate ones she shared with him.

"If he was in a position to get a call," Johnny said, "he would have made one."

"Meaning?"

"If you make his phone ring at the wrong time, you could put him in danger."

"But if it were the right time . . ."

"He would have already called you."

Nadia shook her head. "I was thinking the same thing. But isn't there a chance he can answer but can't dial?"

Johnny thought about it for a moment. "What has greater odds? That he can receive but can't dial, or that he hasn't called because he can't and your ring can only hurt him."

Nadia stared at her phone. "Am I overanalyzing this thing?"

"Probably, but under the circumstances, who wouldn't?"

She chose not to make the call and the phone didn't ring.

They arrived at the hotel at 5:25 p.m. They went to their respective rooms to clean up and rest before dinner.

Johnny took a shower hoping the hot water would rinse him of his frustrations. Bobby and Genesis II were gone. At home he got things done. He did whatever was necessary to protect the ones he loved. He'd framed Victor Bodnar and his twin blond protégés for drug trafficking because they wouldn't have left Nadia alone until the formula was theirs or they were certain it didn't exist. In Japan, Johnny was out of his element. It showed in his lack of results.

Nadia needed more help. More help than he could provide. And now another problem loomed. His week's vacation was coming to an end. He needed to leave on Saturday to be at work on Monday. His boss had generously allowed him to leave on zero notice. Asking for an extension would be the equivalent of quitting. He loved his job and it had taken him years to find a man he could work with. But if he and Nadia didn't find Bobby and Genesis II by Saturday, Johnny would have no choice but to resign. He certainly wasn't going to leave Nadia alone.

They met at the bar at 7:00 p.m. As soon as he saw her he knew something was wrong. He could tell by the clouds in her eyes.

"I called him," she said. "I couldn't resist. I had to know."

"And?"

Nadia's eyes fell.

"What?" Johnny said. "No answer?"

"No. There was an answer."

"And?"

"The person said hello in English, but the voice didn't belong to Bobby."

CHAPTER 23

———— ❄ ————

BOBBY CLUNG TO THE TRUCK'S UNDERCARRIAGE. HIS HEAD rested below the gas tank. Petroleum fumes filled his lungs. Road noise strained his eardrums. The tires kicked up dust. It stung his eyes, blew up his nose, and covered his lips.

At first the dust didn't bother him. He knew how to disengage his senses. Years of brutal training sessions with the Coach had taught him to ignore discomfort. But then he remembered they were in Fukushima. The dust covering his face might be hot. The particles sneaking past his lips and up his nose might be radioactive. He'd seen pictures of the workers from the Chornobyl nuclear power plant who'd been infected after the explosion. Their bodies covered with burn marks. Their inner organs rendered useless. Miserable deaths had followed.

He might have sentenced himself to death the moment he dove under the truck. He'd been born with radiation syndrome but Dr. Arkady had cured him. He'd known kids who'd died in their teens. He had been one of the lucky ones. He'd survived. Now he was infecting himself again. What had he done?

Then he thought of Eva. She was dead. But if that was the case, how could he have seen her in the window? Or had it been a mirage? Had he imagined that the androgynous Japanese boy Nakamura had called Yoshi was actually Eva with her hair cut short? It was possible, Bobby thought. She might have convinced Nakamura to refer to her as a boy to further protect her real identity. Still, Bobby worried her face was a figment of his imagination. One thing was for certain, he was going to find out the truth. If there was a chance Eva was alive, he would accept whatever fate was necessary to see her again.

The truck continued on paved roads for another ten minutes, and diverted onto a grassy field. A wooded lot followed. Bobby absorbed bumps and jackknife turns. When the vehicle emerged on fresh asphalt, the road noise grew. Tires rolled in the opposite direction, and Bobby knew they had left the Zone. Wherever they were headed—an abandoned airstrip or an obscure port—it wasn't going to be a five-minute trip. His arms and shoulders burned. He knew his stamina would be tested like never before. He banished doubt and told himself to live in the moment. The key to pain management was to control his mind. The prerequisite to controlling his mind was visualization.

And so he summoned memories of a fourteen-year-old witch with purple streaks in her hair and matching lipstick. She had two friends who dressed as witches, too. Everyone knew that Bobby lived with her, but she didn't want anyone to see her associating with the school freak. The boy whose mother had been a prostitute. The boy who was rumored to have been born in reactor four. What no one else in school knew was that Eva suffered from radiation syndrome, too. Eva swore him to secrecy, and Bobby kept his word.

Twelve months later, Bobby joined her in secondary school and became the favorite target of the bullies in his class. One afternoon they indoctrinated a new kid who'd just moved to Korosten into their gang. They followed Bobby from school. Introduced him to the new kid as human waste. Told him to watch what they did to radioactive scum. They chased and tackled Bobby. They pounded him with their fists and kicked him with their boots.

Bobby fought back but there were too many of them. He curled into a turtle position and covered his face with his arms. One foot broke through his guard and connected with his nose. Pain wracked his nasal area. A bitterness filled his mouth. It was the taste of blood. He heard someone howl. Realized it was his own voice.

"Hold his legs," one of the bullies said. "I'm going to kick him in the knees until his kneecaps crack. I'm going to paralyze him. Then we'll see how good he skates."

Bobby struggled to get up and run but he couldn't get out of their grasp. One kid pinned Bobby's shoulders. Two others grabbed his legs. A third reared his right leg back and took aim for Bobby's left knee. Bobby would never forget the gleam in that kid's eyes as he prepared to ruin Bobby's legs.

Then the bully crumbled to the ground. Eva stood behind him with a wooden bat. One of the other boys released Bobby's leg.

"Lesbian bitch," he said, and charged her.

She sidestepped him and clubbed him across the shoulder. He fell.

The other two boys froze. Bobby kicked the legs out from one of them. The bully tumbled. The boy who was pinning him down released his grip. Bobby pushed him aside, jumped to his feet, and coiled his fist to strike him. But the kid ran away. The other bullies followed, beaten, bruised, and confused.

From that day on they walked to school together. Word spread that Eva had thyroid cancer. The mean girls in school whispered in the hallways that she'd been born in reactor four, too. It was the same rumor that followed Bobby from school to school. It drew Eva even closer to Bobby. They shared dreams of leaving Korosten. Bobby coveted a life as a professional hockey player in America. Eva revealed her love of animals. She dreamed of being a zoologist.

If bullies and rumors brought them closer together, scavenging made them best friends. Their family faced a crisis. There was no money to buy gasoline for their monthly trips to Kyiv. But the Coach had a plan. There was good money to be made in the Zone. Chornobyl and Pripyat were less than a hundred kilometers away and the Coach had connections. He showed them how to sneak into the Zone to scavenge for vehicle parts that could be sold on the black market.

By their fifth trip they were seasoned pros. Their lithe, athletic frames allowed them to crawl deep into the graveyards and get to parts adults had difficulty negotiating. Their foot speed allowed them to move quickly in and out of the Zone. They shared the adrenaline rush of the danger and savored their scores. When one got stuck or locked in a car trunk, the other freed him or her. Until the night the hunters found them.

There were six of them, to the best of Bobby's knowledge. Members of an elite club who enjoyed hunting the most dangerous game. The first shots from their rifles missed Bobby and Eva. The youths ran through the red forest under cover of darkness. When they circled around the cooling ponds to make their escape, one of the hunters revealed herself and blocked their path. The woman aimed her rifle at Eva. When the gun misfired, Bobby lunged and shoved the woman into the radioactive cooling ponds. Just as Eva had protected him from the bullies two years ago, he saved her from the hunters.

Bobby remembered the moment when they got home that night. He stood outside the bathroom waiting for Eva to come out so he could take a shower and go to sleep. When she stepped out in her t-shirt and sweatpants, her hair was damp and she smelled of lavender. She stopped and looked at him. Usually she looked away quickly but this time she held his gaze. There was something different in her expression. Something more than brotherly affection. Then she kissed him on the cheek. When she pulled away she smiled at him. It was the first time she'd ever smiled at him. It was the last time she ever smiled at him—

The truck veered left. Brakes screeched. Gravity pulled Bobby's body to the left. His torso strained. The truck straightened and slowed down. Bobby's body rolled right back to equilibrium. The truck slowed to a crawl. Bobby tried to remember how long they'd been driving but he'd lost focus.

The smell of petrol grew more intense. The truck stopped beside a rectangular structure. Based on its width, it was the size of a refrigerator. Steel clanged against steel. It was the sound of a fuel dispenser entering a gas tank.

They'd stopped at a gasoline stand.

Footsteps clanged above him. Bobby heard a man's voice. Deep, masculine. Controlled but firm. The sound of flesh slapping flesh followed, and then a muted gasp. He'd hit her, Bobby thought. The driver had hit Eva. Even though she was bound and gagged he'd found it necessary to remind her he would harm her if she dared try to escape somehow.

Bobby suppressed his rage. Children acted on impulse. Adults waited until their emotions subsided. This is what his father had taught him at age twelve. Bobby was not a child. It was questionable if he'd ever been one. Sometimes that reality depressed him. He felt he'd missed out on something during his primary school years. But other times he treasured his life's experience. Few adults could control their emotions as well. His self-control was an advantage in competitive situations. Like this one.

The door opened and closed. A pair of black combat boots hit the ground. A cough and a groan. It was the type of yawn a man emits when he stretches his arms after a long drive. A lock snapped shut. The driver had locked the car, Bobby thought. The combat boots moved.

Pain wracked Bobby's shoulders and arms. It shot up into his brain and overwhelmed him. Only when the driver pulled off the highway did Bobby realize the magnitude of his agony. His daydreams had distracted him. But now that he was on the verge of getting a rest, his life seemed to depend on it, as though he couldn't have hung on another minute if the driver hadn't stopped.

He counted to three to make sure the driver had entered the convenience store. Then he eased himself to the ground and released his grip on the stabilizer bar.

Relief spread through his torso. He stretched his legs. A delicious release of energy tingled his thighs. He savored a moment of joy. He was still alive.

He rolled out from underneath the truck. Rose to a crouching position. Checked his watch. It was 3:17 p.m. They'd been driving for two hours. A rush of adrenaline. He'd hung on for two hours. He would hang on for another two hours if necessary. He could do it. He could and would do whatever was necessary to stay close to Eva.

Bobby circled to the back of the truck. Tried the door but it, too, was locked. Peered into the window but the driver had spray-painted it black. Bobby leaned into a seam between the back door and its frame.

"Eva," he said in Ukrainian. "It's me. Adam. I'm going to get you out of this. Just like that night in the Zone. Do you hear me? Just like that night in the Zone."

Bobby glanced around for a sign in English that might reveal his location but he couldn't find one. Everything was written in Japanese, except for the English added to a sign in the store's window.

Policeman droppings inside.

Bobby reached into his pocket for his mobile phone. He'd hoped to be able to tell Nadia his location.

His pocket was empty. The cell phone was gone.

It must have fallen out during the drive. It could have happened anywhere. Now he had no way to contact Nadia on the go. He had to hope he would find a public phone and have the opportunity to call her.

A shadow flashed in the convenience store. The driver. Bald head and black leather jacket headed for the counter. He could not have looked more Russian unless he'd been wearing a fur hat. He was buying two tall cans of some sort of refreshment, two bottled waters, and three bags of snack food. He dumped his haul on the counter.

Bobby slid back under the truck and assumed his former position. The driver returned and filled the tank with gas. Then he climbed into the truck. Footsteps clanged above Bobby in the cargo space. Bobby guessed he was giving his captive some water.

The engine rumbled. The undercarriage shook. The gear shaft groaned. The tires rolled.

Bobby tightened his grip. He closed his eyes and once again focused on memories of a girl. A girl he'd dreamed of calling his own. A girl who was supposed to be dead and now was sitting bound and gagged above him.

Or so he prayed.

CHAPTER 24

───────────── ❄ ─────────────

Nadia sat down beside Johnny at a corner table in the hotel restaurant. A busboy brought them a tray containing two damp hand towels. Nadia unrolled hers and used it to wipe her hands. Johnny applied his towel to his face, as she'd seen other men do at Japanese restaurants. He breathed into the towel for a moment before wiping his hands clean.

Nadia turned her cell phone to vibrate and placed it on the table beside her. "Whoever answered Bobby's phone had a bit of an accent, but all he said was hello. It wasn't enough for me to place it."

"But he wasn't an American," Johnny said.

"I don't think so. I asked who he was but he hung up. I tried calling two more times but there was no answer."

"What do you make of that?"

"Either the Russians have him and they don't want to talk, or someone else has his phone."

"It might have fallen out of his pocket."

"I hope so."

"Let me give it a shot," Johnny said. He reached out for her to hand him the phone.

"How is that going to be any different?"

"It's not. But it's like opening a jar or something. When your friend or loved one can't do it, you always think you'll have a better shot."

"The problem is, Charles Atlas, we're not trying to open a jar."

A waiter interrupted them. They ordered bottled water, green tea, and a massive assortment of sushi. Shrimp tempura and grilled chicken skewers to start.

Johnny placed the call after the waiter left.

Someone answered. Nadia could barely hear his voice but it sounded like a man. Was it the same man who'd answered when she'd first called?

"Hello," Johnny said. He stared at Nadia as he spoke. "The phone in your hands belongs to a friend of mine, Bobby Kungenook. Would you please tell me who you are and how you got his phone?"

Johnny listened. A frown spread on his face. He pulled the phone from his ear. The sound of laughter emanated from the earpiece. He pressed the phone back to his ear.

"Don't hang up," Johnny said. He repeated his hello a couple more times, then shook his head and ended the call.

"Who was it?" Nadia said. "What did he say?"

"It was a kid."

"A kid? What do you mean it was a kid?"

"Some Japanese kid. Great English, but you could hear his accent when it came to pronounce an L. It sounded just a bit like an R. The Japanese can't pronounce the L."

"What did he say?"

"He said 'Godzilla's fathers are under arrest.'"

Nadia tried to make sense of the words. "What is that supposed to mean? Is that a reference to Bobby?"

Johnny started to chuckle but stopped himself. "No. It's a reference to the movie. The original *Godzilla* is very famous in Japan. It was made here in 1954. Legend has it the producer and director were arrested when they were overheard plotting the story on top of a Tokyo skyscraper. People thought they were terrorists planning to destroy the city. Later, people said it was a miracle the film got made given Godzilla's parents were arrested."

"So what does this mean? Is it code for something?"

Johnny gave her a sympathetic smile. "The phone fell out of Bobby's pant pocket and some kid found it. That's all it means. The kid probably knows some basic English. He's with his friends—that would account for the laughter in the background."

Nadia imagined a kid finding a phone on the road. "If the phone fell out of his pocket and a kid found it, the truck couldn't have been in the Zone, and it couldn't have been on a highway. They had to have pulled off the road. To a rest stop or something like that."

Nadia's phone rang. She glanced at the screen. Looked up at Johnny. "It's Bobby's phone."

Johnny shrugged.

Nadia answered it. "Hello?"

Complete silence.

"Hello?" Nadia said. She could hear frustration creeping into her voice. "Would you please tell me where you found this phone?"

A few seconds of silence followed, and then she heard the same kid's voice. "The oxygen destroyer must not be used!"

"That's a line from the movie," Johnny said. "Hang up."

Laughter poured from the speaker. It sounded as though a room full of kids had exploded.

"Please," Nadia said. "I'm begging you. Tell me where you found this phone. A boy's life is at stake." She waited for an answer.

"Later, Miss Lady," the kid said, and hung up.

"He's just a kid," Johnny said. "He probably wasn't listening to you, and even if he was, just because he knew the line in a movie doesn't mean he understood your question."

"You're right."

Johnny reached out and put his palm on her hand. "You need to relax. We need to eat. Then we can try again. Maybe we'll catch him in a different set of circumstances. Maybe his girlfriend will pick up or something."

He pulled his hand away, and much to Nadia's surprise, she found herself wishing it was still there.

The waiter brought them their beverages.

Nadia sipped her green tea. "I watched the local news in my room."

"I did, too. If you can't understand a word, how could you be sure it was local?"

"All the people in the stories were Japanese."

"Good thinking. Very you. I watched the local news, too. Couldn't understand much more than a word here or there."

"I didn't see any stories about malfeasance in Fukushima."

Johnny raised an eyebrow. "Malfeasance?"

Nadia shrugged. "And I did a thorough search on the web. Nothing there either."

Johnny nodded, then turned solemn. "Nakamura," he said.

Nadia bowed her head and stared into her tea. "Tragic."

"This formula is taking lives."

"It was doing that even before we were sure there was a formula."

"You mean we're sure now?"

"Hardly," Nadia said.

During her first trip to Ukraine, she'd risked her life in pursuit of a treasure that would have allowed her to pay off a mobster who believed she owed him. Her second trip to Ukraine had also put her in mortal danger, but that was to save Bobby from a lifetime jail sentence. Now, the prospect that Bobby, Johnny, and she were all risking their lives for nothing turned her stomach. Her greatest fear wasn't the danger. Her adrenaline served as anesthetic to the risk. Her greatest fear was that it was all for naught, for reasons that were beyond her understanding at the moment.

"If we don't hear from Bobby tonight," Johnny said, "we have to consider our options."

"You mean we have options?"

Johnny picked from a bowl of salty-looking snacks. "Only bad ones. We could go to the embassy and tell them the truth, or some version of it. They would get the local authorities involved. They could check with passport control. The driver must have a Russian name. Probably came in through Narita. How many Russians can possibly have entered the country recently?"

"That will take forever and get us nowhere. By the time we're interrogated and the system starts rolling, Bobby will either be dead or long gone."

"Alternatively, we can search by ourselves. We could hire a detective. I know it's no fun to hear and I'm not trying to get you upset, but he could check hospitals. And presumably he'd have contacts with the police. He could see if there have been any reports about an American boy fitting Bobby's description."

"Usually there's at least one good 'bad option.'"

"Yeah," Johnny said. "In this case they both suck."

"That they do." Nadia caught Johnny's eye. "I want to thank you for what you did back there in the Zone."

Johnny waved his hand as though what he'd done was nothing.

Nadia caught his hand mid-air. His eyes widened.

"Don't underplay it," she said. "You put your life on the line for Bobby. For me. Words can't even begin to cover the debt I owe you."

"No worries. That's why I came along. Fortunately, I had some help from our mystery angel, or things might not have worked out so well."

"He does remain a mystery. Whatever happens tonight and tomorrow, though, I want us to have an understanding."

"What's that?"

"You're on that flight back to Newark on Saturday."

Johnny frowned. Let their hands fall to the table. "And leave you here alone? With Bobby missing? There is simply no way—"

"Yes way. Your boss gave you a week on the spur of the moment. Your colleague took over your cases. You told me yourself it was a stretch to get that week. You promised when you booked the trip that you wouldn't let it cost you your job."

"Yeah, but I never imagined things would go down like this. I can't leave. It doesn't matter . . . It doesn't matter what happens . . ."

Nadia squeezed his hand. "I cannot let you lose your job—"

Her phone rang again. She spoke immediately for fear the kid on the other end of the line would end the call. "Don't hang up. I need to know where you found this phone. Please. It's very important. Do you speak English? Can you understand me?"

A light static buzzed in the background. There had been no such noise during her previous calls. Something was off. Something was different. Nadia pulled the phone from her ear and glanced at the number from which the call was originating.

It wasn't Bobby's phone.

Then a voice sounded. As soon as she recognized it a wave of joy swept through her.

"My English isn't as good as my hockey," Bobby said. "But yeah, Auntie. I can understand you."

CHAPTER 25

───────── ❄ ─────────

BOBBY REMAINED GLUED TO THE TRUCK'S UNDERCARRIAGE for another ninety minutes. The crossbeam farthest away from his head helped him survive the trip. By hooking his knees over it, his arms and shoulders had to support only a fraction of his weight. He diverted his mind with a series of memories and fantasies. The latter included his favorite action sequence, the one where he completed an end-to-end rush and scored the Stanley Cup-winning goal in overtime for the New York Rangers. Not that the uniform mattered that much, as long as it belonged to an NHL team.

He began to smell the ocean halfway through the second leg of the trip. This was his first clue they were not heading back to Tokyo. The second clue was the traffic pattern. The closer one got to Tokyo, the worse the traffic. If they were headed back there, the volume of cars would have picked up after two hours. It didn't. Instead, traffic lightened.

An hour and a half after the stop at the gas stand, the driver exited the main road. He took two right turns and one left, and parked the truck. Bobby was surrounded by tires. He assumed it was a parking lot. Then he heard a long whistle. A man's voice came over an intercom. He spoke with a rhythm and cadence consistent with someone announcing some form of transportation was departing or arriving.

A train station.

Bobby heard a door slide above his head. Footsteps and a man's voice followed. The cabin went quiet for a count of sixty, and then more footsteps sounded. Weight shifted toward the back of the truck. The suspension dipped. Bobby felt the force of gravity pull him toward the asphalt until the shock absorbers kicked in. The back door opened. He heard feet hit the ground behind him. The first set connected with a heavy thunk. The second set kissed the asphalt.

The door shut. Two pairs of legs walked by him on the left. One belonged to a man. Black cotton pants and leather boots. Rubber soles with a thick tread but stylish enough to be worn into a casual restaurant. The second pair of legs belonged to someone slimmer. Blue jeans. Androgynous brown calfskin boots. The legs and the footwear might have belonged to a young man or a woman.

Bobby counted to twenty and slid out from under the truck. He tried to stand up but he couldn't straighten his knees. He squatted down to stretch his thighs and tried again. A delicious pain wracked his thighs, like the kind he experienced at the end of a leg workout.

He followed the driver and Eva into the Joetsu train station. On the way in he took off his hoodie and reversed it. It was gray with light blue trim on one side, navy on the other. He switched it so that the blue was on the outside. He pulled his knit hat over his head to cover his ears. Unfortunately, his sunglasses were in the Global Medical van. The reversal of the sweatshirt and the hat were the only element of disguise available to him. Up close the driver would recognize him. This was going to be tricky. Bobby needed to follow the driver but keep a safe distance so as not to be discovered. That might prevent him from getting a good look at Genesis II to confirm she was Eva.

The inside of the station buzzed with activity. The walls were lined with ticket machines. Bobby took cover behind a vending machine and scanned the main lobby. People stood buying tickets at most of the machines. None of them resembled the driver or Eva.

A sign with male and female stick figures hung on a wall. An arrow pointed toward two doors in the far corner. If Bobby needed a restroom, they did, too. Especially Eva. The driver wouldn't let her use the women's restroom alone, nor would he dare go into one himself. He was attracting enough attention by being the oversized gaijin that he was. His only option was to pull the hood down low over Eva's face and escort her into the men's room as though she were a boy or disabled person who needed help.

Five minutes later the driver and Eva emerged from the men's room, just as Bobby had suspected. The driver guided Eva to a ticket window. Bobby snuck up behind them to hear their destination, then hustled away. Once they disappeared down the platform, Bobby bought a ticket to Takaoka for himself.

"Joetsu line to Echigo-Yuzawa," the agent said. "At Echigo-Yuzawa, transfer to Hakutaka Ten Limited Express. Four thousand two hundred ten yen, please."

Bobby paid with a credit card tied to Nadia's account. He used the restroom, bought a bottle of water and two Japanese candy bars, and boarded the train. He took a seat next to a man in a suit reading a comics magazine. Once the train took off, he devoured his candy bars and drank his water.

He made the necessary transfers. He spotted the driver and Eva once from behind, at the Echigo-Yazawa station. Two hours later he hurried off the last train and caught up to them on the platform heading for the exit. The smell of fish and salt hit him as soon as he followed them outside.

A large ship stood anchored in a port in front of the building next door. A vast sea stretched far beyond it. A long line of people began in front of the ship and disappeared into a side entrance at the other end of the building. They carried bags and cameras. A man in a blue uniform guarded the entrance to the gangplank. A yellow rope stretched across it and prevented the people in line from accessing it.

The driver led Eva into the building. Bobby waited a minute, then snuck inside, pulled his hat low, and watched. The driver purchased two tickets and walked over to a long line. A sign above the line contained a single English word as translation. "Immigration." Bobby circled behind them to the information desk. An English-speaking woman answered his questions. The answers struck fear in Bobby's heart. Afterward, he bought tickets to the boat's destination.

Then he found a payphone and called Nadia.

CHAPTER 26

N ADIA HELD THE PHONE TO HER EAR. SHE GLANCED AT Johnny across the dinner table. "Bobby," she said.

Johnny's eyes lit up. He leaned forward. Nadia didn't have the speakerphone on and Johnny wouldn't be able to hear, but he still moved closer to the phone. There was no hiding his genuine affection for the boy.

"How are you?" Nadia said. "Where are you?"

"In a town called Takaoka," Bobby said. "At a pay phone in a ferry building. I lost my phone."

"I know. Are you hurt? Are you all right?"

"I'm a little stiff but I'm good."

A dozen questions raced through Nadia's mind. She performed some quick mental triage. "Are you in danger?"

"Nope." He hesitated. "At least I don't think so."

Nadia imagined him looking around. He was a self-aware and cautious kid. He could take care of himself.

"No," he said. "I'm safe. I'm sure of it." His voice was peppered with ebullience. He sounded better than safe. He sounded excited. "I've been worried about you."

"You've been worried about me? Are you kidding me? I'm the one who watched you dive under that truck and grab hold of it. How long were you under there?"

"Not sure. Two fifty, maybe three hundred miles."

"Are you serious?"

"Yeah, but we stopped at a gas stand so I got a break."

"Why did you do something so reckless? You could have been killed so easily. What were you thinking?"

"I couldn't let that truck get away. It was that moment that comes in life, you know? Where you have to take a stand and say, no matter what it costs, no matter what the consequences, this is something I've got to do."

"For a formula that may or may not exist?"

"No." He took a breath. "For Eva."

"Who?"

"Eva."

His friend from the Zone in Ukraine. The girl who'd died from surgery complications. Nadia remembered Bobby's stories about her. They'd been inseparable. "What about her?"

"I think I saw her."

"You think you saw Eva?" Nadia softened her voice. She feared the kid had lost it. Maybe he'd become delusional during his ordeal hanging under a truck for who knew how many miles. "Where?"

"Back in Fukushima. As the truck was pulling away. I caught a glimpse of Genesis II. Of the other boy. Except he wasn't a boy. He was a she. A girl with short hair. And she was Eva."

Nadia imagined Bobby seeing Genesis II's face. Had he really seen her or was she a figment of his imagination. "Are you . . . are you sure?"

Bobby hesitated. "Yes. Absolutely."

Nadia tried to make her delivery as gentle as possible. "You sound like you had to think about it."

"No. Not at all." He sounded angry and defensive. "I'm sure. I'm one hundred percent sure."

"Okay," Nadia said. She let a moment go by. "I believe you. But listen. If you have any doubts, it's okay to tell me. We promised to be honest with each other. Remember?"

A moment of silence passed. Bobby took a deep breath. "I was sure when I saw her. Then time passed and every time I caught a glimpse of her—at a gas station, in the train station, on the train—I never got a chance to see her face again. Today has been crazy. I'm so tired. And now I'm like . . . I'm not sure of anything anymore."

"I understand," Nadia said. "You're exhausted. You're traumatized. Like you said. As soon as you get some rest you'll remember better. The important thing is you're safe." Nadia saw the waiter approaching. "Hold on a second, some food is being delivered."

A waiter delivered a plate of steaming grilled chicken skewers and an enormous platter of shrimp tempura. Johnny kept his eyes planted on Nadia's the entire time as though he were interpreting her conversation with Bobby by reading them.

"Tell me about the trip to the ferry building," Nadia said. "In detail."

Bobby told her about the support beams under the truck, the stop at the gas station, and the train rides. Nadia marveled at his determination, endurance, and resilience. She'd known he was athletically gifted, but his ability to survive such long drives while hanging onto the bottom of a truck seemed like a remarkable feat. For the first time since she'd met him in Kyiv, Nadia wondered if Dr. Arkady's treatments for radiation sickness had given him a permanent physiological boost of some kind. All those months of watching him play hockey, the bursts of speed that left teammates and opponents in the dust, his victory against one of the fastest professional hockey players in a race at the rink in Central Park, he just seemed gifted. Now, he seemed more than gifted. He seemed special.

"Where are the driver and Genesis II now?" Nadia said.

"You mean where are the driver and Eva?"

Nadia detected the pain in his voice. She'd offended him by suggesting he was imaging things. She regretted her choice of words. "Yes. Sorry. Force of habit. Where are the driver and Eva?"

"They went through immigration about ten minutes ago. But the boat doesn't leave for another forty-five minutes."

"Immigration? Where is this boat going?"

Bobby's answer came out in a throaty whisper, as though he were trying to sound impassive but couldn't contain his nerves. "Vladivostok."

A bolt of anxiety wracked Nadia. Vladivostok. Siberia. The largest Russian port on the Pacific Ocean, close to China and North Korea. Home of the Russian Pacific Fleet. Neither of those characteristics, however, bothered her that much. It was the mere thought of Bobby stepping onto Russian, Ukrainian, or any type of former Soviet soil that stood her nerves on end. He'd suffered enough during his young life. He was an American now. He belonged in New York. He belonged with her.

"Are you sure?" Nadia said. "Does the boat make multiple stops? Is there any chance they're going somewhere else?" Nadia tried to conjure a more palatable destination but realized she was fantasizing. The men who'd taken Genesis II had been Russian. The driver was Russian. They were going back to Russia.

"It's the Far Eastern Shipping Company," Bobby said. "Ferries run to Vladivostok and South Korea. This one's going to Vladivostok. It takes two and a half days. It cost forty-eight thousand yen, which is about five hundred dollars."

"Cost? As in the past tense? You bought a ticket already?"

"Yup. I put it on your credit card. We should probably talk about that."

"Don't worry about my credit card. I'll call and get my credit limit boosted. And I'll start using another one. But you are not getting on that ferry. You're going to stay put right where you are. Johnny and I are going to rent a car at the hotel, get a driver if we need to, whatever it takes. And we're going to come get you. Right now."

Johnny's lips parted in mild surprise. Then he closed them and nodded.

"Sorry, Auntie," Bobby said. "Can't do it."

"Can't do what?"

"I can't wait for you."

"Sure you can. Not only can you, but you know it's the smart move. You're acting on emotion right now. You saw Eva, you don't want to lose her. Again. So you want to follow. I understand. Believe me, I understand. But you're just a . . ." Nadia stopped herself before she said he was just a kid. That wouldn't help her agenda. And besides, he was mature and resourceful beyond his years, and he knew it. "You're just one man. Your father would have been the first to tell you to wait for help. There's a reason he coaxed me into coming to Kyiv to get you. He didn't want you to make that trip to America alone. And now here you are, a year later, trying to do exactly what he didn't want you to do. Be smart about this, Bobby."

"You're right. My father would say it was a dumb move. Because everything was about money for him. And this isn't about the money. It's not about the formula, and it's not about the money. Not anymore."

"But you're acting on emotion. You know that. And deep down you know how dangerous that is."

Bobby considered her comment. "My decision to follow may be emotional. But that doesn't mean I'm not cool in the moment. Do I sound emotional to you now?"

No, he didn't sound emotional. He never sounded emotional. He rarely showed any emotion in the best or worst of times. "No, you don't sound emotional. That's the problem. You're too cool for your own good."

He chuckled. "Damn straight, Auntie."

Nadia knew she was losing the argument. If Bobby got on that boat she might not see him again. She simply had to find a way to stop him.

A thought hit her. A ray of hope. "Wait. Oh my God. We've forgotten the obvious."

"What?" Bobby said.

"You're going to Russia, right?"

"Yes." He sounded uncertain.

"Getting into Russia is not the same as getting into Ukraine," Nadia said. "An American citizen like you—with an American passport to prove it—can get into Ukraine without a visa. But to get into Russia, you need a visa. How are you going to get through immigration without a visa?"

An audible sigh of relief. "You don't need a visa if you're taking the ferry from Takaoka."

"Who told you that?"

"The woman at the information desk, here at the ferry building. If you're planning to stay in Russia for less than seventy-two hours, you don't need a visa to get on the ferry. My guess is it makes business easier and helps with tourism."

Great, Nadia thought. There was a career for the kid in international relations if he survived this ordeal and the hockey thing didn't work out.

"I didn't want to say this, Bobby, but you leave me no choice. I forbid you to get on that boat." Nadia didn't hear a sound on the other end of the line but she could sense him tensing. "Do you hear me? Are you listening? I'm your legal guardian, and I'm telling you you're not getting on that boat."

He remained silent for a few more seconds. When he spoke, he sounded like a surgeon giving his nurse the most familiar instructions. "I need you to go to Kyiv for me."

His delivery was so relaxed, his request so unexpected, Nadia was rendered speechless. "What?"

"I need you to go to Kyiv. You could investigate over the phone but there's no substitute for looking a person in the eyes, you know? My father taught me that, too."

"You expect me to go to Kyiv? Just like that? I don't even know what to say to you."

"You're the only one who can do this. You're the only one who can help us. Genesis II is not a boy, she's a girl. And the girl is Eva.

That means she's alive, not dead—obviously—and she might have the second part of the formula. I need you to go to Kyiv to find out if she really died. To look into the whole thing using her as your angle of investigation. You didn't consider her last time you were in Kyiv digging around into the past."

"While you're following her and her captors all over Siberia? Are you even listening to yourself?"

Bobby continued talking as though she hadn't interrupted him. "If you confirm she's alive, or can't confirm she's dead, I need you to go to the Division of Nervous Pathologies. That's where Dr. Arkady treated us. He's dead, but he had an assistant. Her name was Melnik. Mrs. Ksenia Melnik and she had a son, too. They may know more about Eva, the formula, everything."

Nadia still hadn't accepted the reality that he was going to get on the boat to Vladivostok. The thought of him telling her what she should be doing infuriated her, and yet with each passing second, she saw the logic in his words. She couldn't stop him from boarding the boat. While he was at sea, she could ask some valuable questions. Especially if she could get to Kyiv quickly, and then somehow catch up with him.

"I'm going to be on the boat for two and a half days. That gives you time. When I get to Vladivostok, I'll try to buy a cell phone. If I can't find one, there's got to be plenty of pay phones. It's a huge city. I'll call you one way or another, for sure. Just remember. The trip takes two and a half days. So I won't be in touch until Sunday morning at the earliest, wherever you are." He paused for a moment. "Okay, I better get going."

"Wait," Nadia said. "Not so fast—"

He resumed talking in his cool, clinical voice. "You're a forensic security analyst, Auntie. You're the best investigator no one knows about. You can tear companies apart to reveal the truth like no one else. Same goes for people."

"No. I meant not so fast because I need you to repeat the name for me. Ksenia who?"

Bobby repeated the details about Ksenia Melnik and her son.

"You take care of yourself," Nadia said.

"You too, Auntie."

"Make sure you call me."

Nadia heard a click before she finished her sentence. When Bobby didn't answer, she knew he'd hung up. A fleeting sense of anxiety washed over her. He was going back to Russia on his own. To *Russia*.

Johnny had started digging into the food. He pulled chunks of chicken from a skewer onto a plate with his chopsticks. "Bottom line," he said, "the kid's still alive. You got to pause and give thanks for the major gifts of life."

The phone rang.

A surge of hope swept through Nadia. Maybe the man wasn't taking Eva to Vladivostok. Maybe Bobby had misread the situation. Nadia hit the RECEIVE button without even looking at the screen and pressed it to her ear.

"Bobby?" she said.

But it wasn't Bobby. It was a Japanese man speaking broken English. He said his son's friend had found a cell phone at a gas station and this was the most frequently dialed number. He wondered if Nadia knew the proper owner and how he could go about returning the phone to him.

Nadia asked him to ship it to their hotel in Shibuya along with his address so she could reimburse him for the postage and include a reward. He declined the reward like a classy Japanese gentleman. She thanked him for his kindness.

"Oh, hell," she said, after hanging up.

Johnny pointed toward the plates of food with his chopsticks. "Try some appetizers? Mighty tasty. Can't get shrimp tempura like that in Kyiv. Can you?"

CHAPTER 27

—————— ❄ ——————

T HE PAMPHLET AT THE FERRY STATION BOASTED A PICTURE of a luxurious ship with a massive swimming pool. Even if he had swim trunks, Bobby knew he couldn't afford the risk of exposing himself, literally and figuratively. Still, he enjoyed a quick little daydream, where the driver accidentally fell overboard and he and Eva had the pool to themselves. The rest of the passengers were passed out drunk from vodka and paid no attention to them. What followed in the pool was an even more unlikely fantasy, though it had helped him endure the trip beneath the truck. In fact, he would have sacrificed all hope for its becoming reality to confirm she was still alive and secure her safety.

Bobby found a convenience store and a food kiosk in the ferry building. He bought a travel kit containing a toothbrush, toothpaste, a comb, a razor, and shaving cream. It also contained a mask, the kind painters wore in America, and sick folks wore in Tokyo. A rack of cheap sunglasses offered protection from ultraviolet rays and prying eyes. Bobby ran straight to the rack as soon as he saw it. He tried on a few pairs and settled on a wraparound design that athletes and kids his age might wear. They were a bit flashy, but he looked even stranger when he tried on the aviator designs adults might wear. His father had warned him not to out-think himself. Sometimes the best disguise was being oneself.

He bought a six-pack of bottled water and enough packaged food for two days. He knew from his experience on the Trans Siberian Express not to expect anything but boiled water on the ferry. Perhaps they would have food but it would be expensive. By bringing his own supplies he would arouse less suspicion. He might actually look like a regular commuter, someone who knew how to save a dime. He also bought a notebook, a pen, and two t-shirts from a souvenir stand, and a duffel bag. He stuffed his purchases into the bag so he appeared to have some luggage.

Once he was finished shopping, Bobby converted his yen into rubles at the currency exchange desk. Nadia had changed 500 dollars into yen for him. Even though he had a credit card, she didn't want him traveling without local currency in his pocket. He'd used the credit card to make his purchases so he had 460 dollars worth of rubles left when he made the second conversion. The currency traders made a nice living. Eleven more conversions and he'd be left with no money even though he hadn't spent a dime.

A wall in the ferry building contained ads from several hotels in Vladivostok. Bobby noted the cheapest one. He entered it as his destination on the proper Russian immigration form. He told the immigration officers he was on vacation with his aunt who was back in Tokyo. He was writing an article for his school blog about the students' most unusual experiences. It was a contest, with the winner earning a place on a prominent New York City travel magazine's blog. Boy did he want to win that contest. Such a victory could help a kid get into a good college. The top colleges were so competitive in the States, he told the officer, among other random observations about his high school experience. He spoke in English, enunciating carefully to hide any trace of his Russian fluency, not pausing to take a breath so as to frustrate the officer as much as possible.

It worked. The immigration officer's face turned eggplant as Bobby yapped away. With a long line of people waiting behind Bobby, the immigration officer stamped his passport and let him pass.

Bobby found the driver and Eva sitting in a waiting area in front of a window facing the pier, their backs to the main lobby. No one could see their faces upon entering the waiting room, and those who walked past them to enter the pier had their eyes on the ferry. Eva rested her head on the driver's shoulder. To a casual observer, it looked like an affectionate gesture from a daughter, wife, or lover. To Bobby, it spoke of needles or pills and a heavily sedated state. He resisted the temptation to try to catch a glimpse of her face. His goal was to follow them and not to be seen, he reminded himself. He would not be helping his cause by confirming she was Eva if the driver recognized him. The driver had a cell phone. He would call his associates. They would kill Bobby on Russian soil, dissolve his corpse in acid, feed it to pigs, or toss it into the foundation of a new high-rise in Vladivostok. No, Bobby thought. *Keep to yourself.*

Eva was Genesis II, he thought. She simply had to be.

When boarding started, Bobby watched the driver and Eva climb the gangplank and disappear inside. He waited five minutes to let them find their seats and minimize the risk he'd bump into them. Only then did he make his way onboard.

One side of the ferry resembled an open sardine can filled with used Japanese cars. They nestled so closely to one another that there was barely any room to open their doors. Bobby wondered how someone could manage to squeeze in and out, as it appeared that only a stick figure would be able to slither behind their wheels.

If the parking lot was a revelation, the swimming pool was a major disappointment. It bore as much of a resemblance to the picture in the pamphlet as Pripyat did to the utopian city built for the nuclear workers in Chornobyl. There were no lounge chairs or side tables with umbrella drinks. Patches of rust covered the handrails. The diving board had been snapped in half. Strips of cracked and peeling paint dangled along the sides and bottom of the basin. The pool itself wasn't filled with sky blue water. Instead it was crammed full of motorcycles. A five-foot plank rested beside the shallow end, no doubt serving as the ramp to get the motorcycles in and out of the pool.

The passenger side of the ferry was actually worthy of a brochure. Probably not a luxury cruise brochure, but certainly one for ferries. An immaculate lobby the size of a ballroom greeted passengers. Stairs led to the second floor where the first- and second-class cabins were located. Bobby was certain the driver had secured such a room for himself and Eva. The thought of him spending two nights with her sent chills down Bobby's spine, but he soothed himself with logical reasoning. He couldn't overtake the man when he was locked in a private room on a boat in the middle of the ocean. He had to bide his time. He had to concern himself with his stealth and her survival.

Most passengers congregated in the restaurant. Bobby took his sunglasses off so as not to arouse attention, and put his mask over his nose. He pulled his hat down low to his eyes and glanced at his reflection in a lobby window. He looked like a sick young man acting in accordance with Japanese customs, keeping his germs to himself to prevent his fellow passengers from getting infected. The knit hat reinforced the notion that he had a cold. Even Russian passengers would pay him no mind. If they were on the ferry, they were probably regular commuters. They likely understood Japanese culture by now, and wouldn't glance at the kid with the mask twice.

The restaurant resembled a secondary school cafeteria, with a room full of tables and two serving lines along perpendicular walls. There were plenty of noodle soups and teriyaki dishes for purchase. Bobby was reminded this was a Japanese operation and not a Russian one.

A second-class berth would have cost two thousand dollars and put him at risk of accidentally sharing the same room as the driver and Eva. For both these reasons he had no choice but to buy a second-class B ticket. It was a nice sales tactic. There was no third-class seat. Just two versions of second class, even though the B class was essentially general admission. He would share sleeping quarters with a hundred or more other passengers in the tatami mat room. A tatami mat was a traditional form of Japanese flooring made from rice straw. Pillows and blankets were provided.

Bobby spent his first day in the restaurant, going on deck to get a breath of fresh air as other passengers did the same. He kept to himself, and clung to groups of men when he needed to move about. Although he doubted the driver would emerge from his cabin except to get food, and he was confident in his disguise, he planned his movements to minimize the risk of being seen.

The reason the ferry was filled with cars and motorcycles became apparent the first night on the ship. Russian dealers bought used cars and bikes in Japan and sold them in Vladivostok. Bobby counted nine dealers and an equal number of vodka bottles at their table. They downed shot after shot, toasting Toyota, Nissan, the Emperor, the Japanese hostesses who could milk a man's wallet and glands dry, and the genius who planted those beautiful cherry blossoms.

Bobby was reminded of something a teammate on the Fordham Prep hockey team had told him. The kid's father owned a car repair shop with an export business on the side. According to him, used Lexuses were scarce in America because they were routinely shipped to Moscow.

Bobby drifted in and out of sleep during the first night, never catching more than an hour of consecutive shut-eye without being woken up by ship and human noises alike. Mechanical devices creaked and groaned. A few old men got up to use the bathroom in the middle of the night. The drunken Russians showed up around 2:00 a.m. Someone farted so loudly Bobby thought it was the engine backfiring until the stench of rotten eggs hit him.

Boredom set in during the second day. It mixed with a queasy anticipation of the unknown that awaited him in Vladivostok. The combination left him neither sleepy nor alert, but rather strangely unsettled. As he sat idling in the restaurant, Eva preoccupied him even more. Action and planning diverted his mind. In their absence, he thought of nothing and no one else. His imagination was consumed with the image of the face he'd seen through the truck's window in Fukushima.

Shocked, scared, confused. More mature then he remembered her. Cheekbones more pronounced, porcelain skin a bit damaged from the sun. The eyes—the sweet puppy-dog look completely incongruous with her tough, self-reliant personality—meeting his. Conveying her fear, looking for a connection . . . a flicker of recognition, a parting of her lips . . . And then the truck drove off.

Bobby had never seized the opportunity to tell her what he felt in his heart before she supposedly died. The mere thought of doing so was absurd. They'd never discussed their feelings about each other. Besides, for years she hadn't even acknowledged his existence. The thought of weirding her out by revealing his true affections for her sounded like the dumbest move a man could make.

And yet he regretted not doing so. For if there were a sliver of a chance that she shared his affection, that would mean more to him than anything else. More than his hockey career, his American citizenship, more than life itself.

If given another opportunity, he wouldn't make the same mistake twice.

The sound of footsteps interrupted his daydream. Heavy boots marching toward him. The sound was close, too much so for him to escape. Bobby cursed himself. He hadn't been focused. And now someone had snuck up right behind him. Bobby didn't turn, though. Instead he hoped he was mistaken and that man was simply walking toward the window to take a look outside.

The footsteps stopped behind him. For a moment there was no sound, and Bobby thought that maybe he'd guessed right. But then Bobby felt a boot connect with the leg of his chair. It was just a poke, to wake him out of his apparent slumber. The man spoke in a baritone, his voice rough from years of cigarette smoking.

"Hey, kid," he said in Russian. "Don't I know you?"

CHAPTER 28

---※---

JOHNNY ATE SUSHI AS HE LISTENED TO NADIA'S SUMMARY OF what Bobby had told her on the phone. She rubbed one chopstick against the other as she briefed him. This wouldn't have been unusual in most Japanese restaurants, as it was common practice to remove any loose slivers of wood before digging into food. But they were eating at a swanky hotel eatery. The chopsticks were made of polished wood and painted with a rich black lacquer. There were no slivers to remove. Nadia was rubbing them together because she didn't have a pair of stress balls to squeeze.

But by the time she was done, Nadia was nibbling on a giant shrimp caked with golden batter. This didn't surprise Johnny. He knew how her brain worked. Recounting everything she'd heard gave her the opportunity to digest it all. She analyzed implications, calculated the upside and downside of various strategies. Johnny was sure she had a strong idea of what she planned to do next.

To Johnny it was a no-brainer. They needed to get to Vladivostok ASAP.

"He's sure Genesis II is Eva?" Johnny said.

"No. He wants to be sure, but he's not. And neither am I. Nakamura referred to Genesis II as a 'he,' and Yoshi is a boy's name, right?"

"Wrong."

Nadia lifted her eyebrows.

"It's androgynous. Yoshi could be a boy or a girl. I knew one of the latter when I was an exchange student. Nakamura might have referred to Genesis II as a 'he' to keep her real identity all the more secret. Nakamura just met us. A smart man would keep the truth to himself until he was sure he could trust us, until it was absolutely necessary to reveal Genesis II's real identity, including her sex."

Nadia considered his theory. "Nothing's changed then. We can't assume anything about Genesis II. We have no clue if he actually saw Eva or not."

"No. We don't. Did you ask Bobby if he was being followed?"

Nadia dismissed his question with a wave of her chopsticks. "He was under the truck when he left Fukushima. Stayed there for most of the trip. How could anyone have picked up his trail?"

"Exactly," Johnny said. "He was under the truck when he left Fukushima. Said another way, he got under the truck in Fukushima. And before he got under the truck, he was standing on a street in the Zone of Exclusion outside a house where he could have been seen."

Nadia gave him an incredulous laugh. "By whom?"

"Who threw the boomerang?"

Nadia froze. "The angel."

"Presumably he was standing behind you and Bobby. That's the only way to explain the trajectory of both boomerangs. When you both looked back, you didn't see anyone. But he could have been there, right? He could have been watching."

Nadia shook her head. "It didn't occur to me. I keep forgetting about the angel. Which is amazing."

"No it's not. You're human. That was an emotional conversation. You did a great job staying cool in a situation where you had no control over what a kid was going to do. Anyone could have missed an angle or two."

Her eyebrows shot up. "Are you saying I missed something else?"

"No. I was just saying."

"You're right. I guess it's possible he was being followed. And we might be tempted to think it's a good thing."

"I hear you. Saved him once, save him again."

"Right. But there's no such charity in the world, let alone in Russia. The angel is after the formula, let there be no doubt. Bobby is carrying half of it—we had no choice to appease Nakamura. Genesis II may or may not have the second half."

"Either way he needs Bobby," Johnny said.

"So do I."

"Then what are we waiting for?"

Nadia checked her watch. "I'm waiting until 10:00 p.m."

Her use of the singular pronoun stung Johnny. It was a sign her plans didn't include him. He waited for her to elaborate but she kept staring at her watch instead.

"You plan to bring me up to speed on why you're waiting for fifty minutes to go by, or are you going to make me sit here like your personal secretary waiting for her majesty to decide when I'm worthy of being informed?"

Nadia frowned. "Sorry, I was thinking."

"Why the fifty minutes?"

"It was something Bobby said."

"What?"

"He said he'd be on the boat for two and a half days. Actually, it doesn't leave for forty-five minutes. So it's two days, twelve hours, and forty-five minutes."

"And?"

"He said that would leave me enough time to go to Kyiv and make inquiries."

"What of it?"

"It's a crazy idea, isn't it? Think about it. Logistically, it's impossible to do it on commercial airlines."

"Why? Departure times? How do you know until you look into it first?"

"Flight time from Tokyo to Kyiv is twelve hours. Flight time from Kyiv to Vladivostok is ten hours. That's twenty-two hours flight time in the air. That excludes check-in, getting through customs, immigration. All that fun airport stuff."

"Call it four hours more for that stuff. Twenty-six hours travel time. Bobby's going to be in the boat for sixty hours. That leaves you . . . thirty-four hours. That leaves you with a day and a half in Kyiv."

"You're assuming the proper departure times exist. That I can time all my business to get to the airport on time."

Again with the singular pronoun. Johnny wished he didn't care so much. No matter how closely they bonded she always reverted to being an individual. "You're right. I'm assuming you're not screwed at the airport. Like I said, you won't know until you check, and even if the logistics work, there's risk."

"No," Nadia said. "There isn't just risk. There's a guarantee of failure."

"Why?"

"Because if I come into Russia on a commercial airliner I have to go through the normal immigration procedure. I won't be on the ferry from Takaoka like Bobby. They won't let me into Russia for seventy-two hours without a visa."

"You need a visa." Johnny shook his head. "I forgot about the visa."

"It's the adrenaline. Look at me. I forgot about the boomerangs. I forgot about the angel."

"So what are you saying, you fly back to Takaoka and get on the ferry? That doesn't make sense. You'd be two and a half days behind." It was a stupid thought, a stream of consciousness. He regretted even suggesting it.

"No ferries. And no commercial planes."

"Then what? You have a private submarine?"

"No. But I have a friend who has a private plane."

A flash of envy passed through Johnny. Simeonovich. The man

with all the toys. The man Nadia wouldn't trust when she went to Ukraine to dig into Bobby's background. First, he was Russian, and Russians and Ukrainians had a history of adversity. Second, he was a Russian oligarch. Apparently one of the more honorable ones, but he himself had admitted to Nadia that by American rules of law, all oligarchs were criminals without exception. It was impossible to conduct business in the countries that comprised the former Soviet Union without offering bribes.

"So what, you're going to trust him now?" Johnny said.

"To some degree, yes. I have no choice."

"You're kidding me. With this?" Johnny looked around to make sure no one was listening. Leaned across the table and lowered his voice. "You're going to trust a guy who lives for money with the formula?"

"I'm not sure I'll need to go that far for him to help me."

"You think he's going to let you fly in his plane from Tokyo to Kyiv and not expect you to feel some obligation toward him?"

"He has an office in Tokyo but the odds his plane is here are zero. No, I think he's going to charter a plane for me to get to Kyiv. Then let me use his plane from there."

"And you're comfortable with this? Because before, you weren't too keen on confiding in him."

"The thought of owing him doesn't bother me so much anymore. I like him. I . . . I trust him."

Johnny noted the slight hesitation in her voice and her choice of verbs. "You sound as certain as Bobby was that he saw Eva. You expect him to do this for you without knowing what you're after?"

"I must sound pretty arrogant right now, huh?"

Johnny shrugged. It wasn't so much arrogance as it was feminine confidence, the kind a woman projected when she knew a man held a fascination for her, and was prepared to do whatever was necessary to get her. Whatever that meant. Johnny wanted to tell her she was making a mistake. That a man who measured his happiness by counting dollars, euros, or rubles would inevitably let her down. If she brought Simeonovich closer, he would find out about the formula and choose it over her. But there was no sense in doing so. Johnny would only sound like a jealous fool.

"It's not about humility or arrogance," he said. "It's about Bobby, and it's about the formula. You have to use all the resources at your disposal. All of them. If you have access to a private plane, and you trust you can handle the man who's lending it to you, you have to go for it."

Nadia considered his statement and nodded.

"Back to the original question," Johnny said. "You're waiting for fifty minutes to go by because of the time difference. Where are Simeonovich's headquarters? Moscow?"

"Forty-six minutes. But who's counting. Yeah, Moscow. Moscow is five hours behind Tokyo. So it's 4:14 p.m. He prefers not to get personal calls until 5:00 p.m., when his workday is done. Everything rolls to voice mail before then. Thus the wait. I could call his business and have him interrupted, but I know the man. It will work better if I'm patient."

"What if he's somewhere else? In the UK or the US?"

"He knows the time changes. He'll still know I respected his schedule." Nadia shrugged. "What can I say? He's a billionaire. He's eccentric."

"Self-important."

"Semantics. In my experience with the super rich, as an analyst for hire, once a man's net worth goes north of a hundred million dollars, inhibitions melt away pretty fast."

"The emperor sheds his kimono." Johnny recalled using the line with Nakamura. Sounded like emperors were stripping all over the place.

Nadia managed a laugh. Her eyes went to her watch again, then to Johnny, the food on the table, and back to him. They lingered on him. Johnny felt helpless when she stared at him, like he did in the courtroom when he was waiting for the verdict on an impossible case, one where he didn't have a chance to impose his will on the final outcome.

"I better eat some of this fast and get to my room," she said. "I want to be packed and ready to go. Just in case he says yes."

"Sure."

"I'm sorry to rush through dinner like this."

Johnny barely heard what she said. He was coming to grips with what they weren't discussing. That she needed him to go away now.

"I know it's presumptuous of me," Nadia said. "I mean, it's nuts, right? I'm just assuming he's going to charter a plane for me . . . "

Her eyes were alive now, similar to how she'd described Bobby's voice on the phone. And Johnny would not be part of it. If she was successful in getting Simeonovich to help her, he was not invited. Their unspoken understanding was that he would be going back to New Jersey. Johnny wouldn't dare suggest tagging along. She appreciated him, maybe even loved him in a platonic way. But she needed more help than he was capable of providing. The man who could provide it wouldn't want him around, and Nadia understood the reality of the situation. In addition to that, she genuinely didn't want Johnny to lose his job by extending his vacation, especially not if she had an oligarch at her disposal.

The waiter delivered the bill on a tray. Nadia and Johnny had an understanding that she was paying his expenses for the trip. Johnny still tried to pay for the meal out of pure chivalry, but Nadia grabbed the tray with the bill from his hands. Johnny knew that her checking account was temporarily flush from the fat fee she'd earned from the securities analysis she'd performed for Simeonovich. Johnny watched her stack some yen on the tray to cover the bill and the tip.

People didn't touch money in public in Japan. When a person needed to hand currency to another, he used an envelope. Money was considered filthy, both literally and figuratively. The Japanese were right, he thought. Money was a filthy thing, especially when it came from Russia. Johnny didn't trust the bastard. Not one bit. They had no rule of law in Russia. Why would anyone trust a man who knew how to manipulate the law to his own benefit?

They left the restaurant and rode the elevator together.

When they got to Nadia's room, she looked at him. Her eyes turned large and moist.

"You're too good to me, Johnny Tanner," she said. "I'm never going to be able to thank you properly for everything you've done for me. For Bobby and me. For us." She kissed him firmly on the cheek.

Johnny went back to his room and called his credit card concierge to check the flight schedule from Tokyo to the New York metro area. He didn't need to wait for Nadia to tell him what Simeonovich would say. They both knew the outcome of her call just as surely as they knew what had just transpired in front of her hotel room.

She'd given him the big kiss good-bye.

CHAPTER 29

THE CO-CAPTAIN OF THE GULFSTREAM G550 EMERGED FROM the cockpit every half hour to see if Nadia needed anything. The sleek jet seated nineteen people, but she was the only passenger.

"Will we be stopping to refuel?" Nadia said.

The co-captain was an American in his fifties, with a gray crew cut and a lean physique. His military looks inspired confidence. He shook his head. "Nope. The G550 has a range of six thousand, seven hundred fifty nautical miles. The flight from Tokyo to Kyiv is about five thousand miles."

Simmy had purposefully chartered a jet that could cover the distance non-stop. He didn't want her to waste any time. Nadia pictured him telling his assistant—the condescending one with the sculpted cheekbones that she'd met on his yacht less than a month ago—to make sure she chartered a plane that met all of Nadia's needs. A warmth spread over her body.

The co-captain said, "I'm guessing you didn't make the charter yourself?"

"How can you tell?"

He chuckled. "The same way I can tell whoever chartered this plane is very fond of you. Kind of obvious."

Nadia lowered her voice to make her next question sound more discreet. "How much for a jaunt like this?"

He shrugged. "Figure about ten thousand per thousand miles."

"Fifty thousand?" Nadia swallowed. "That much?"

"Unless your friend is a good client. Then he has his own contract, his own rate. It's negotiated."

"My friend has his own plane. It just wasn't in Tokyo."

The co-captain smiled. "Good news then."

"What's that?"

"Your friend loves you. It was at least fifty grand."

Nadia had called Simmy at precisely 5:00 p.m. Moscow time. It was his private mobile phone. Only his most trusted friends and associates had the number. He answered the phone without emotion, then turned enthusiastic as soon as he heard her voice.

Nadia explained the urgency of the situation. Bobby was in danger on a ferry headed to Vladivostok. Nadia needed to get to Kyiv to investigate some matters and get to Vladivostok before Bobby arrived. She had approximately fifty-seven hours before Bobby arrived and the clock was ticking. He'd offered to help her before. She hadn't accepted. Now she needed his help. In the most grandiose, inappropriately expensive way imaginable.

It was a preposterous request. And yet Nadia was certain he would say yes. First, she'd saved him tens of millions of dollars with her analysis by preventing him from overpaying for a company whose books had been cooked. Second, fifty thousand dollars to him was the equivalent of fifty cents to her. It was a mercenary's observation, but it was the truth. Third, he wanted her and Nadia knew it. A woman knew a man's intentions based on the look in his eyes, his body language around her, his manner of speech. Whether she was an object of temporary fascination or something more serious, she had no idea.

But the prospect of either one thrilled her as much as telling a Russian oligarch about the existence of a formula scared her.

Oligarchs became who they were because of their insatiable appetite for wealth. A radiation countermeasure would be worth billions. If he learned of its existence, could she trust him not to try to acquire it for himself?

No. And yet, now she had no choice.

Before offering to arrange transportation from Tokyo to Kyiv, he'd asked only three questions.

"Are you in danger?"

"Yes. Someone tried to kill me today."

"Is Bobby in danger?"

"Yes. The same people tried to kill him. He's following one of them into Russia."

"Will you tell me the complete truth about what this is all about if I meet you in Kyiv?"

"No."

"No?" His voice rang with disbelief.

"No. I'm going to tell you the truth now. I need to investigate a few things in Kyiv as soon as I get there. And I need your help to make the necessary arrangements ahead of time. Otherwise I won't make it to Vladivostok in time."

She gave him a brief summary of everything that had transpired in Japan. She also told him about the origins of a potentially revolutionary formula, her discovery that it was only partially complete, and the e-mail that had led them to Fukushima. She told him about Eva, too. She had to. Eva was the focal point of her investigation. She was the reason Nadia was going to Kyiv. Nadia told him everything he could possibly want to know. Except for one thing.

"Are you going to tell me what this priceless formula is about?"

"Yes."

"When?"

"When I'm done with my investigation in Kyiv."

"I'll be accompanying you personally during your investigation."

"Then you'll have to know earlier so our meetings make sense. I'll tell you all about it during the drive from the airport."

"You're going to trust a Russian?"

"Yes."

"I'm so happy to hear you say that. It means two things."

"What's that?"

"You are an American after all."

"And?"

"There's hope for us yet."

He told her he was taking his private plane to meet her in Kyiv.

When she arrived in Kyiv at 5:15 a.m. on Monday, he was waiting for her at the terminal in Boryspil Airport. He wore a tan suede jacket over a black mock turtleneck. A day's growth on his beard added mischief to his appearance. He'd appeared freshly shaved in his pinstripe suits when she'd met with him before. His transformation left Nadia wondering how he looked in pajamas.

He kissed her on both cheeks and escorted her to his Range Rover. It was the white one in front of the two black ones surrounded by six soldier types with crew cuts and cinderblock shoulders. He held the rear door open for her and climbed in beside her. One of his men took a seat behind the wheel and drove them out of the airport.

"I left the limousine at home," he said. "I hope this is comfortable enough. Given we're going to be asking some questions in some questionable neighborhoods, I thought it best to take the vehicle that commands the most respect. You probably drive one of these yourself in New York City, don't you?"

"Range Rover? Me? Oh, sure."

The closest she'd come to Range Rovers was on the Triboro Bridge heading in and out of Manhattan, when they passed her with an implied sense of superiority. But when she climbed into the plush leather cabin, she had to admit she could get used to driving in the fast lane.

"You said someone tried to kill you. And your boy has taken off in pursuit of them. Tell me everything."

Nadia told him about what happened in the Zone of Exclusion without getting into details about why they were there. She saved that part for her discussion of the formula, which she suspected was imminent.

"Did you find Ksenia Melnik?" Nadia said.

"The woman that worked at the Division of Nervous Pathologies in Kyiv," Simeonovich said. "Yes. My people found her."

"Where is she?"

"I will tell you. And I will take you to her if you like, although I think you'll change your mind about wanting to see her. But first, you must fulfill your promise to me. You must tell me what this precious formula is about."

Nadia felt her temperature rise. The magnitude of her imminent revelation hit her. She realized for the first time that she feared she might be on the verge of betraying all mankind. The formula could theoretically be used to save a nation's population after a nuclear attack. In a nuclear exchange, one group of people could heal while another died. She was about to reveal the possible existence of such a formula to a Russian. Her ethnic distrust, planted by her immigrant parents, had been reinforced by headlines during the Cold War. Ronald Reagan's bluster about the evil empire. Stories of oppression behind the Iron Curtain. Was she about to make one of the biggest errors in judgment in mankind's history?

No, she decided. Men had tried to kill her and Johnny. One of them was holding Genesis II hostage. Those men were also Russian. They were unequivocally evil. If Bobby made a mistake and revealed himself, they might have the entire formula in their possession, if it existed. Simmy was an international business figure with a reputation for integrity, at least where Russian oligarchs were concerned. Aligning herself with him to fight the other Russians was a no-brainer.

"You had me look into records at the Division of Nervous Pathologies," Simeonovich said. "The radiation research center.

That was a strong hint. An ambitious man might draw some earth-shattering implications from that alone."

"Even a man blinded by his ambition is right once in a while."

He chuckled. "Are you saying I'm driven only by money?"

"No. I'm saying even you're right once in a while."

"American women. Are they all so insolent?"

"No. Just the ambitious ones."

Nadia turned sideways to face Simeonovich. She described the formula in detail, including her visits with Eric Sandstrom, the radiobiologist at Columbia University. She told Simeonovich about Dr. Arkady Shatan and the treatments he administered to Eva and Bobby. There was no reason for Nadia to hold back. If Simeonovich had found Ksenia Melnik, he knew that she'd worked for the brilliant, reclusive, and dead former Soviet scientist.

Simeonovich glanced at Nadia occasionally, but mostly stared at the seatback in front of her. He listened without interruption and maintained a stoic expression until she finished speaking. When she was done he glanced at her casually, as though she'd just finished giving him the weather forecast.

"Who else knows about this?" he said.

"Johnny Tanner knows everything," she said. "He's on his way to the States. And the people who fought us and took Genesis II hostage probably know something." Nadia remembered Victor Bodnar. Nadia didn't know how much the old thief knew, but it was irrelevant. He was in Riker's Island prison and going to stay there for ten years.

"Anyone else?"

"No—" The memory of a flying boomerang popped into her mind. "Wait. There's the angel. He may or may not know about the formula, but he was following us for a reason."

"Angel?" Simeonovich appeared confused. "What angel?"

Nadia rolled her eyes. "Oh my God. I forgot to tell you about the angel." She recounted how two boomerangs saved their lives.

"And you didn't see anyone?"

"Not a soul."

"Extraordinary." Simeonovich sounded like an Englishman. Native Russians who spoke fluent English often did so with a British flair. That England was held in the highest cultural regard across the former Soviet Union undoubtedly contributed to this.

He turned to his driver and spoke in rapid-fire Russian. He told him to inform the men in the other cars that there were two other interested parties. One was a group of Russians. Based on their actions in Japan, they were armed, trained, and serious. There was no reason to suspect they had any idea Nadia was in Ukraine. The second might be one or more men who favored the use of boomerangs. Their ethnic origin was unclear.

The driver said, "Unclear but certain."

Simeonovich grunted in agreement.

"What does that mean?" Nadia said.

"Boomerangs are used to herd reindeer in Siberia," Simeonovich said. "Your angel is most likely Siberian. Quite possibly a Yakut from the Yakutia Republic. They are great herders. Experts with the boomerang."

Nadia glanced at him out of the corner of her eyes. "You're from Siberia, too? Chukotka, wasn't it?"

Simeonovich crinkled his brow as though amused by her implication he might know the angel. "Yes. Chukotka is near Yakutia. I'm sure this man and I would have been practically neighbors, if it weren't for the fact that Yakutia is the world's largest subnational territory, and only slightly smaller than India."

"Point taken," Nadia said. "Now tell me why you think I might not want you to take me to see Ksenia Melnik?"

"Because she's dead."

"What?"

"Robbery-homicide."

Nadia felt deflated. Her best lead gone. "That's a bit coincidental, don't you think?"

He shrugged. "Who's to say? Such acts of violence are not uncommon. A delivery man sees something valuable. A break-in follows. These criminals are not the smartest men in the library. They assume the woman is gone, but in fact she's still there."

"Wait," Nadia said. "She had a son. Bobby told me so. His name is—"

"Denys. Denys Melnik. We're going to go have a chat with him now."

Nadia checked her watch. "It's only 5:20 a.m."

"He's an early riser."

"How can you be sure?"

"Because we're going to wake him up."

CHAPTER 30

———— ❄ ————

THEY DROVE TO KYIV. A WINDING ROAD REVEALED COBBLE-stone streets, old mansions, and monuments. Nadia recognized Podil, the oldest part of Kyiv. She remembered her dinner at the River Palace, Simmy's private club. The circumstances had been equally daunting. Bobby had been facing life in prison on a murder charge. Simmy had hired her to analyze a company for him and she couldn't refuse. She'd needed the money. At the same time, it created an opportunity for her to go back to Chornobyl and unravel the mystery behind the murder charge. But as ominous as the prospect of Bobby at Rikers Island jail had been at the time, this was even worse. At least there was a rule of law in America, even in one of its more notorious jails. In Russia, anything could happen. There was no roll call for inmates in the morning. Bobby could vanish if the wrong people found out he was following Genesis II.

They arrived at a Victorian home on a hilltop above the River Dnipro.

"How old is he?" Nadia said.

"Nineteen."

"What do you know about him?"

"He's going to inherit the equivalent of 210,000 dollars from his mother's death, and her generous pension. He's set for a few decades. He can live in her apartment and pursue his dream of making it to the PHL."

"PHL?"

"Ukrainian Professional Hockey League," Simmy said.

Nadia's head snapped toward him. "Hockey?"

"Very popular in Ukraine and Russia. Thousands of boys play as children in hope of making the pros. I know your boy Bobby is an accomplished player. I wouldn't be quick to draw any conclusions just because this kid plays amateur hockey."

"I wasn't drawing any conclusions. Just noting the coincidence. Both boys hung around Arkady Shatan. Both play hockey."

Simmy shrugged.

"What else?"

"There's no record of Denys Melnik being treated for radiation illness."

"You're sure?" Nadia said.

"Yes. The records have been computerized. One of my team analyzed them earlier this morning."

"Even if he wasn't treated, he hung around the office, and he was his mother's son. She could have talked. He might know more than he's willing to share. Or, he might not be willing to share what he knows."

"He'll share what he knows," Simmy said. "I wouldn't worry about that."

Simmy's confidence buoyed Nadia's spirits. For the first time since she'd met Bobby two years ago and endured a harrowing trip back to the States with him, she had a powerful, resourceful man at her side. Not that Johnny wasn't resourceful. But Simmy was rich. There was resourcefulness, and then there were *resources*. There was no substitute for the latter when one needed to extract information and travel quickly across a continent.

Nadia started to get out of the car, but Simmy pulled her back in.

"My men will make sure he's awake and dressed properly." He

winked. "They'll even put a pot of coffee on. Then we can go inside in a civilized manner."

Ten minutes later they sat in a parlor facing a frazzled teenager in a t-shirt and warm-up pants. Denys sat in a dining room chair that had been placed in front of a sofa. Slippers covered his otherwise bare feet. That was interesting, Nadia thought, because it suggested a certain amount of finesse on the part of Simmy's crew. Did the boy slip them on, or did they insist he sit before them with feet covered? He'd appeared more irritated than afraid when Nadia and Simmy walked in, at least until he saw the oligarch's face. Then his expression turned to one of awe and disbelief.

Simmy stretched his palm out toward the sofa. "May we sit down?"

The boy nodded, jaw agape.

Nadia and Simmy sat on the sofa. The two men who'd come in first stayed in the kitchen. The smell of coffee wafted into Nadia's nostrils. She sniffed twice to make sure she wasn't imagining it. She wasn't. They really were making coffee.

"Please accept our condolences on the loss of your mother," Nadia said. "Sorry to disturb you so early in the morning, but we have some urgent questions we need to ask you."

"I told the cops everything I know," Denys said. "Have you talked to them?"

His eyes darted in Simmy's direction. He swallowed as though he were nervous, leaving little doubt that he wasn't speaking the truth. Nadia knew when someone was lying to her from years of interrogating financial executives.

Obviously Nadia hadn't spoken to the police. She prepared to give him a vague answer, one that would encourage him to rehash everything he'd told them. But Simmy interrupted her.

"I've talked to the cops," he said.

Nadia shot him a look of surprise.

He gave her a stoic look in return, and smiled at Denys. "Let me tell you what they told me."

Simmy described the night of the burglary and murder. The most interesting part of the story was Denys's insistence that he hid in his bedroom closet during the entire event. He told the cops he shut the door behind him, put his headphones on, cranked up the music, and didn't hear a thing. Nadia knew from experience that the Kyiv police had more cases than they could investigate. It wasn't surprising to her that they neither had the time nor the inclination to challenge his story. As she watched him try to stay impassive while Simmy spoke, Nadia strongly suspected he knew more than he'd told the cops. His breathing was too shallow, his pallor too stark. There was something else about his appearance that struck her as notable, but she couldn't figure out what it was.

"Was that accurate?" Simmy said, when he was done.

"Pretty much," Denys said.

"Now tell us the rest," Nadia said.

"Excuse me?"

"Tell us the rest," Nadia said. "Tell us what you didn't tell the police."

Alarm registered on Denys's face.

"You might make it in the PHL," Simmy said, "but you'll never make it as a poker player. Do you want some coffee?"

One of the two men had poked his head in from the kitchen. He held a steaming pot of coffee in his hand.

"No," Denys said.

"No, you won't make it in the PHL?" Simmy said.

The kid frowned. "No. I mean no I don't want any coffee."

Simmy nodded at his man. "He'll have some. Bring three cups." He turned to the kid and dropped his chin for emphasis. "I have some connections in the PHL."

Denys laughed. "Yeah. That's what the other guy said."

Simmy frowned. "Other guy?"

"What other guy?" Nadia said.

"The guy who said he knew Wayne Gretzky and pretended to be a scout."

"*The* Wayne Gretzky?" Nadia said.

A wise-ass smile spread across Denys's lips. "Is there another?"

Simmy cleared his throat just a touch slower than one normally might have for emphasis. But when he spoke his tone was relaxed, his pitch even. "Please watch your manners, son."

Denys zipped his lips and turned eggplant. Evidently he realized that pissing off an oligarch wasn't conducive to rapid career enhancement.

"This man who pretended to be a scout . . . he asked you the same questions?" Nadia said.

"Yeah."

"What was his name?" Nadia said.

"He said his name was Max Karl. But when I asked around, no one's ever heard of a scout by that name."

"Max Karl," Nadia said, speaking to herself but out loud. "Karl Max. Karl Marx."

"What did this imposter look like?" Simmy said. "Other than a communist." Simmy glanced at Nadia with an amused look. "Obviously he must be a communist."

Denys described a man most Americans would have considered to have Eskimo features. That was a bogus word used by Americans to describe the Inuit and Yupik people of the polar region in Alaska and Siberia. Nadia knew this from her unplanned trip to Alaska last year. Given this man had spoken Russian, he was most likely Siberian.

Nadia glanced at Simmy. She knew they were both thinking the same thing.

The boomerang. Siberian reindeer herders used boomerangs. The man who'd thrown the boomerang and saved her was the same man who'd pretended to be a hockey scout. The angel had paid Denys a visit.

"And what did you tell him?" Nadia said.

Denys told them that after he heard the men come into the apartment, he hid in the closet without his headphones. He heard cajoling, shouting, and muffled voices. He only heard one sentence clearly. It was followed by the sound of a muted gunshot.

Nadia repeated what he'd heard. "'You'll find what you're looking for in Fukushima, Japan.' That's what your mother said?"

"Yes."

That would explain how the angel had known to go to Fukushima, but it didn't account for his timely arrival right when Nadia needed him to be there. Nor did it explain his motives. Nadia got so caught up in this discovery it took her a minute to realize that Denys Melnik did not appear to be grieving. There were no signs of tearstains on his cheeks. No hint of a sleepless night.

"We're sorry to disturb you at such a difficult time," Nadia said. "I'm sure you're still hurting."

Denys shrugged. "Yeah, sure. She was my mother, right?" He glanced at Simmy again and wet his lips. "But life goes on. Don't worry about it. Ask away."

Once again Nadia had the strange sensation that she was missing something. Something right in front of her nose. "What else did you tell the other guy?" she said.

Denys hesitated. Glanced at Simmy.

Simmy didn't hesitate. He knew a transaction was in the works. "I really do have connections in the hockey world." Simmy pulled out a business card and handed it to him. "And this is my real name. And my word is good."

Denys told them about a photograph his mother had once shown him in an antique book. Nadia asked him if they could have a look at the book. He nodded at an empty bookcase. The men had stolen her collectible books, presumably to make the murder look like a robbery. Denys said the photo depicted six men and one woman in the Siberian mountains. They were called the Zaroff Seven and they wore a certain type of gold ring. One of the men who'd killed his mother had been wearing such a ring. Denys had seen it through the crack in the door to his room before hiding in his closet.

Nadia's blood pressure rose. She and her brother had an encounter with two members of the Zaroff Seven in Chornobyl's Zone of Exclusion a month ago, when she'd gone to Ukraine to investigate the backstory behind the murder charge against Bobby in New York. They'd tried to kill her, but ended up dying in a fire themselves. Those men had worn similar rings.

Simmy sat stoic through the discussion of the Zaroff Seven. She wondered how much he knew about them, if he was intimately familiar with their story. Now the Zaroff Seven knew about the formula. What else could they have been looking for in Japan if not Genesis II? If they knew about the formula, they knew about Bobby.

The men brought a tray of coffee and sugar cookies. Simmy rubbed his hands with delight. Twelve hours ago she'd been in Japan. Now two polite men who looked as though they could rip a man's head off with their bare hands, while apologizing with the utmost decorum for doing so, were serving her coffee in a kid's house. A kid whose mother had just been murdered. And Simmy was completely unaffected by what was happening around him.

He munched on a cookie and sipped his coffee. Glanced at Nadia and tapped his watch. "I know," he said. "We better take the cookies to go."

Simmy extended his hand to Denys. As the kid shook it, Nadia followed the trail of red from his cheeks to his Adam's apple. And then she saw it. The object that had stirred her senses. She must have caught a glimpse of it a few times but remained so focused on extracting the necessary information from Denys that it had escaped her attention.

A thin gold necklace hung around his neck. A bump protruded beneath his v-neck t-shirt. When he leaned over to shake Simmy's hand, the object attached to the necklace popped in and out of sight.

It was a gold locket, identical to the one Bobby's father had given him on his deathbed, the one that contained half the formula for a radiation countermeasure.

As soon as she realized what it was, Nadia knew she could not and would not leave the apartment without it.

CHAPTER 31

❄

B OBBY CLOSED HIS EYES AND WILLED THE STINKY MAN WITH the baritone voice to go away. It was a silly thought, and yet he couldn't help himself. He was physically and emotionally exhausted. He couldn't handle any more problems. He wanted to be left alone.

But the man kept kicking the leg of his chair, pushing Bobby toward the window, inch by inch. The man had been sitting at a long table with eleven other Russians. Bobby had heard them toast the Japanese carmakers so he suspected they were the car dealers. This man was one of them.

Two possibilities dawned on Bobby. First, the man was mistaken. Second, he knew Bobby's true identity, and they'd met in Ukraine. If the latter was the case, there was only one place where they could have met. Used car dealers were scavengers, like the ones who had once foraged the vehicle graveyards of Chornobyl for spare parts. Either way he wasn't going to get away pretending to be asleep.

The car dealer booted his chair again. The force of the kick vibrated through Bobby's body.

"Turn around and answer me, boy," he said. "Don't make me ask you again."

Bobby rose to his feet, pretended to cower against the wall, and faced the car dealer. Bobby's hat covered his shorn ears. His comfort mask hid his nose and lips. He recognized the car dealer as soon as he saw him. Three years had passed since he'd last sold him some engine parts from an ambulance buried deep in Chornobyl's mechanical graveyard. He hadn't aged well. He'd lost ten pounds of muscle mass and gained twice that amount around his waist. His sunken cheeks suggested his drinking and smoking were quickly sucking all the life out of him.

The car dealer was the scavenger of scavengers. He relied on others to do the dirty work and profited by knowing the end buyers. Getting rid of him would require some effort and guile, otherwise Bobby would be exposed as a runaway from Ukraine living under an assumed identity. With that realization, a rush of adrenaline stiffened Bobby's nerves. For the first time in over twenty-four hours, he was awake and alert.

"Why are you kicking me?" he said in English. "Who are you and what do you want from me?"

The car dealer reeked of nicotine and body odor. He narrowed his eyes as though he couldn't believe whom he was seeing. A flicker of recognition flashed in his face.

"Take that mask off." Still speaking Russian.

"Leave me alone."

"Take it off."

"What are you saying? I don't speak Russian. English. Only English."

The car dealer reached out to grab the mask.

Bobby stepped back to the window. "Leave me alone or I'll scream for help. I will."

"Take that mask off or I'm going to rip that hat off your head."

Bobby enunciated slowly as though he were exasperated with their supposed language barrier. "I can't understand what you're saying."

"I'm going to rip that hat off your head so your disgusting half-ears are there for everyone to see. And then everyone will see you for the human scum that you are, and whatever con you have going will be over before you can collect."

Bobby tried to look nervous, as though the car dealer's threat was resonating.

The car dealer wiped his nose with his shirtsleeve. "No? Suit yourself. I would have liked to have been your partner on whatever it is you have cooking here, but I like a good freak show just as much." He lunged for Bobby's hat.

Bobby sidestepped him and deflected his arm with the outside of his own hand. The car dealer slammed into the wall. He retained his balance, swore under his breath, and turned toward Bobby.

"What was born in the Zone should stay in the Zone," he said. "Next best option? Throw it overboard." He lowered his head and started toward Bobby.

Bobby raised one hand, pulled his mask off with the other. "No. Stop," he said in Russian.

He kept his voice low, as the car dealer had, and quickly looked around the restaurant to make sure they hadn't attracted attention. Some of the men at the car dealer's table were watching, but as soon as Bobby removed his mask and the dealer stopped charging they laughed and returned to their card game. The other forty or so people in the cafeteria were engaged in their own conversations. They weren't paying attention to what was happening in the corner.

The car dealer's eyes lit up. "It is you. Adam Tesla," he said, using Bobby's old name from Ukraine, the one he'd been born with. "Deformed, derelict, and deranged. Still playing hockey?"

"Hockey?" Bobby tried to sound sarcastic, like a kid who was trying to hide his fear. "Sure. There's a nice rink in Vladivostok. I'm headed there now for a pickup game."

"Sure you are. And I'm Yul Brynner's long-lost son. I'm going to his birthplace in Vladivostok to claim the family inheritance.

Now do you want to stop bullshitting me, or do you want me to jump up on a table and tell everyone who'll listen that they're on a ship with a piece of radioactive scum?"

"I'd rather you didn't."

"Finally you say something that makes sense."

"So we're done here, right? Nice to see you again, can I go back to my nap?" Bobby reached for his chair.

"That's funny. You were always good for a laugh. Not because you were funny. How could you be? You barely said ten words over the course of how many transactions? More than ten. How many pieces did you sell me from the Zone? Was it closer to twenty?"

Bobby shrugged. He'd sold him twenty-four different vehicle parts, from starter engines to full sets of wheels. Each time he'd been petrified he was getting infected with radiation again. Each time he'd prayed it was the last. To the best of his knowledge he hadn't been infected again, and he executed his last theft with Eva five days before she died.

"Doesn't matter now," the car dealer said. His face took on a sunny disposition. "The important thing is we're friends."

"We are?"

"Of course we are."

The car dealer was changing tactics. He must have realized that if he hoped to profit from whatever he imagined Bobby was scheming, bullying wouldn't help him achieve his goal on a ferry. His mistake was that he hadn't thought of that from the start. Not that Bobby wouldn't have seen through him immediately. He would have had more respect for him, though.

The car dealer slapped him on the shoulder. "We're good old friends. No, wait. That's not true. We're not just good old friends. We're the best of friends." He pulled Bobby's chair back to one of the tables. "Come, my friend. Come sit down with me and tell me a tale."

He wiped the smile off his face to make sure Bobby knew he had no choice. As soon as Bobby stepped toward him he resumed beaming. He grinned at Bobby as though it were his turn to speak, but Bobby knew better than to open up so quickly. He had to make sure the car dealer believed he was coercing him into revealing why he'd been in Japan and why he was on the ferry.

"Are you hungry? Have you been eating? You're looking a little peaked, my boy. In fact, that was my first thought when I set eyes on you and thought I knew who you were. That looks like my old friend Adam Tesla and he doesn't look well. I wonder if I can help him."

"Lucky for me I ran into you."

"Lucky. Yes indeed. You've had bad luck most of your life, haven't you, Adam? But now your luck has changed. Something to eat?"

"No. I'm fine."

"Something to drink, perhaps. Coca-Cola?"

Bobby raised the bottle of water he kept by his duffel bag.

The car dealer looked around to make sure no one was listening. Then he pulled his chair closer to the table and leaned into Adam. "So tell me, what's the deal?"

Bobby frowned. "What do you mean?"

The car dealer rolled his eyes. "Takaoka. Vladivostok. This ferry. You're working an angle. It's money. I can smell it off you the way I could smell you're from the Zone even if I didn't know you." He tapped his nose with his finger. "A middleman can smell the money. It's his gift."

"I'll take your word for it. Me, I don't have any gifts."

The car dealer turned serious. "You used to have two gifts, far as I can remember."

Bobby raised his eyebrows. Two gifts. For the first time, he didn't know what the car dealer was talking about.

The car dealer stared beyond Bobby. "You could skate, my boy." Nostalgia peppered the car dealer's voice.

His sincerity prompted Bobby to forget they were adversaries. At least for the moment.

"I used to watch you during the games on the cooling ponds. My God, could you fly. And handle the puck. No one ever saw a kid handle the puck the way you did."

Bobby was reminded of his year at Fordham Prep and all the practice he was missing. The stakes notwithstanding, a melancholy washed over him.

"That was your first gift," the car dealer said.

"I didn't know I had a second."

A sympathetic look flashed on the car dealer's face. Once again Bobby was left at a loss. The car dealer was clearly being sincere. Bobby actually felt a genuine connection with the man. They'd both done business in the Zone. They'd both seen the hideous effects from radiation sickness handed down through generations. And they'd both profited from the wasteland the disaster had produced.

"Your second gift was your biggest one," he said.

Bobby shook his head, modestly disturbed that he wasn't able to keep one step ahead of the car dealer.

"The girl. The beauty who tried not to be one. The one with the legs that went from Kyiv to Minsk. What was her name again?"

"Eva."

"The first time I met the two of you—tractor transmission, I think it was—she acted more like your sister. Last time you both did business with me? A month before she died. Last time I saw the two of you together? I could tell that she loved you."

Bobby lost his breath. "How?"

"The two of you stepped out of her father's car. You walked up to me with the goods. A wind was blowing. You both started shivering. You offered her your coat and she looked at you as though you'd insulted her."

"I remember that." Bobby could picture her glare, offended that he dare suggest she couldn't handle the weather as easily as a man.

"She gave you a look, the kind a strong woman gives to a man. But you walked behind her and draped the coat over her shoulders anyways. And when you stepped forward to hand me the box with the goods, she looked at you again."

"She did?"

The car dealer nodded. "I saw her. I saw her look at you. I saw the look on her face, and I knew right then."

"What?"

"That she loved you."

Bobby let the words echo in his ears a few times, then reminded himself that the car dealer had an agenda. He was trying to soften him up. Still, Bobby was certain the man wasn't creative enough to have made up the story. It was much easier for him to summon a memory, and for that reason, Bobby had no doubt he was telling the truth.

"I heard she passed away," the car dealer said. "Sympathies."

Bobby nodded. If only he knew what was really going on.

The car dealer cleared his throat. "But that is the past, and there's nothing we can do about it. Let's look to the future. Tell me. What are you doing so far away from home? You can't possibly be on your own, can you? What's the score?"

The car dealer knew that Bobby's deceased father had been a notorious thief with connections all over the former Soviet Union, especially Siberia.

"Electronics," Bobby said. "It's big. When my father died, some friends of his gave me a job. I moved to Vladivostok. They sent me to Japan to meet with a guy. They didn't want to take the risk of leaving the country themselves. You know, with their pasts and all that."

"So much responsibility. You need an advisor. Lucky you ran into me. Do you keep your money at home or in the bank?"

It was blackmail. Plain and simple. The car dealer wanted to get paid for not revealing Bobby's true identity.

"At home," Bobby said. "My father taught me the safest place to keep my money was in a sack with dirty underwear. Most thieves are men, and most men don't like digging through another man's stinky skivvies."

"Your father was the wisest of the wise men. He taught his son well. We will stay close to each other the rest of the trip. That way we can learn from each other."

"Great idea," Bobby said.

He needed another great idea soon, one that would let him escape from the car dealer and follow Eva and the driver when they arrived at Vladivostok.

CHAPTER 32

---※---

NADIA WAITED FOR A LULL IN THE CONVERSATION BETWEEN Simmy and Denys. They had segued into a debate over which of the two reigning Russian stars in the NHL was the better player, Ilya Kovalchuk or Alexander Ovechkin. Nadia had heard Bobby talk about both of them with his friend Derek when they watched games in her apartment. She knew they were two of the golden boys of professional hockey, but she had her eye on something with a more tangible golden hue: the necklace hanging around Denys Melnik's neck.

She tried to think of a clever way to approach the topic but couldn't conjure one. That left her no choice but to be painfully direct.

"That's a nice-looking necklace you're wearing," Nadia said.

Denys lowered his chin and grasped it. He pulled the locket out from beneath his shirt. It looked identical to the one Dr. Arkady Shatan had given Bobby's father, who in turn had passed it on to him. But Nadia couldn't be certain until she held it in her hands.

"This?" Denys said. "My mother gave it to me. She said Dr. Arkady made the locket himself. I guess he was one of those Renaissance men. He could do anything. The guy was a genius."

"Do you keep something special inside it?"

Simmy studied Nadia. He kept a straight face, but Nadia sensed he was wondering about her motives for asking the question.

"No," Denys said. He narrowed his eyes, pulled the tiny clasp open, and revealed the inside. "I used to have a picture of my girl inside but we broke up." He shrugged. "It's empty now but I still wear it. I don't know why. I guess I just got used to having it around my neck."

"May I take a closer look?"

"Sure." Denys slipped the necklace off his neck and handed it to Nadia.

As soon as Nadia palmed the locket she knew it had come from the same mold as the one Bobby's father had given him. Same oval shape. Same depth and dimensions. Same contours.

"May I open it?"

"Sure."

Nadia opened the tiny clasp. The locket was empty. Its interior mold was also identical. Nadia smiled at him. "I'd like to buy it from you. I collect lockets."

Denys made a disapproving sound. "I don't want to sell it. Dr. Arkady made it. I used to hang out in his office waiting for my mother to finish work. He was a weird guy but he was always nice to me. I guess the locket has sentimental value."

"Sentimental value," Simmy said. He pulled his wallet out of his pocket. "You can't put a price on it, except you can put a price on everything, can't you?"

Nadia examined the locket further. There was no evidence of any etchings beneath the gilding, but there hadn't been any such signs on Bobby's locket either. The only way to be certain was to remove the gilding. What were the odds this locket contained some part of the formula? Close to zero, Nadia thought. But she had to know.

"Listen," Denys said, eyeing Simmy's wallet. "I really don't want to sell it."

"I like your style, my boy," Simmy said. "You're a good negotiator. There's a career for you in business once you hit forty and your illustrious hockey career comes to a glorious end." He cracked the billfold open.

Nadia reached over and put her hand on top of his. She added sufficient pressure to close the wallet. Simmy cast a look of surprise at her. She gave him a quick, firm smile. Just because he'd shelled out fifty grand for an airplane rental for her didn't mean she was going to rely on him to cover every expense.

"Denys, please," Nadia said. "I can't explain why, but if you sold this locket to me it would mean a lot to me. I'm pretty sure this isn't real gold. It's just made of steel with a nice coat of gold paint on top of it."

"Yeah," he said. "I know. My mother told me it was more a keepsake than anything valuable." He glanced at Simmy's wallet and turned back to Nadia. "What kind of price did you have in mind?"

"How about one hundred American dollars?"

Denys nodded as though it was a fair offer and lowered his head for a moment. When he raised it again he was blushing. "How about two hundred?"

Nadia gave him a traveler's check for two hundred dollars, thanked him, and said good-bye.

"I need a knife," Nadia said, on the way to the car.

"Music to a man's ears," Simmy said, "when a woman asks him for a knife. What for?"

"To scrape the gilding off this locket and see if there's anything etched beneath it."

"You don't need a knife to do that."

"I don't?"

"No. You need one of my men to do it while we watch."

They climbed in the SUV. One of Simmy's men used the serrated edge of a hunting knife to strip the gilding from the locket. When he was done, he wiped it clean with a bandana, and handed it to Nadia.

Nadia examined the entire surface of the locket. There was nothing etched beneath it. She rolled her fingers over the bare iron and imagined running her fingers over the tiny indents that existed on the locket Dr. Arkady had given Adam. She wondered whether Genesis II had the same locket as Bobby or Denys Melnik. She wondered how Bobby was doing.

Simmy's driver started the car and drove.

"I'm afraid you're out of luck," Simmy said.

Nadia considered his statement. "Not entirely."

"How so?"

"We've discovered an identical locket. That means there are at least two of them. And we learned that Arkady Shatan made them himself. There very well may be a third."

"Genesis II?" Simmy said.

"Yes."

"Or shall we call her Eva?"

"I don't know. Let's not get ahead of ourselves. That's what I'm here to find out, right?"

"No. That's what *we're* here to find out."

"Right. Sorry. That's what *we're* here to find out."

Simmy's reminder that he was now equally vested in her mission to meet up with Bobby and discover once and for all if a formula existed stirred mixed emotions. Without his assistance, she wouldn't be in Kyiv. With his assistance, she was now indebted to another person.

One she still wasn't certain she could trust.

CHAPTER 33

———— ❄ ————

CARS CRAWLED ALONG THE STREETS OF THE CAPITAL OF Ukraine. Pedestrians marched on sidewalks toward trains and businesses. Nadia never ceased to be amazed at how well the people of Kyiv dressed. It was a source of cultural pride, an old-school European custom. Day or night, people dressed up whether they were going to work or out for a coffee. The per capita income in Ukraine was approximately 3,600 dollars, less than one-thirteenth of that in America. You wouldn't have known it by looking at the sidewalks. The people were honest, friendly, and worked hard just to survive. Their pride in themselves and their country showed by the way they carried themselves in public.

Nadia glanced at her watch for the second time since they'd left the apartment six minutes ago. Simmy finished a call with his assistant. He'd kept his voice low. As a result, Nadia couldn't overhear everything he'd said. But she was certain she'd heard him use the word *detective* twice.

"It's not going to work," he said, after he hung up.

"What's not going to work?"

"Checking your watch every minute is not going to make the time go by any slower." Simmy chuckled. "Trust me, I've tried this several thousand times."

Nadia looked away, pretending to be irritated. "Don't be ridiculous. I'm not checking my watch every minute." She sighed. "I'm checking it every three minutes."

"Pardon me. I'm sure that will be much more effective."

"Let's confirm my timetable one more time," Nadia said. "The flight from Kyiv to Vladivostok will take eleven hours. How far is the Vladivostok airport from the ferry?"

"About fifty kilometers. Call it an hour and a half to allow for traffic." Simmy glanced out the window and made a sour face. "Not this kind of traffic. Just traffic."

"Call it two hours to be on the safe side. That's thirteen hours' travel time. Kyiv is eight hours behind Vladivostok. That means I have to be on a plane no later than 4:00 p.m. to meet the ferry at 1:00 p.m. And that leaves little to no cushion for unexpected delays."

"There will be no unexpected delays. We will be on my jet well before 4:00 p.m. You have my word on that."

Nadia squeezed his arm. "Thank you."

"We're going to save time by doing two things at once."

"How are we going to do that?"

"You and I are going to the Central Clinic," Simmy said.

The Central Clinic was one of Kyiv's finest hospitals. Simmy had discovered that Dr. Arkady Shatan had been affiliated with it. That's where he'd treated patients who'd required hospitalization. Logic dictated that Eva would have been admitted and treated there before she supposedly died.

"And my men are going to go to the Civil Registry Office. That's where recent birth, marriage, and death certificates are kept. They will look for the birth and death certificates for one Eva Vovk."

"Vovk," Nadia said. She'd met someone in Chicago with that last name, so it wasn't entirely uncommon. But it was certainly most memorable. It was the Ukrainian word for wolf. "That was her last name?"

"Yes. You said she lived with her uncle in Korosten and that he was a former member of the Soviet National hockey team back in its glory days. We traced her through him. She was the only Eva in the secondary school, and her address in school records matched that of the uncle. Same last name, too."

"So the uncle was on her father's side."

Simmy said, "Why does that matter?"

"Not saying it does. Just noting it for the record."

Simmy rolled his eyes. "Forensic analysts."

"That's right. That's why you pay them the moderately big bucks."

"Moderate?"

Nadia shrugged. "Compared to the oligarch's typical payday. Very moderate."

Simmy donned a look of mock irritation and shook his head. "Still insolent."

"You've arranged for someone to help us navigate our way through the hospital?"

"Yes. Nothing commands respect like a detective's badge and a gun."

"Except for money."

"Depends on where the gun is pointed. He should be waiting for us when we get there. Which would be five minutes from now if it weren't for this damn traffic. In the meantime, tell me again what you know about the Zaroff Seven and what your connection is to them?"

"Me?" Nadia said. "I was going to ask you that."

"You asked me about them a month ago and I told you. They were former Soviet administrators who cashed in their political connections and used the system to get rich during privatization."

"You mean they pilfered state assets."

"From a Westerner's point of view, yes. From a Russian's point of view, they used the system to their advantage. Boris Yeltsin created the rules for privatization. Blame him."

"He's dead."

"That shows you what a waste of time it is to blame people. As I told you before, the Zaroff Seven were remnants of old Russia. Of the Soviet Union and the lawless transition that followed. Individually, they weren't so powerful as to be intimidating, in business or in politics. But collectively they had capital and political clout. And they had the ear of the president and the prime minister."

"Aren't they one and the same man?"

"Exactly. Two offices. Two ears. One man."

"You used the past tense. The Zaroff Seven don't have that kind of clout anymore?"

"No. It appears there are only three of them left. Two died of natural causes. Two others vanished under mysterious circumstances a month ago. Right around when you were asking me questions about them." He narrowed his eyes. "You wouldn't know anything about their disappearance, would you?"

"Me? Don't be ridiculous."

Nadia knew the two men had died in the fire at her deceased uncle's house, but she didn't know where the babushka had buried the bodies. A neighbor's root cellar, she supposed. And one of the two original deaths hadn't been natural. Bobby had pushed the sole female member into the cooling ponds while defending his and Eva's lives.

"It's obvious they've found out about the formula," Simmy said.

Indeed, Nadia thought. What had begun for them as a search for comrades had turned into a treasure hunt.

"Once they discovered there was a formula," Nadia said, "they zeroed in on Arkady Shatan's assistant, Ksenia Melnik, the only person alive with intimate knowledge of his work. Based on what her son told us he heard, she sent them to Japan for the second half of the formula."

"What about the first half of the formula? What about the part only you and Bobby have?"

Nadia told Simmy about the Russians who'd showed up at her apartment in New York and the ones she'd evaded at the airport. "They were after the formula, I'm sure."

"All right then," Simmy said. "It's much easier to fight a battle when you know your enemy. The driver who lifted Genesis II. The man Bobby is following. The odds are high he's with the Zaroff Seven."

"Which means Bobby's following the men who want to capture him."

"I like this boy's style. He's fearless. When he decides he wants something, there's no stopping him. He reminds me of someone."

"I wonder who."

"Men like the Zaroff Seven. Old-school Russian nationalists who think the Soviet Union should be re-created. They may not care about the beneficial implications for a countermeasure to radiation. The medical implications, for instance. They may see it more as a military application that would help them achieve their ultimate goal. Colonize the independent states that once made up the Soviet Union under Russian leadership. Return the new Russia to superpower status."

"I doubt the president and prime minister of Russia would disapprove of that agenda," Nadia said.

Simmy didn't comment. How could he? The president and prime minister was an old-school strongman in disguise. He'd permitted Simmy to accumulate his businesses, wealth, and power. Without his approval, Simmy wouldn't have succeeded to the same extent. If the president and prime minister changed his mind and disapproved, Simmy could find himself convicted of corruption or embezzlement charges and serving an indefinite prison sentence like other oligarchs before him.

They arrived at the hospital at 10:10 a.m. A detective was waiting for them in the lobby. He had a picture of Eva with him. It was a headshot taken three years ago. Stringy black hair and purple lipstick. Carved cheekbones with small facial features. Too extreme, too Slavic to be called gorgeous. Yet definitely distinctive. Nadia could picture them at school, the two social castaways with no one but each other to rely on.

"This picture was in the system," the detective said. "From her dosimetric passport. The radiation treatment unit was supposed to update it every year. But this is the most recent one."

The detective established his credentials. A nurse searched a computer system for records of admission for one Eva Vovk. She found one such record. It corresponded to the week prior to Eva's death. The orthopedist who'd treated her was not due to arrive for another forty-five minutes.

"I hate to waste time sitting around," Nadia said, "but in my experience a phone call is not as reliable as an interview. The only way to tell if a man is telling the truth is by studying his extremities. That's where the tells are. The lips, the Adam's apple, the hands, the arms, the legs."

"Adam's apple," Simmy said. "Who would have thought? And all this time I thought you were staring at my lips."

"Of course you did. Humility is not a prerequisite to the oligarch's major."

Simmy frowned. "Excuse me?"

"Never mind," Nadia said. "It doesn't translate that well from English."

He raised his eyebrows. "More insolence?"

Nadia laughed. "Pretty much."

"Good. I like it when you're insolent to me."

"You do?"

A little smile spread across his lips. "Within reason, of course."

"Ah, within reason. And who decides what's reasonable?"

"The less tolerant person, of course. The needier one with more limitations."

"Ooh. This is getting good. And which of us is that?"

Simmy studied her, smile still etched in his face. "I'm not sure. I think we're pretty similar. We like to think we have no needs or limitations . . ." He lowered his voice for effect. "But it's a lie."

"Is it?" It was. If loneliness implied need and limitations, Simmy was right. "Huh. I guess that'll have to remain a mystery for now."

"Yes." Simmy raised his chin and looked away with a contented expression. "For now."

They sat in the waiting area. Simmy's man brought tea and ham sandwiches from the cafeteria. Nadia ate her lunch, unsure when she would have the opportunity to eat again. The doctor showed up on time at exactly 11:00 a.m.

"I remember Eva well," he said. "She'd been a swimmer her first year in secondary school. Set all sorts of school records at a ridiculously early age. Incredible physical specimen. A true athletic talent. I remember asking her why she quit and she said because it wasn't fair. She said she had an unfair advantage. She said she was stronger than the others because of the treatments her personal physician had been administering to her. That was nonsense. If anything she suffered from a weaker immune system based on the usual regimen prescribed for thyroid cancer. I asked her if she got along with her teammates and she said no. They hated her. Didn't like being in the water with her. That's the real reason she quit. Problems with socialization. It's not uncommon for Chornobyl children."

"What did you treat her for?" Nadia said.

"Initially, an open fracture to the left fibula. They said it was a hiking accident. She slipped and fell down a mountain."

Nadia pictured her falling as she tried to run away from the Zaroff Seven with Bobby. "Who said?"

"She and her uncle."

"She needed surgery?" Simmy said.

184

"The surgery was successful, but this type of break—where the bone protrudes through the skin—is very susceptible to infection. She returned within a week in bad shape."

"She didn't respond to antibiotics?" Nadia said.

"I wouldn't say that. I wouldn't say that at all."

"You wouldn't?" Simmy said.

"Oh, no. Her fever had dropped and she'd stabilized before she was released."

"She was released?" Simmy said.

Nadia said, "She didn't die here?"

"No. I heard about her passing a week later, but she didn't die here."

"Why did you release her?" Simmy said.

The doctor's jaw tightened. "Because I had no say in the matter. It was her uncle's right to sign her out to another doctor's care."

"What doctor?" Nadia said.

"A man by the name of Arkady Shatan. Dr. Arkady Shatan. Eva Vovk died a few days later under his supervision."

CHAPTER 34

NADIA AND SIMMY RETURNED TO HIS CAR AFTER THEIR meeting with Eva's orthopedic surgeon. Nadia waited until Simmy was seated beside her before checking her watch. She wanted to make sure he noticed her doing so to reinforce her sense of urgency. In her experience, the super-rich boasted short attention spans and mercurial personalities. They were also risk takers content to push timetables to the limit.

"It's 11:35," she said. "Four and a half hours left. And that's if I want to push it. And I don't want to push it."

Simmy's driver handed him a computer tablet from the front seat. Simmy took the tablet and cast a bemused look at Nadia. "Push it? When did I ever suggest I wanted to push anything with you?"

Nadia blushed.

"When someone tells me something," Simmy said, "I remember it. I don't need to hear it twice. And when I give my word I'm going to do something, my word is good. I'm going to have you in Vladivostok on time."

"I didn't mean to offend you," Nadia said. "It's just that dealing with you is even harder than dealing with the president and prime minister of Russia."

"This I have to hear."

"Same idea, fifty percent more complicated."

"How so?"

"You are oligarch, client, and friend. Three men, two ears. That's fifty percent more man per ear than the president and prime minister of Russia."

"Is that true?"

"Certainly. It's a matter of mathematics. Talking to you is— by definition—fifty percent more complicated."

"No. Not that. Is it true we're friends? And I don't mean by American standards for friendship between a man and a woman."

"What are the American standards?"

"You get the benefit of my private plane. I get the benefit of your beauty and your insolence."

"That doesn't sound like any kind of friendship I've ever had."

"I should hope not. You're a woman, and you don't have a private plane. At least not yet."

"I like the sound of that last part. And yes, we've become friends by universal standards."

"What are those?"

"There are times we would rather be together than apart."

Simmy chuckled. "Always the analyst. Not exactly heart-melting, but remarkably accurate."

"Get me to Vladivostok on time and my heart will be yours." The words escaped Nadia's lips before she could stop herself.

Simmy's eyes twinkled. "Has any man ever had more incentive?"

"Always the deal maker. Not exactly real and true, but remark-ably sweet."

Nadia pictured her father telling her it was the formula the Russian wanted. She was merely a distraction. What her father never could have contemplated was that perhaps the rich man was merely a distraction for her, too. The reality was she simply wasn't sure what Simmy meant to her, beyond being her current salvation and a source of excitement.

He shook his head and studied the computer. "My men found Eva's death certificate. Cause of death was sepsis. From the infection. They also checked the cemeteries in Korosten. It was the logical place for her uncle to bury her."

"And?"

"They found her. Same name, dates of birth and death match."

"That doesn't necessarily mean her body is in that grave," Nadia said. "If her death was staged. If her uncle was trying to protect her from the Zaroff Seven seeking revenge for the death of one of their own. Even if Bobby killed the woman in self-defense, Eva might have been at risk. Her uncle might have taken drastic measures to compel the Zaroff Seven to forget about her. She might still be alive. The grave might be empty."

"It might. That's why we're going to take a ride and pay our respects."

"Our respects? To whom?"

"To the man who makes the burial arrangements, the one who oversees the actual burials, and the deceased."

"You want to dig up the grave?"

"Don't you?"

"I . . . I guess so. Will they let us?"

"My men have already come to an arrangement with him."

"An arrangement?"

"Yes. An arrangement."

Nadia didn't want to unearth a grave and disturb the dead, but excitement and urgency supplanted her misgivings.

"Is there a birth certificate?" she said.

"I'm sure there is, but they haven't found it yet. For whatever reason it appears there's more order in death than in life in Ukraine."

Nadia examined the death certificate. Her uncle was listed as the surviving relative. Eva had not been married, the injury had not taken place at school or at work, and no autopsy had been performed. And why would there have been an autopsy if Eva had died from an illness? Or if she hadn't died at all? Nadia scrolled through the pages to find the signature.

The death certificate had been signed by Arkady Shatan.

Eva's death had been staged. Nadia was sure of it. Such a ruse was the stuff she'd been dealing with ever since a man had been shot in the streets of New York and whispered a cryptic clue in her ear a year ago. Dr. Arkady and Eva's uncle had wanted the world to believe Eva was dead.

And they'd succeeded.

The driver covered the hundred-mile trip from Kyiv to Korosten in less than two hours. They drove past the city limits to the Old Cemetery. The driver pulled up to a square stone building on cemetery grounds. The second SUV parked beside them. A rectangular wooden shed wobbled beside it. The door to the shed was open. A lawnmower lay on its side. A bald man with a heavily lined face emerged from behind it. Grease stains blackened his hands. Caution shone in his eyes.

One of Simmy's men introduced himself as the man who'd called him that morning. They had a quick chat in hushed tones. The cemetery man nodded throughout the talk. When they were finished, Simmy's man slipped him an envelope. The cemetery man opened it to check its contents. Nadia watched him fan through a stack of hryvnia. He nodded again. Through the entire process, the cemetery man remained stoic.

Simmy and Nadia followed the cemetery man inside the building. Two of Simmy's men trailed behind them.

They entered a bare-bones office with simple wooden furniture. Scratches and stains marred the desk. A thermos, telephone, and calendar rested atop it. The chairs facing him had no cushions and looked equally worn. Binders lined a bookshelf. Dust covered the notebooks.

The cemetery man reached for one of them. It was the only notebook not covered in dust.

"I recognized the name as soon as he called and asked me about her," the cemetery man said. "Eva Vovk. Name like that. Who could forget? Lot four. Plot two hundred forty-six. I know all the names. One thousand two hundred forty of them. These people are my friends. The gravestones talk to me. They talk to me, you know?"

Nadia traded glances with Simmy.

The cemetery man grinned. "You don't believe me, do you? Probably think there's something a little wrong with me."

"No," Nadia said. "We all have at least one special skill."

"That's right, that's right," the cemetery man said. He scrunched his eyes together. "What's your special talent, honey?"

"A lady never tells. Who delivered the body to you? Was there a funeral home involved?"

The cemetery man cracked the notebook open to an earmarked page. "No funeral home. I can't remember how the body got here. It just showed up."

"Was the body in a casket?" Nadia said.

The cemetery man shrugged. "Where else would it have been?"

"But if there was no funeral home involved, where did the casket come from?"

"How would I know? The recently departed arrived in a casket. They all do. It's none of my concern where the casket came from."

"But it didn't come from a funeral home," Simmy said.

"Is there an echo in here?"

Simmy glared at him.

"No. It didn't come from a funeral home," the cemetery man said. "I have it written right here. Received directly from hospital."

"Hospital?" Nadia said. "What hospital?"

"I don't know what hospital."

"Are you sure it was a hospital?" Simmy said.

The cemetery man considered the question. "I guess not.

Maybe I just assumed she came from the hospital, given there was no funeral home involved."

"Was there a burial ceremony?" Nadia said.

"There was a small gathering. I wouldn't call it a ceremony."

Nadia said, "How many people?"

"Three."

"For a man who doesn't remember everything, you seem pretty sure of that."

"That's because of her uncle. The departed's uncle. I knew who he was as soon as I saw him. Staroslav Vovk. Defenseman on the Soviet National hockey team during the seventies. Became an assistant coach later on. I used to watch all the games. He did not age well. Happened to a lot of Soviet athletes once they faded from the headlines. Most people wouldn't have recognized him, but I was a real fan. I used to watch all the games, you know."

"Who else was there?" Nadia said.

"Some city type," the cemetery man said. "Tall, crazy hair going in every direction, spoke real intelligent. Definitely an educated man."

Karel, Nadia thought. The botanist she'd met in the Zone a year ago. He'd been friends with Bobby's father, Damian, and Dr. Arkady. He'd helped Nadia and Bobby escape Ukraine, then died a year later. He'd been a friend of Bobby's, which meant he'd also known Eva. His attendance was to be expected.

"And?" Simmy said.

"A short old man with a cane. Didn't say much. He paid the bill."

"If he paid the bill, you must have his signature somewhere," Nadia said.

"I have better than that," the cemetery man said. "I have his name right here as the contact for the burial."

He showed Nadia the ledger. The contact's name was Dr. Arkady Shatan. Nadia tilted the ledger so that Simmy could see it. He read the ledger but showed no emotion.

"No priest?" Nadia said.

"No. There was no religious ceremony."

That didn't necessarily mean anything, Nadia thought, but it was unusual. Most Ukrainians were Orthodox Christians, and there was a strong contingency of Catholics in Western Ukraine.

"The doctor said a few words," the cemetery man said. "A few raindrops fell—I remember because no one was shedding any tears so the heavens opened up to show some sympathy for the recently departed—and that was that. They left."

"Any visitors since then?" Simmy said.

"None. Not a single person."

"How can you be so sure?" Nadia said.

The cemetery man glared at her as though he were offended. "Because she would have told me."

"Excuse me?" Simmy said.

"The spirit of the departed. Eva Vovk. She would have told me. The dead, you see, they speak to me."

"They speak to you," Simmy said.

"Who else do they have to talk to?"

"I see your point," Simmy said. He pretended to scratch his forehead, shielded his face, and rolled his eyes at Nadia.

The cemetery man replaced his ledger on the shelf.

Nadia and Simmy went outside.

"I find it hard to trust a man who believes he speaks with the dead," Simmy said.

"As opposed to the corporate men you deal with every day?" Nadia said. "In Russia, England, and America? The ones who run our corporations, with such sterling ethics?"

"I trust them even less."

"He was lucid, he remembered details about the burial, and he didn't hesitate when he answered questions. He sounded reliable to me, up until the bit about talking with the dead. Eva died of an infection. Why no funeral home? Why no visitation hours? She had to know other people. Teachers, people who took care of her growing up. People who would have wanted to pay their final respects."

"Don't be so sure. She was a child of Chornobyl. You yourself said they were social outcasts. And maybe the uncle couldn't afford the funeral home."

"You may be right about that. Still, no priest strikes me as suspicious, too."

"Not me. She was an orphan. She was buried by two scientists and a former hockey player and coach. If the latter three weren't religious, why would they want a priest? Why would they pay for a priest?"

"Always the financial angle," Nadia said.

"Financial challenges are the reality here. That makes it one of the most important angles. My men arranged for him to raise the casket as soon as he arrived this morning. A quick ride and all will be illuminated."

They drove deeper into the cemetery. Mounds of dirt surrounded a plot. A closed casket rested beside it. The cemetery man arrived in a dilapidated truck with cracked sea-foam paint and blotches of rust. A young protégé with an obvious affinity for beer climbed out of the truck with him. They worked the latches on the casket.

Simmy took an audible breath beside Nadia. "No offense intended, Nadia. I understand your sense of urgency and the danger of Bobby's current situation. But I must be honest."

Nadia raised her eyebrows, unsure of what he intended to say.

"This is more exciting than buying low and selling high."

Nadia breathed a sigh of relief. She feared he was going to confess the entire business was a giant nuisance. "I suspect that depends on just how low you bought and high you're selling."

Simmy cocked his head to the side and nodded. "Yes. I guess you're right."

The cemetery man and his protégé opened the casket. Nadia took a breath and stepped forward.

A human skeleton rested inside.

"Broad pelvis, narrow collarbone, small frontal and temporal bones," Simmy said. "Looks like a woman to me. And there's evidence of a break in the left fibula."

Nadia saw the broken bone below the knee. It brought back memories. She'd stabilized a broken tibia for a distressed hiker on the Appalachian Trail during a three-day Ukrainian Girl Scout survival test. Both bones belonged to strangers she'd never met. The difference was this one would never heal.

She appraised Simmy with a fresh perspective. "Did you work in a morgue?"

"No. My platoon stumbled on a mass grave in Siberia when I was in the Army. I watched and listened when the forensic technicians came. So much for your theory. There lies a woman. There lies Eva Vovk."

Nadia stared at the skeleton. How could she be sure it belonged to Eva? Nadia wished she had more time to investigate further.

A voice startled her from behind.

"You're right on the first count," the cemetery man said, "but wrong on the second."

Simmy regarded him with curiosity. "How so?"

"A girl definitely lies there, but she is not Eva Vovk."

"Why do you say that?" Nadia said.

"Because this girl speaks to me. I told you. When I tend to her lot."

Simmy gave Nadia another skeptical glance.

Nadia said, "And what does she say?"

"That she has finally found peace now that she is alone."

Nadia waited for him to follow up, but he didn't add anything. "And?" she said.

The cemetery man shrugged. "And nothing. That's all the proof you need the girl is not Eva Vovk."

Simmy looked amused and confused. "How is that?"

"Eva Vovk. Her last name means wolf. Wolves travel in packs. No wolf would ever say she was at peace now that she was alone. A wolf would only find peace with others like her. I'm not educated like you two and I may just move dirt for a living, but this I guarantee you. That is not the body of Eva Vovk."

CHAPTER 35

N ADIA AND SIMMY COMPLETED THEIR BUSINESS AT THE cemetery in twenty minutes. They were back on the road to Kyiv by 1:55 p.m. That left them two hours until Nadia' self-imposed deadline for her plane to depart for Vladivostok.

"Not only will my driver make up time on the ground," Simmy said, "my pilot will make up time in the air."

He excused himself while he called his assistant to get briefed on what had transpired since he'd last talked to her half an hour ago. Such was the life of an oligarch. He ran a multi-billion-dollar empire. He demanded performance and held his employees accountable. He didn't micromanage them but he stayed informed so that he understood the business. Charities, pension funds, other businesses depended on him. Nadia had worked for such men in New York City. They were consumed with their work. In Nadia's experience, such men had to maintain an exhilarating pace for fear of coming to rest and realizing the magnitude of their unhappiness in their lives.

Simmy finished his call and hung up.

"I'm not convinced it's Eva's body in the casket," Nadia said.

Simmy appeared distracted. "Pardon? Oh. Yes. I see. Would you like to spend the night so you can talk to the recently departed and ask her yourself?"

"Very funny. Dr. Arkady and Eva's uncle were relevant in the Soviet era. A scientist and a hockey star. If they weren't powerful, they were at least well-connected. Maybe they maintained their connections. Maybe one of them knew someone that could have provided him with a similar-looking corpse. Or sold him one. Maybe they were able to stage a burial with an actual body, someone who died of an accident or natural causes, perhaps another orphan or a homeless girl. It wouldn't be too hard to break a fibula, either, to make the illusion even more convincing."

"You've been watching too much American television."

"I barely watch any television. But I'll admit that the bit about the wolf not wanting to rest alone did resonate with me."

"Oh that's much more comforting." Simmy sighed. "Are you pleased with what you were able to discover under such difficult time constraints?"

"Yes. Denys Melnik was hugely helpful. We know it's the Zaroff Seven who've been one step ahead of us. They think there's a formula, and they'll kill to get it. They killed his mother and she was the last person alive with knowledge of whether Dr. Arkady completed the formula. You'd have to believe the answer is yes. She sent them to Japan for a reason. We also know he made the locket Bobby wears around his neck. Denys Melnik had a copy, and so does Genesis II. The question is, if it is Eva's remains in the casket, who is Bobby following? And who is Genesis II?"

"The answers may be in Siberia, and the road through Siberia will begin in Vladivostok."

Nadia checked her watch out of sheer instinct. Simmy laughed and shook his head, as though she were a cynical being who simply refused to believe one of life's simplest truths, that the oligarch always got what he wanted, that nothing could interfere with this agenda.

Except for the government that ran the country where his plane happened to be waiting for him.

When they arrived at Boryspil Airport, they sailed through

a special immigration line for VIPs and boarded Simmy's plane at 4:07. Only seven minutes past her deadline. Nadia was beyond impressed. Her thoughts turned to Bobby as she prepared for the plane to taxi down the runway for takeoff.

But it never left its gate. Fifteen minutes later Simmy asked the pilot for a reason behind the delay. The pilot said it had to be routine. Nadia remained calm despite the sinking feeling in the pit of her stomach. With each passing minute, the odds of meeting Bobby's ferry at the dock diminished. Still, she clung to hope. Pessimism never won the debate, the horse race, or the war.

When the pilot killed the engine, she knew her hope was misplaced.

The pilot joined them in the cabin, a grim expression on his face. "This runway is closed for an hour."

"Then move us to another runway," Simmy said. "What's the problem?"

"No planes are allowed to move."

Simmy hadn't bothered to secure his seat belt. He snapped to his feet. "Said who?"

"Air traffic control, obviously. VIP government departure. Probably the prime minister. Or the president. The VIP runway goes on lockdown. Standard procedure. They don't give advance warning for security reasons."

A few choice words of profanity escaped Simmy's lips. He wheeled to the back of the plane where four of his men were playing cards. He eyed the one who'd made the arrangements with the cemetery man.

"Get me the MVS," Simmy said.

"Is it wise to ask the Minister of Internal Affairs for a favor when you know he's not going to be able to grant it?" the man said. "Given one of his superiors is on his way to the airport to catch a plane right now?"

Simmy's voice rose a few decibels for the first time. "Do I pay you to ask me questions?"

"Yes, boss. You do."

"I do, don't I?" Simmy said. "I also pay you to think. There's got to be something we can do."

Watching Simmy become animated for the first time ever had the opposite effect on Nadia. If he was upset, there was no need for her to stress. In fact, her optimal course of action was to help keep Simmy calm to ensure his fury didn't cause him to enrage some airport official and result in an even longer delay.

Nadia patted his seat cushion with her palm. "Come sit with me and tell me tales of Siberia. A wise man once taught me patience is like virtue. You need it when you want it the least."

Simmy looked prepared to shed his dress shirt, don his cape, and fly to Vladivostok after dropping a bomb on the traffic control tower first. He thought for a moment. By the time he sat down beside Nadia, he'd returned to his stoic self.

"Who was the wise man who taught you this?" Simmy said.

Nadia remembered the first time she saw Victor Bodnar in his apartment, looking like an old cigar that could never be extinguished. "No one important," she said. "Just an old thief."

Simmy took Nadia's hand and squeezed it. Lines sprang to his face as he looked her in the eyes.

"My pilot will try to make up the time, but if we're late I will make this up to you. I have friends in Siberia. It is a vast place but a boy from America cannot go unnoticed. He cannot survive without the help of others."

He's not a boy from America, Nadia thought, *and he knows people in the region. People who might help him.*

Nadia squeezed Simmy's hand back. "There's nothing for you to make up. Bobby is resilient, and he'll call me on my cell phone as soon as he gets the chance. Besides, worst case, how late can we possibly be? It's not like he'll have a day's head start. More like an hour or two, at most, right?"

Simmy nodded, but it seemed more an obligatory gesture than sincere agreement. He released Nadia's hand.

Nadia smiled, but deep down she didn't believe a word she'd just said. Vladivostok was in Siberia, and Siberia was the home of *gulags* where many of her Ukrainian ancestors had perished for anti-Soviet behavior such as speaking Ukrainian or writing poetry.

It always was and would be a place where people disappeared forever.

CHAPTER 36

———— ❄ ————

THE FERRY ARRIVED IN VLADIVOSTOK ON SUNDAY MORNING. The car dealer stood beside Bobby at the front of the line to disembark.

"I know you have to take care of your car inventory," Bobby said. "Here's what we should do. I'll give you my address, and I'll go on ahead and prepare your money. Then when you're done . . ."

The car dealer looked incredulous.

"No, no," Bobby said. "That's ridiculous, right?"

The car dealer laughed. It was the scratchy growl of a lifetime smoker.

"It makes it sound like I'm trying to ditch you," Bobby said. "And I'm not." Bobby stood quiet for a moment, and then became mildly animated as though a great idea had occurred to him. "You know what's better? I'll stay with you. How about that? You have to process your car inventory, right? Get your documents straightened out with the authorities. I'll stay with you until you're finished, and then we'll go to my place together." Bobby pretended to be enthusiastic by sealing his suggestion with a nod and a smile.

"Sure," the car dealer said. "That's a great plan. It gives you the opportunity to make your escape during all the chaos. Nice try, boy." He slapped Bobby on the shoulder. "Don't worry about my cars. My colleagues will take care of my cars. You and I are going to do what best friends do. They stick together and enjoy a cold beverage after an exhausting trip. We're going to pass through immigration. I will go first. You will be behind me. Soon as you give me my money, I'm going to buy you that beer."

Bobby dropped his head and raised it just as quickly. It was a flash of dismay, something he'd perfected in front of the mirror for those instances when he had to inadvertently reveal he'd been duped. As though he'd let his emotions slip and only a practiced eye could have noticed it. He saw the car dealer's lip turn up a smidge. He thought Bobby was disappointed. The car dealer thought he'd gotten the better of him. It was the exact reaction Bobby was trying to provoke.

By positioning himself at the front of the line, Bobby knew the driver and Eva were somewhere behind him. The density of the crowd prevented him from turning around and trying to spot them. There was no place to hide, too big a risk the driver might see him. The only risk to his plan was that he would be delayed at immigration, and the driver and Eva would sail through via a different line.

After the ferry docked, the passengers made their way off the gangplank into the building. Signs instructed the passengers to form two lines. The lines to the far left were for Russian citizens. The ones to the right were for foreign nationals. The twelve people ahead of Bobby and the car dealer headed straight toward the local line. The car dealer put his hand on Bobby's back and nudged him to the left to become the thirteenth. Bobby stepped to the right, slipped away from his touch, and bared his American passport.

"I need to use the other line," Bobby said. "But I'll be waiting for you on the other side."

The car dealer stared at the blue passport.

"And no beer for me. I don't like alcohol. Slows my legs down. But you can buy me a lemonade. After I give you your money."

Bobby left the car dealer standing open-mouthed and blinking rapidly. Bobby removed his comfort mask and bolted to the second line for visitors to Russia. When he saw the United States passport, the immigration officer looked twice at Bobby. He asked Bobby about the purpose of his visit to Russia, and how long he was planning to stay. Bobby gave him the same story about being on a grand adventure and writing for the school newspaper. He showed him his return ticket to Japan, scheduled to depart in forty-eight hours, well within the seventy-two hour limit. The immigration officer took his paperwork and entered some information into a computer. It took him less than thirty seconds to do so, but by the time he returned the passport to Bobby there was a line of twenty arriving passengers behind him.

"Welcome to Russia," the immigration officer said.

After he heard these words and knew he was free to enter Vladivostok, Bobby added the spiel he'd been rehearsing in his mind.

"There's one more thing. A man walked up to me on the ferry. I think he mistook me for a Siberian native. That's not surprising, you know, because of my background, my face. I was born in Alaska. He asked me if I wanted to buy a gun. He said he and his friends had a lot of guns. He said they had them stored in the cars they were bringing over from Japan. In places the cops would never look. He said they were selling guns to something called the Sibiryak movement, to help them free the slaves from Russian imperialism. I have no idea what that is. Maybe you do. I don't want to be wasting your time. Maybe this is none of my business . . ."

The Sibiryak movement sought to unite Siberians across all ethnic backgrounds to pursue common social and economic interests. This was a socially acceptable way of saying some Siberians wanted independence from the rest of Russia. It reflected the tensions between Siberian people and those from urban areas such as Moscow, and the difference in living standards.

The immigration officer asked Bobby some questions. They resulted in him repeating the entire story.

"Where is this man?" the immigration officer asked.

Bobby pointed to the car dealer, who was looking right at them from his place in line. He was eighth now, Bobby counted. The local line was moving four times as quickly thanks to Bobby's fiction.

The immigration officer picked up a phone, waited for a voice on the other end of the line, and rattled off an abbreviated version of what Bobby had just told him. Then he hung up and pressed a button under his desk.

Ten seconds later, three men in gray uniforms burst out of a side door carrying rifles. A sour-looking man in a black suit followed. Two of the men with rifles flanked the line for locals. The third followed the black suit. They marched to the line for foreigners. The immigration officer whispered into the ear of the man in the black suit. The latter cast an ambivalent look at Bobby, and then a considerably more disapproving one at the car dealer.

The man in the black suit asked Bobby to step forward and wait beside the booth. Bobby complied. The man in the black suit told the immigration officer to continue with the next passenger. Then he motioned to the remaining guard and approached the car dealer.

Bobby spied the look of concern in the car dealer's expression. Gone was the arrogance of ten minutes past, when he thought he was about to earn a year's wages in a day. It was replaced by fear. The man in the black suit was probably FSB, the secret police of the Russian Federation, successor to the KGB.

The man in the black suit asked the car dealer for his passport. The two guards who'd been flanking the line moved in and surrounded him. The man in the black suit spoke again. The car dealer shouted back at him.

People hushed. They turned their attention to the commotion in the locals' line. Even the immigration officer who had helped Bobby stopped reviewing the next arrival's passport. Like everyone, he was entranced by the prospect of an arrest or, even better, a fight. Anything to relieve the boredom of the job.

Bobby slipped out the front door.

The streets of Vladivostok left no doubt Bobby was back in Russia. It smelled of petroleum and cabbage instead of sea salt and fish. The shops and commercial buildings surrounding the ferry building appeared in desperate need of renovation. A gray sky loomed above. Bobby couldn't tell if it was a function of smog or clouds.

He found a café with a view of the ferry building's entrance. He stepped inside and remained beside the door. The waitress was busy taking orders from new arrivals. His watch said 8:15 a.m., but the clock on the wall told him it was already 10:15 a.m. Bobby hated forward time changes. They left him with the sense he'd lost two hours of his life, and he detested the thought of losing a minute.

He adjusted his watch for the two-hour time difference. He spotted a payphone on the other side of the lobby and thought of Nadia. She would be worried. If only he had time to call her.

The sound of coarse Russian reminded Bobby of his location. He was back in a place where the rule of law didn't exist the way it did in America. Musicians were jailed for criticizing the government. The media pedaled propaganda or risked stiff consequences. A kid on his own chasing a girl held captive by powerful people could vanish if he were caught.

The sight of the driver and Eva exiting the ferry station cleared his mind. Eva was her usual self, sedated, leaning against the driver, head held low, face obscured. The driver looked around. His eyes settled on something. Bobby followed his eyes.

Two men in suits sliced their way through the crowd toward Eva and the driver. They weren't beefy types in black leather jackets. Instead they looked like corporate executives who ran marathons. Dark pinstripe suits with gel in their hair, both in their early thirties, Bobby thought.

One of them exchanged a quick word with the driver. The other put his arm around Eva and guided her toward the street.

They moved with a sense of purpose. The men with the pinstripe suits helped Eva into the back of a black Mercedes SUV, the type with the grille in the front that looked like a quasi-military vehicle.

Bobby lowered his head and ambled past the SUV toward the taxis behind it. The line was twenty people deep, which did not bode well for those who were waiting. Bobby had experience with taxis in Ukraine, though. He ignored the attendant and the line of people and marched straight to the last cab in line.

The cab driver tried to wave him off. Bobby heard passengers by the curb hurling insults at his back. He ignored both of them and climbed into the back of the taxi.

"Imbecile," the cab driver said. "There is a line. Get out of my car. Get out of my car now."

Bobby flashed a thick roll of rubles. Summoned his finest fluent Russian. "Follow that Mercedes jeep," he said.

The cab driver's eyes widened. "You look too young to be a spy." He paused as though gathering courage. "Are you a spy?"

"Sure. Aren't you?"

The roll of money exerted its gravitational pull. The driver's eyes yielded to it, and then whipped around toward the windshield.

"Your wish is my command," he said. "Should we hang back and avoid being seen?"

It was not the first time a cab driver in Vladivostok, home of the Russian Navy, had been told to follow someone.

"Yeah. That would be best."

They drove for an hour and seven minutes. The Mercedes' destination became apparent ten minutes before its arrival. A small passenger plane made its descent through the clouds on the horizon. A bulky cargo plane climbed toward the same clouds five minutes later.

They were headed toward the airport.

Bobby suppressed a sense of hopelessness and reminded himself of what his father had taught him. It was a mantra among the *vor v zakony*, the secret organization of professional criminals in the countries of the former Soviet Union that dated back to Stalin's days. The greatest opportunities presented themselves when all hope was gone.

The Mercedes drove to a special terminal for private planes. A guard opened an electronic fence. The SUV drove past it and the guard closed the gate behind it. Bobby paid the driver 1,500 rubles, the equivalent of fifty dollars. It was probably a rip-off, but there was no time to haggle. He walked inside the terminal like he owned the place with no plan in mind.

There was a small waiting area. A floor–to-ceiling window offered a view of the terminal and its runway. Bobby watched the men and the girl he thought was Eva board a sleek private jet.

Thirty seconds later they took off for a destination unknown.

Bobby watched the ground controller through the window. As he returned to the terminal, Bobby pulled the duffel bag from around his shoulder. He gripped it with both hands and waited for the ground controller to arrive at the door.

Bobby rushed toward the door. He took deep breaths to make himself appear to have been running.

The ground controller stepped inside the terminal to find Bobby sucking wind and looking frantic. The ground controller appeared startled. He looked at Bobby uncertainly.

"I'm looking for a private plane with three men and a young woman," Bobby said. "It's supposed to leave here any minute."

"It just left," the ground controller said.

"Oh, no," Bobby said, closing his eyes as though disaster had struck. "My boss was on that plane." Bobby raised the duffel bag. The ground controller looked at it. "I was supposed to give this to him." Bobby shook his head. "I'm a dead man."

The ground controller shook his head. He appeared sympathetic. He understood there was a 50 percent chance Bobby was being serious. In these parts, if a man said he was dead because he didn't deliver a package to some people who owned a private jet, he might not be kidding. The ground controller wanted to help him, Bobby could sense it.

Bobby raised his eyebrows. "Maybe if I get it to him today I'll still be okay. Maybe he'll understand I got stuck in traffic. If I'm only a few hours late. Where is the plane going?"

"Irkutsk."

Irkutsk was also one of the largest cities in Siberia. About half a million people lived there, similar to the population of Vladivostok. It sat below the Angara River, forty-five miles below Lake Baikal, the deepest, largest, and oldest body of freshwater in the world. Bobby's father's Siberian friends had told him about Lake Baikal. The part of the lake known as the Baikal Riviera contained sprawling mansions popular with government officials, wealthy oligarchs, and organized crime leaders, not that those three categories were mutually exclusive. Lake Baikal was also four hundred miles long and forty miles wide. It would not take long for a party of four to disappear without a trace. Bobby needed to get to Irkutsk quickly, while there was still some trail left to follow.

"When is the next flight to Irkutsk?" Bobby said.

"Ten thirty tonight."

"That late? Nothing earlier?"

"No."

"Nothing at all?"

"Nothing."

"Any private planes leaving earlier? Maybe a cargo plane, for instance?"

The ground controller started to shake his head and stopped. He studied Bobby the way a man did when he was trying to decide if he could trust another.

"It's my life," Bobby said. "And I can pay."

The ground controller studied him some more. "I may know a man who's delivering a load to Irkutsk today. He has a good heart. He's the kind of man who might want to help a youngster out of an unpleasant jam." He cleared his throat. "You have money, you say?"

Bobby paid the ground controller the equivalent of fifty dollars. He paid a pilot another one hundred dollars for a ride in his plane to Irkutsk. The plane was filled with crates of consumer goods imported from China, Korea, and Japan. Bobby sat in the far back in a jump seat. Across from him was another such seat.

The plane left the airport at 12:30, an hour after the private plane had departed with Eva. A few minutes before departure, the pilot came in the back to make sure Bobby was secure in his seat. He also brought another passenger with him, a scruffy looking man with Siberian features. Bobby kept his disappointment to himself. He'd been looking forward to some solitude, and maybe a few hours of sleep. Once he landed, he wasn't sure when he'd be able to get some rest again.

But the man strapped himself into the jump seat opposite Bobby and put him at ease. It was quite remarkable, Bobby thought. The guy seemed to be able to read Bobby's mind.

"Don't worry, my friend," the Siberian said. "I won't bother you during the trip. I need some sleep myself. I have some good buckwheat bread here. And a few bottles of lemonade. Have some with me? The grains will relax your mind. Help you sleep."

Normally Bobby would have said no immediately. In fact, he would have been wary of the stranger. But there was nothing threatening about him, and Bobby couldn't escape him for the next four hours if he tried. He might as well make the best of it, and not antagonize someone who could potentially help him once they landed. Besides, he was hungry. And the previous talk of lemonade had left him with a taste for it.

"Do you live in Irkutsk?" Bobby said.

The Siberian smiled. "I do." He pulled some bread and two bottles of lemonade from his own duffel bag. "My name is Luo. What's yours?"

CHAPTER 37

B Y MID-AFTERNOON, JOHNNY REGRETTED HAVING GONE straight to work from the airport.

He'd left Japan on Friday morning. The flight took less than thirteen hours, which happened to be the time difference between Tokyo and New York. He arrived in Newark at about the same time he'd left Tokyo, 7:00 a.m. A blue sky, the sound of the English language, and the absence of boomerangs flying through the air boosted his spirits. He was still alive, he had his career, and his girl was in good hands, or at least super-wealthy hands. On top of that, the sun was peeking through a puff of cloud when he got in line for a taxi. What the heck did he have to be depressed about?

Johnny went directly to the office and resumed working on an immigration case. After lunch he went to Superior Court to meet a new client. He needed two cups of coffee with shots of espresso mixed in to keep his eyes open the rest of the afternoon.

Shortly after 4:00 p.m., he walked to the parking garage near the courtroom and climbed into his car. His phone rang. He held his breath as the number of the party calling him appeared on the screen, hoping it belonged to Nadia. It didn't. It belonged to his boss.

"How are you holding up?" his boss said.

"On fumes," Johnny said.

"I need you to do something first thing tomorrow morning."

"On a Saturday?"

"Yeah. Client's request. He's on the job today, off tomorrow."

"A cop?"

"Yeah. Local. He's under investigation for an indictable. I don't know the details. I'm hearing they may file charges against him any day." The state of New Jersey referred to cases where the accused could be punished by more than one year in jail as indictable offenses, not felonies, the way most states did.

"You know my preference where cops are concerned." Representing cops did nothing to improve one's reputation with those who regularly needed criminal lawyers.

"Yeah, and I don't like whitefish but my wife serves it twice a week. Besides, you haven't heard the rub yet."

"Which is?"

"The guy asked for you personally."

"You're kidding me. What's his name?"

"Richard Clark."

Johnny searched his memory. "Don't know him."

"Well, he knows you. Says he knows you real well. He's going to meet you at the Tropicana at 9:00 a.m. for breakfast."

The Tropicana was a diner in Elizabeth. "Now you're talking. I'm having pancakes and you're buying."

Johnny hung up. Much as the prospect of a tall stack with bacon on the side made his mouth water, the cop's request for Johnny to represent him left him uneasy. The cop knew something Johnny didn't, and he knew it would bother him until he learned exactly what it was.

When Johnny got home, the only thing on his agenda other than eating and sleeping was pulling out his world atlas. Last year he'd kept track of Nadia's location on the atlas when she called him during her trip to Ukraine. Maybe he'd be able to do the same this year. Maybe she would call him tonight, he thought.

But she didn't.

CHAPTER 38

---※---

BOBBY DEVOURED A FIST-SIZED CHUNK OF BUCKWHEAT bread and washed it down with a bottle of Leninade. It was a pink-lemonade-flavored soda, a bit too sweet for his taste under normal circumstances, but these weren't normal circumstances. He craved sugar. Once he started drinking, he couldn't stop. He knew the craving was a function of the stress of the last forty-eight hours. He knew this because he'd experienced the same sensation while being bullied at school, whipped during hockey practices with the Coach, and scavenging with Eva. Sugar soothed his mind.

The label on the bottle consisted of a hammer and sickle, the communist symbol for peaceful labor. The red star on the neck of the bottle represented military service and the Red Army. Beneath the star was an invitation. "Join the Party!"

Bobby realized that Luo was staring at him.

"I knew a fellow who wore that same expression," Luo said.

Bobby's fellow passenger hadn't said a word since introducing himself. Instead, they'd sat quietly as the plane took off. Bobby had closed his eyes to meditate. When he cracked them open to spy on Luo, he saw that the Siberian man also had his eyes closed. After the plane leveled off at cruising altitude, Luo had shared his Leninade and bread.

"What expression is that?" Bobby said.

"Disapproval. The Leninade not to your liking? A bit sweet, is it?"

"No. It's fine. I like it very much. I was just thinking that we're flying over Siberia, where fifteen million people suffered in the labor camps—the *gulags*—and more than a million died. My father was sentenced to a *gulag* for twelve years." Bobby looked at the bottle. "And here I am, drinking a soda that makes fun of the man who started it all, the one who gave birth to Soviet communism."

"Would you rather be drinking Stalinade?"

Bobby managed a chuckle.

"Putinade?"

"The more questions you ask, the less thirsty I get."

"Look at it this way. You're drinking Leninade only because the Soviet Union collapsed and the individual republics freed themselves. If Soviet communism existed today, you wouldn't be drinking that soda. And we wouldn't be here. Which raises the question, why are you here?"

Bobby's guard immediately shot up. He could hear his father's voice in his ear. *Be wary.* This man who called himself Luo had said he wanted to sleep. Now he was asking personal questions.

"Same reason as you," Bobby said. "I need to get to Irkutsk."

"I know that, but what were you doing in Japan?"

"How did you know I was in Japan?"

"I was on the ferry with you. You don't remember me?"

Bobby had studied faces. If Luo had been on the ferry, he would have seen him. Unless Luo was trained to avoid detection, and he hadn't wanted Bobby to see him.

"No," Bobby said. "I don't remember you."

"That's no surprise. I blend in with an Asian crowd. Because there's almost nothing special about me. You know what the only special thing about me is?"

Bobby didn't bother answering.

"The self-awareness that tells me there's nothing special about me at all."

Bobby was starting to think the truth was to the contrary.

"So why Japan?" Luo said. "Why the ferry? And why a cargo ship to Irkutsk instead of a commercial airliner?"

"I thought you weren't going to ask questions. I thought you were sleepy."

"Must be the Leninade. Makes me inquisitive. How about that? Must be the sugar, you know? You on business or studies? You look more like a student to me."

"Yeah, I'm a student. And if it's all the same to you, I'd like to get some rest."

"Sure. I understand. Get some rest. If I keep chattering, don't mind me. It's just that bootleggers and drug dealers have been known to use cargo planes to get from Vladivostok to Irkutsk. Sometimes there are cops waiting at the airport in Irkutsk. Sometimes they interrogate the pilots and the passengers. I know some of those police. I'd hate for any misunderstandings to ruin your trip. Irkutsk police station. Prison cell. They're not recommended tourist destinations. Sometimes paperwork gets lost, a judge goes on holiday, a person can get lost in that prison cell."

Bobby realized that Luo could be a cop. Evading his questions might antagonize him. Instead of ignoring him, Bobby told Luo the same story he'd told the immigration officers about competing in a writing contest. It had sounded reasonable then, but not as plausible now on a cargo plane traveling from Vladivostok to Irkutsk. Still, Bobby sold it as best as he could.

Luo smiled and nodded like a good listener. On the surface he acted as though he believed the story, but Bobby's instincts told him otherwise.

"You know what I think?" Luo said.

"What?"

Luo grinned. "I think you're going to win that writing competition."

214

"I hope so. What about you? What's your business? Why were you on the ferry?"

"Oh, come on. You know the answer to that."

"I do?"

"Sure. It's obvious, isn't it? I was following you."

A hot flash seized Bobby. He waited for shock to pass. It didn't take long. Three seconds, maybe four. He was used to it. Adversity likes to strike when its victim least expects it. He composed himself, considered Luo's claim that he'd been following him.

Impossible, Bobby thought. Only Nadia and Johnny had seen him slide under the truck in Fukushima. The other men were dead or seriously injured. If no one followed him then, how could anyone have picked up his trail when he'd been hidden under a car for over two hours? How would anyone know to be at the gas or train stations?

But there was no sense in disagreeing with the man, so Bobby asked the obvious question. "Why were you following me?"

"Because I'm pursuing a treasure."

The formula. Luo knew about the formula. That still didn't explain where he'd picked up Bobby's trail—

The boomerangs.

Luo was the angel! He was the one who'd saved their lives.

"I have no idea what you're talking about. What treasure?"

"The girl you used to scavenge with in the Zone. Her name is Eva. They say she's dead, but I think that's a lie. I think she's alive. And you either know where she is or you're looking for her, too. You see, I am her father. And she is the treasure I seek."

CHAPTER 39

LUO STUDIED ADAM TESLA'S REACTION. HE'D BEEN IMPRESsive from the moment Luo had met him. Cordial but not engaging. Responsive but not revealing. The sound of Eva's name, however, had caused him to freeze. It had injected an intensity into the boy's eyes.

"I don't know any Eva," Adam said.

"I was a soldier in the Russian army. On leave in Moscow. Eva's mother was a student at a university. She was studying nursing. I met her. We became sweethearts. I did well in the Army. I liked the structure. I liked the action. We exchanged letters, but I rarely came home. I only saw Eva three times before her mother died. She was two. Her aunt and uncle took care of her from then on. The war in Chechnya broke out. I lost touch with them. But I never forgot. I have this picture. She's so young you may not recognize her but take a look anyway."

Luo fished a photo out of his wallet. It was a picture of Eva and her mother when his daughter was two years old.

Adam glanced at it. He revealed no emotion. He handed the photo back to Luo.

"Why do you think she's alive?" Adam said.

"Because a wolf only finds peace with others."

Adam frowned. "Excuse me?"

216

Luo laughed. "Something the groundskeeper at the cemetery told me. I went to visit her grave. The groundskeeper told me what he knew. I got curious. I went to your old school. Asked some questions. The two of you had become inseparable. There were rumors you scavenged in the Zone. I went there and spoke to a guard. He's ex-military, too. Guards in the Zone hear stories after the fact. I bribed him. He told me he heard something about the Zaroff Seven and a pair of scavengers that fit your descriptions. He also told me an American woman had been seen in the Zone twice in the span of a year. I found her driver, a professor named Anton Medved, and the scavenger who'd brought her in. A man named Hayder. The babushka, the Division of Nervous Pathologies, Ksenia and Denys Melnik. They all pointed to a treasure. Something priceless in the hands of a boy and a girl. And now here we are. Both looking for the same thing. Except I don't care about money. I only care about the girl."

Adam studied him. "I only care about the girl, too."

"Then we should discuss a partnership."

"But if you were following me the entire time, you had to have seen her face. You had to have seen the driver and the girl. On a train, in one of the stations, in the ferry building. You had to have seen her face."

"Obviously I knew you'd jumped under the truck for a reason—"

"Then why didn't you walk right up to her and look in her eyes? Why didn't you pretend to bump into them or something like that?"

Luo hung his head. "I did."

"And?"

"I didn't recognize her. I thought it would be like the cinema, you know? I thought I'd see some part of her mother or me but I just wasn't sure. The driver kept her so wrapped up in that hood I wasn't even sure she was a girl. And I couldn't try again or he'd become suspicious. My best move was to keep following you. Be patient. You know about patience, don't you?"

"I know about patience. But how is the situation better now? We don't even know where she is anymore."

"I'm not worried about that. I'll find her. And I will be better off because we won't be in a public place. And their guard will be down. They won't be expecting me. They won't be expecting us."

"Us?"

"Two men stand a much better chance than one."

"Why should I trust you?" Adam said. "How do I know you're really Eva's father? How do I know you didn't make all this up to earn my trust so you can get the other treasure? The one everyone else wants. How do I know you're not lying?"

"That's the beauty of the situation. It doesn't matter if I'm lying or telling the truth."

"Why not?"

"If I'm lying, and I'm not Eva's father, and all I want is this other treasure, our interests are still aligned. It will do me no good if you are harmed, and it will do me no good if she is harmed. We can still help each other."

"Meaning, I can trust you no matter what, up until that moment in time when I won't be able to trust you at all."

Luo grinned. "Couldn't have said it better myself."

"My father had a name for this type of scenario."

"What did he call it?"

"A fool's bargain."

"Your father was a wise man. We are all fools for falling in love. I fell in love once. That love produced a child. And then you fell in love. With that child. Most men are fools until they die, and those who aren't are already dead."

"I would prefer to stay alive. The thing is, even in a fool's bargain, there has to be some token of trust to get the relationship started. If I give you my trust, what will you give me?"

Luo shrugged. "What do you want?"

"What else do you have in that bag besides Leninade?"

"A toothbrush, some soap, a towel, some bottled water, some reindeer jerky, and these." He pulled out three boomerangs. "Ever use one?"

Bobby shook his head.

"Then they'll be of no use to you."

Luo put the boomerangs back in the bag and placed it on the floor. He lifted his left pant leg. A ten-inch knife pressed against his calf. He unstrapped the holster and offered it to Bobby.

"It's a G10 handle—the stuff they use for structural supports—and a high-carbon Damascus blade," Luo said. "It never let me down in the tundra or the battlefield. Check it out."

Adam took the holster. He slipped the knife from its sheath. The midnight blue handle seemed to mold to his hand.

"You like it?" Luo said.

"I don't like guns or knives. But I like this one."

"I thought you might. Keep it."

"Really?"

"As a token of good faith."

"Thanks."

"Make sure you don't strap it too tight."

"I thought I'd just keep it in my bag."

"Not a good idea."

"Why?"

"Two reasons. You may need to drop your bag to defend yourself. And if you get caught, your bag will get searched before your legs."

"What do you have strapped to your other leg?" Bobby said.

Luo looked up but didn't answer. For the first time, Adam had asked him a question he hadn't expected.

"Let's hope you don't have to find out."

Adam attached the holster with the knife flush on his calf.

"No," Luo said. "Put the knife to the outside of the leg. Secure both Velcro straps tight but not too tight. Make sure it's comfortable."

Bobby stood up and walked around. "What do you do for a living?"

Luo grinned. "I thought you didn't want to talk. I thought you wanted to get some rest."

"I do. But sometimes a question nags at me and keeps me awake."

"I get that, too. I'm a retired soldier living on a pension. Sometimes people hire me to find people for them. In this case, I hired myself."

"Do you have a mobile phone?"

Luo reached into his knapsack and pulled out a cell phone. "Coverage could be spotty as soon as we get away from Vladivostok. If you need to make a call, I'd make it now."

Adam sat down. Luo handed him the phone.

"So tell me," Luo said. "And be honest. If you had to guess now, do you believe I am who I say I am?"

Adam shrugged. "Doesn't matter. Our interests are aligned." He paused before adding a final thought. "For now."

Luo smiled, closed his eyes, and reclined his head against the wall. "Smart boy."

CHAPTER 40

———— ❄ ————

N ADIA RECEIVED A CALL FROM BOBBY MIDAIR BETWEEN
Kyiv and Vladivostok.

It lasted only ten seconds. The pilot told them that altitude was not the problem. Cell phones were built to transmit a signal up to ten miles, and an altitude of 30,000 feet was the equivalent of six and a half miles. The problem was that the plane was moving quickly. On land, a call might be facilitated by a network of three towers pointing in different directions. In a plane, the caller might lose access to two of those cell towers before the call was completed.

Nadia tried calling the number from which Bobby's call had originated but she couldn't get through. Nor did the phone ever ring again.

"Cargo . . . Irkutsk . . . father."

Those were the defining words Nadia had heard.

"You're the forensic analyst," Simmy had said. "What do you think?"

"The key words are cargo and Irkutsk. There are two possibilities. Cargo is leaving Vladivostok for Irkutsk. Or cargo is arriving from Irkutsk to Vladivostok."

"That one seems rather obvious."

"Given Genesis II is the cargo," Nadia said, "and the cargo was moved via ferry from Japan to Vladivostok, it makes less sense that it's coming from Irkutsk. More likely it is going to Irkutsk. That means Genesis II is being taken to Irkutsk."

"Agreed. But would a boy who is in love with a girl—and we can assume that Bobby is acting as though Genesis II is Eva—would he refer to that girl as cargo? English is not my first language, but in Russian, no man would ever speak about a woman this way. No matter what his age."

"No, he wouldn't. I still think cargo is heading to Irkutsk, but Bobby's use of the word wasn't in reference to Genesis II."

"Then what was he referring to?" Simmy said.

"Maybe it was part of a phrase. What word might Bobby have spoken after cargo? Ship? Truck? Plane? Aren't they the most obvious?"

"Especially in a port city. Especially in Vladivostok. A ship is unlikely. Irkutsk is accessible by the Angara River but that would be slow. So would a truck. My guess is they're moving Eva to Irkutsk via a cargo plane."

"That's possible," Nadia said.

"The question is where is Bobby?"

"We don't know. The only conclusion we can be comfortable with is that wherever he is, he's headed to Irkutsk."

"What about the last word you heard?"

"Father?"

Simmy nodded.

"That makes no sense. Can't be Bobby's father. He passed away last year. Can't be Eva's father. He told me she's an orphan. The only thing that makes sense to me is that I misheard him and that he said 'farther.' As in, 'If you're in Vladivostok, you need to go farther west to Irkutsk.' Or, 'Don't land in Vladivostok, keep going farther.'"

"Either way, we need to reroute for Irkutsk."

"It's logical but not a sure thing."

"It's not realistic to expect a sure thing, "Simmy said. "But the odds are a touch better than you suggest."

"You sound like you know something I don't."

Simmy pressed a few keys on his tablet computer. "I had my people do some research into the three living members of the Zaroff Seven. The richest and most powerful one, Constantin Golov, has a mansion on Baikal sixty kilometers from Irkutsk."

"Lake Baikal?"

"There is only one Baikal. His mansion is outside a town called Listvyanka. Very popular with men of means in Russia. Some rich Azeri oilmen have built their castles there, too. The higher echelon of the Russian business world is a relatively small place. Employees change companies. People talk. My men learned from a good source that Golov is there now. And the other two Zaroff Seven members are on a vacation at an unspecified location at this very moment."

"Irkutsk," Nadia said.

Simmy nodded. "Irkutsk."

Simmy pressed a button for the copilot to come out. When he did so, Simmy told him to reroute for Irkutsk. The copilot spoke Russian with an unfamiliar regional accent. Nadia had to consider his words twice to understand him. The linguistic distraction reminded her of Bobby's choice of language on the phone.

"Oh my God," she said.

Simmy dismissed the copilot. "What?" he said.

"He's not alone."

"Who's not alone?"

"Bobby."

"Why do you say that?"

"He spoke English to me. We don't speak English to each other. We speak only in Ukrainian, unless there are English-speaking people present and we don't want to be rude."

Simmy frowned. "So what are you saying? There's an American with him and he didn't want to offend him?"

"No. On the contrary. He's travelling with a Russian and he didn't want him to understand everything he said to me."

Simmy considered the situation. "The operative word was *Irkutsk*. That transcends language. Everyone would understand that."

"True," Nadia said. "If *Irkutsk* was the operative word."

"What else could it have been?"

"Some other word. Something else he said that I didn't hear."

CHAPTER 41

---·❄·---

BOBBY SAT IN THE PASSENGER SEAT OF THE *BUHANKA*, A CROSS between a minivan and a military jeep. Luo guided it along the two-lane highway from Irkutsk to Listvyanka. A series of steep descents followed protracted climbs of similar height. At each peak, the Lake flashed silver and blue on the left, only to vanish as Bobby's line of sight fell below tree line.

The buhanka reminded him of his escape from Russia a year ago. One of his father's friends had used one to transport him over a long stretch of treacherous terrain. Bobby recalled his trek along the Road of Bones in the Kolyma region of Siberia, where snowcapped mountains and a desolate forest stretched for hundreds of miles. Bobby took comfort knowing the buhanka was indestructible, but it still would take them only so far. The castle where Eva had been taken by her captors was probably heavily guarded. They would have to park their car rental in the forest and cover the final half mile on foot.

They'd arrived at the Irkutsk Airport at 5:10 p.m. Luo had insisted Bobby wait outside the domestic terminal while he made inquiries inside. A Siberian man could approach a fellow countryman working as ground crew more comfortably than if he were a party of two. Bobby's presence would attract additional attention. Alone, Luo would not have to make explanations.

Bribes were a way of life. He would simply offer money for information, he said.

A cloud of steam formed in front of Bobby's nostrils. The frigid air cleared his sinuses but left him trembling within a minute. Temperatures remained well below freezing into May, especially at night. He needed something heavier than his windbreaker.

Bobby tried calling Nadia with Luo's phone while he waited but she did not pick up. He did, however, leave her a voice mail. He feared she hadn't heard any part of their previous call because it had ended abruptly. As a result, Bobby left Nadia a detailed account of what had transpired since he'd arrived at the ferry building in Vladivostok. Bobby used up the entire time allotted to a single message, and had to call back to complete his story. When he was done, he surprised himself when he admitted something else to Nadia in the second voice mail. The words rolled off his lips in a stream of consciousness.

"In my brain, I know I'm not supposed to believe that Luo is Eva's father. But in my heart, for some reason, I have an urge to trust him. But don't worry Auntie, I'm just telling you how I feel. In the end, you're the only one I trust."

Luo emerged from the terminal less than half an hour later.

"A woman, two men in suits, and a roughneck arrived in a private jet two hours ago. The plane's registered to a private company named Baigal Industries. Baigal is the ancient Yakut word for sea, ocean, and Baikal. It's probably a shell company. People with private planes value their privacy. That's why they built their homes here in the first place."

"But do you know where they went after they landed?"

Luo rubbed a piece of paper between his fingers. "That I do. It's called the Swallow's Nest. It's a re-creation of a famous castle built on a cliff on the Crimean coastline. Near Yalta, in the south of Ukraine. The man knew the terrain well. He drew me a map. It's right on Baikal about twenty kilometers past Listvyanka. Which is a total of ninety kilometers from here."

"Who owns it?"

Luo shook his head. "No names. He didn't offer. I didn't ask. A man says a name out loud. Someone overhears it. Next thing you know he's gone without a trace. But he drew me a map."

"How can you be sure he told you the truth?"

"He got paid. He knows I know where to find him and I made it clear my face would be the last one he ever saw if I had to return."

They rented the buhanka at the airport and drove through the city center. They passed a shopping mall as though they were in New Jersey. A mall. In Siberia. It was surreal.

Luo stopped at a western-style sports store called Fanat. It offered camping, hiking, and fishing equipment. Some of its inventory was specially tailored to leisure activities on Baikal. Luo picked out the necessary equipment. They bought cold-weather hiking jackets, too.

"I want to pay for my share," Bobby said.

Luo smiled. "You're a good kid but I've got it."

"No. I insist. My father didn't raise me to be a freeloader."

"Are you paying cash or by credit card?"

"I'm low on cash. Has to be credit card."

"That's what I thought. If you use your credit card, and someone with resources has been searching for you, they'll know where you are." Luo patted him on the shoulder. "You can pay me back when we're done."

Bobby's gut told him that opportunity would not arise. He didn't know why. It was just one of those ill feelings a person had now and then.

As they drove toward Listvyanka, Luo proposed a plan of attack. Bobby listened and asked questions. It didn't take long for him to realize how low his odds of success would have been if he were alone. Bobby hadn't allowed himself to dwell on logistics up until that point. He didn't want logic to stop him. He wanted his heart to propel him to Eva regardless of the risk. He thought he would use his guile and athleticism to free her and escape. Now he knew he'd been purposefully fooling himself to maintain his momentum.

Luo expected the first leg of the trip—the part they were covering by buhanka—to take less than two hours. Fifteen minutes into the trip, Bobby made a startling realization.

"This road is perfectly straight," Bobby said. "There are no twists or turns."

Luo chuckled. "Not a single one."

"Yeah. It's like someone took a ruler on a map, drew a straight line from Irkutsk to Listvyanka, and told the engineers to cut through the mountains even if that wasn't the cheapest way."

"That's exactly what they did."

"You're kidding me. Why?"

"It was 1960. The peak of the Cold War between the USSR and the United States. Diplomats for both countries arranged a visit for the American president, Eisenhower. His itinerary included a stop in Irkutsk and a visit to Russia's sacred sea—Lake Baikal. There was no road from Irkutsk to Baikal, so the government set out to build one. A proper one."

"In a straight line."

"To prove to the West that neither cost nor nature would prevent them from creating the most direct route between two points."

"And what did the American president think?"

"He didn't," Luo said. "He never went on the trip."

"Why not?"

"Right before he was supposed to depart, an American U2 spy plane—the pilot's name was Powers—was shot down over Russia. The thaw between the two countries turned into a deep freeze again."

"That's too bad," Bobby said.

"Yes. It's too bad for President Eisenhower. He missed seeing one of the Earth's most perfect creations. You ever visit Baikal?"

"No. I saw it from a train once."

"Lake Baikal is twenty-five million years old. Its water is so pure you can drink it. It's filled with organisms that keep it pure. It is home to hundreds of otherwise extinct species, like the only freshwater seal known to man."

"Why?" Bobby said.

Luo shrugged. "I don't know. It's the sacred sea. That's just how it is."

"No. It reminds me of Chornobyl today. Nature has returned because man left. That must be why Baikal is so special. Man is absent. He hasn't screwed it all up yet. The minute he arrives, he will. It's what he does."

"Not Baikal," Luo said. "Even man cannot ruin the sacred sea. Earthquakes are a bigger risk."

"Earthquakes?"

"Baikal sits on the deepest continental fissure on Earth. It's almost as active as the ones in the seas of Japan. There are hot springs around the lake. And there are earthquakes."

Bobby glanced at Luo, the memory of Fukushima still fresh in his mind.

"There are a dozen every year," Luo said. "That may account for some of the legends of Baikal."

"Legends?"

"Right now, the lake is still frozen. But in the summer, ships are devoured, vessels vanish. It happens every year. Last one I heard about was a Japanese crew of four aboard a boat called the Yamada. They were experienced sailors. Weather was fine. They vanished. Fishermen say the lake swallowed them whole."

"I have a hard time believing that," Bobby said.

"And then there are the mirages."

"What kind of mirages?"

"The water is crystal clear. Fishermen swear they've seen trains, castles, and ships at the bottom of the lake."

"That sounds like nonsense to me. Unless there's a scientific explanation."

"There may be. Scientists say when warm air rushes in over the cold water, they mix with the sun to produce light rays with fantastic forms. This type of phenomenon can cause magnetic disturbances, the kind that can cause navigation systems to stop working. The mirages, the disappearance of ships. They're all part of the same thing. The mysteries of the sacred sea."

"Fortunately for us, there's no warm air."

Luo grabbed the handmade map resting between them. "And our navigation system is a bit dated."

They weren't the only ones driving along the sacred sea in a straight line. Bobby counted twenty-four cars going in the opposite direction during the trip. Two cars passed them in the same direction. Both contained a single occupant, an unidentifiable male driver. There was no sign of passengers inside either car that passed them.

They arrived in Listvyanka at 7:45 p.m. Streetlights illuminated the road. An empty harbor lay to the right. The frozen lake shone for a few yards beyond it before yielding to darkness. Old wooden homes sat clustered on the right side. Smoke billowed from their chimneys. A dozen cars filled the lot of a restaurant. A couple trudged from a Soviet-looking jalopy toward the front door wearing only sweaters. It must be spring for them, Bobby thought.

The center of town was no more than three hundred yards long. Buildings vanished in the side-view mirror. The forest reasserted itself.

The main drag gave way to a neat gravel road. Luo took a left at the first fork onto a crude dirt road. The trail twisted and turned through the forest. The buhanka negotiated the turns effortlessly. Fifteen minutes later they arrived at a second fork. Weeds and brush covered the road to the right. A chain-link fence blocked access. Private property and danger signs hung on the fence and the trees at each end. The fork to the left was a ninety-degree turn toward the lake. It was narrower but contained tire treads instead of vegetation.

Luo took a left per the instructions on the map and descended to a clearing at the edge of the frozen lake. There was room for a pair of cars or pickup trucks. Luo took the entire parking spot.

"Fisherman's wharf," Luo said. "Just like the man said. The castle is one and a half miles away. That's why the fork to the right is the road untraveled now. It used to lead to high ground. Beautiful views. Popular with tourists. Now it's billionaires' row. The uninvited are unwelcome, and I bet you the closer one gets, the more ominous the warnings."

"Until a man with a rifle appears in front of you."

"And behind you. Which is why we will go via the road where there are no warnings."

They took their gear from the back of the buhanka and walked to the edge of the ice. Six boulders faced the lake for viewing or fishing purposes. Luo and Bobby sat down and changed into their skates. A third pair of skates remained in a box in a shopping bag.

"I'll carry Eva's skates in my knapsack," Bobby said.

Luo didn't bother looking up. "I know you will."

Bobby took her skates out of the box and put them in his knapsack. He squished his high-top basketball shoes on top of them and slipped the bag onto his back. Secured his headlamp onto his forehead by tightening the strap around his head. Luo had just finished tying his first skate by the time Bobby was ready.

"You laced those skates pretty fast," Luo said. "As though you've done that before."

"Just once or twice."

Bobby imagined a mad scene at the castle. Guards running in one direction, while he and Eva escaped in the other. They'd skated together before in a hockey rink in Korosten. She'd been a competitive swimmer and was more comfortable in open water, but she was competent on ice, too. The wind would be at their backs, and their futures in front of them.

They would fly side-by-side across the ice, and never be separated again.

CHAPTER 42

N ADIA STARED OUT THE WINDOW OF THE PLANE. THE IR-
kutsk Airport was located in the middle of the city. Lights
illuminated a sprawl of brick tenements and a low-level cityscape.
The bridges over the Angora River added a welcome dose of aes-
thetic appeal to an otherwise gray and foreboding descent.

"Living standards have improved in major Russian cities,"
Simmy said. "Especially since oil went north of a hundred a barrel. Out here, though, not so much. You can tell by the look of the
city. Money trickles in from Moscow. There's some resentment."

They landed at 7:30 p.m. Evidently money had trickled in for
a new domestic terminal. Its contemporary steel frame and floor-
to-roof windows gleamed in the night. Nadia counted the seconds as the plane taxied toward its gate.

Her mobile phone chimed. Once, twice, three times.

Voice mail.

She accessed it and found three messages waiting for her. All
from Bobby. She listened to them, one by one.

Relief washed over Nadia when she heard he had indeed
taken a cargo plane to Irkutsk. By the time she finished listening
to the messages, however, reality had set in. The first two messages were two and a half hours old. The third was still two hours

old. That meant he had a two-hour head start. And Bobby's final two revelations disturbed her.

"What did he say?" Simmy said.

"Give me a sec. I want to try to call him."

Nadia tried calling Bobby. He didn't answer. Instead, her call rolled into voice mail again. She left him a message regarding her whereabouts and asked him to call her immediately.

Nadia gave Simmy an abbreviated account of Bobby's trip from Vladivostok to Irkutsk.

"He did say 'father' after all," Nadia said. "Not 'farther.'"

"Whose father was he talking about?" Simmy said.

"Eva's."

"I thought he was dead."

"So did I. Apparently that was just a story her aunt and uncle made up. To minimize the pain of the mother dying and the father being absent."

"Or so this man says. How did he find Bobby?"

"Apparently he followed him from Fukushima. He was the angel. The man with the boomerangs. He hitched a ride on the same cargo plane in Vladivostok."

"It's a bit suspect, but then again . . . We weren't a hundred percent sure Eva herself was alive, and now this man appears . . ."

"Makes you think she really is Genesis II."

Simmy raised his eyebrows and tilted his head. "Did Bobby say what their plan was? Do they know where Eva is?"

"He said they took her to a castle. Some billionaire's estate called the Swallow's Nest. Have you heard of it?"

"The one in Crimea? Of course. Some knockoff in Siberia? Good Lord no. Every idiot with a mansion likes to put a name on it, and it's always something painfully unoriginal. It must be Golov's estate. The Zaroff Seven. They're all there waiting for her."

"And now Bobby is on the way there, too."

"And if there are two parts to the formula, they will soon possess both of them."

"Bobby said he and this Luo were stopping for supplies."

"What kind of supplies?"

"He didn't say. But I'm guessing they have some sort of plan. I'm presuming they're going in on foot. Not driving up to the front door."

"The way we are."

"We are?" Nadia said.

"This is the new Russia," Simmy said. "We're a civilized country no matter what you Americans believe. We're a country of businessmen. Businessmen resolve their differences by negotiating. So we'll negotiate."

"Sounds optimistic to me, but I like it."

"You have no choice but to like it."

"That too. I would like your plan even more if we knew where we are going."

"Not to worry. This is the new Russia but some old habits die hard, you know what I mean? Where there is a bribe, there is a way."

Two vintage Toyota Land Cruisers idled on the tarmac. Nadia followed Simmy into a truck with one of Simmy's men. Two others carried the six oversized duffel bags from the plane's cargo area into the back of the second truck. Based on the strain on the men's faces, the bags appeared heavy.

"What's in the luggage?" Nadia said.

"The usual overnight stuff, you know."

"No. I don't know. Enlighten me."

Simmy stared at his computer. Nadia glanced at it. A map popped up. A serpentine route emboldened in red began at Irkutsk and snaked its way to a large blue area. He hit a key and driving instructions appeared.

"You know, the usual stuff," Simmy said. "Pajamas, brandy, toothbrush. And shaving cream. Never forget the shaving cream."

"That looks like some heavy shaving cream."

Simmy rubbed the whiskers on his beard. "A man likes to be able to clean up well on a moment's notice. When you rough it to Baikal, you never know how dirty you're going to get."

"You sound like a man who knew where he was going when he packed."

"No. I sound like a man who was taking precautions. One of those bags has a ski jacket for you. The sleeves may be a bit long and it may be a bit loose in the waist, but it will keep you warm if we have to spend any time outdoors."

"But most negotiations take place indoors, don't they?"

Simmy smiled. "Like I said. I'm an optimist by nature. But even an optimist takes precautions. Especially in Siberia." He checked his watch. "They have an hour and a half to two hours' head start. But they stopped to shop, and they are approaching by foot. Probably from a considerable distance. That gives us a chance to catch up." He patted the front seat. "Let's go, let's go."

The driver gunned the engine.

They took off toward Lake Baikal and Listvyanka.

CHAPTER 43

L IGHT SPILLED FROM THE CASTLE ONTO THE ICE IN THE DIS-
tance. Bobby guessed they were three hundred yards away.
Luo had turned off his head light when the castle had come into
focus, and Bobby had done the same. The ice in front of them
was still black, but now that the castle was in sight they couldn't
risk detection.

Bobby glided along the ice at a fraction of his top speed. Luo
was a decent skater, but he wasn't seventeen years old or a professional hockey prospect. Bobby could hear him inhaling through
his nose and exhaling through his mouth. He could sense the
older man's lungs straining. But he persevered. There was an aura
about him, a sense of determination. Much as Bobby knew he
shouldn't trust anyone, he found himself drawn to the man.

The skating revived Bobby's body, mind, and soul. He felt
most comfortable on the ice. Always had. Perhaps this was a
function of his speed. He could separate himself from any human
being on ice, in a way he couldn't at school when he was being
bullied or ridiculed. Or maybe it was a function of the ice itself.
It was cold, hard, and impenetrable, the way he'd needed to be in
Chornobyl and Korosten. The way he'd need to be to rescue Eva.

Fifty meters away, Bobby and Luo skated to a tree by the side
of the lake. They stopped, rested, and looked. The Swallow's Nest

sprang from the top of a hill overlooking Lake Baikal. It was rectangular in shape with four levels. The highest point was a circular tower, built in the shape of a rook. The tower hung above the water on the edge of the cliff. The other three levels of the castle beyond the tower dropped to successively lower depths. Bobby guessed that the lowest floor was at ground level, but that part of the castle was too far inland to see.

A vibration startled Bobby. Something in his pocket was moving. It vibrated again.

It was Luo's phone. Bobby realized he'd never given it back. He glanced at Luo. Another reason to trust him, or to be seduced into doing so.

"Answer it," Luo said.

Bobby took off his gloves, removed the phone from his pocket, and glanced at the screen.

"It's a voice mail," Bobby said.

"It has to be for you. I didn't give that number to anyone."

Bobby listened to the voice mail. It was from Nadia, confirming she'd received his message and informing him she was in Irkutsk. Bobby gave Luo the details.

"She's on her way here with her rich Russian friend," Bobby said. "And other men. She said to wait until they get here."

"You can try calling her," Luo said. "There's cell service here for sure. We're close to Listvyanka. And the billionaires would make sure there were towers. But we're not waiting. Every minute counts. We can't be sure Eva will be alive when they get here. And I don't trust men I don't know."

"But you trust me, right?"

"I've spent some time with you. I know your heart."

Bobby tried calling Nadia. He got a signal immediately, but the call rolled to voice mail.

"She's on the road from Irkutsk," Luo said. "Out of signal's reach."

Bobby left a message with his current location.

Luo pulled a pair of night binoculars from his knapsack.

"We know the guards will be focused on land," he said. "After all, the lake is frozen. No boat can gain access. That doesn't mean they don't patrol. I'm sure they patrol. But that's not where they'll concentrate their resources. We need to watch, wait, and see."

They stood in place for what seemed like an eternity. Bobby skated small circles behind Luo to keep his legs warm. Thirty-three minutes later Luo dropped the binoculars to his side.

"Fifteen minutes," he said. "A guard walks around and checks the lake side from the deck surrounding the tower every fifteen minutes. In twelve minutes—give or take—the guard will make his way toward the front. He takes stairs down to the third level. It's a massive structure so once he's on the other side of the building he'll be out of earshot. And the wind will be whipping pretty good up on that hill. That will help us with any incidental noises we make, too."

"So we'll have fifteen minutes to skate the last hundred meters, change into shoes, and scale the tower."

"No. We'll have less than fifteen minutes to skate the last hundred meters, change into shoes, and disappear inside the observation tower. And that's assuming it's open. I can only see a bit of the third level beyond the tower. There's a window and room behind it, but if we go down the stairs in that direction we risk being seen."

"At this temperature, I doubt someone left a window open."

"Probably not. The tower is our best bet. But if it's locked, we'll have no choice. We'll have to look for glass to break. Or pray that some other door is open on a lower level. I'm less worried about entry than I am about the surveillance cameras. The first twenty feet of the cliff can be scaled, but the next thirty are a near-vertical drop, so we'll be out of sight on the wall. But there are cameras on the observation deck beneath the tower."

"How can we disable them?"

Luo told him his plan. Then he let Bobby take a look through the binoculars. The ascent from the lake to the castle's foundation was as Luo described. Steep but not vertical. Stunted trees, shrubs, and grasses covered the initial ascent. From there the climb would turn vertical, with the railing around the observation deck adding another four feet. Bobby focused the binoculars on the castle's observation tower. He found the two cameras pointed at the deck and tried to picture himself racing past them.

The guard appeared on schedule. He wore a suit and tie and carried a gleaming black rifle over his shoulder. His mouth was moving as though he were speaking to someone. When he shifted to the side, Bobby could see a wireless microphone wrapped around his ear. He peered over the tower and around it. Three minutes after arriving, he sauntered to the other side of the tower, down the stairs to the third level, and out of sight.

Bobby and Luo raced to the bottom of the castle. The final fifty meters took them less than a minute.

The lights from the castle were pointed at the lake at a forty-five-degree angle. They cast a glow twenty yards out onto the lake and provided just enough light for Bobby and Luo to be able to see what they were doing.

They changed into their shoes and their rope-climbing gloves. They left their skates and ski gloves near Bobby's knapsack close to the ice. They didn't need the extra weight on their backs, and they wouldn't need the skates until they retraced their steps with Eva. Once their shoes were secure, they climbed up the cliff to the base of the Swallow's Nest. Bobby put the principles of hockey to work to negotiate the steep wall. On ice, he was less concerned with where the hockey puck was now, and more focused on where it would be next. On the cliff, he employed the same strategy, looking beyond his next step at all times toward his final destination at the bottom of the tower.

Still, by the time Bobby ascended at the point where the cliff turned vertical, Luo was already pulling the climbing rope out of his knapsack. The old man had beaten him up the hill. Unlike

Bobby, he didn't need to visualize anything. He knew the optimal path through sheer instincts.

"You've done this before," Bobby said.

"Just once or twice."

The climbing rope contained knots at eighteen-inch intervals for better footing and reduced slippage. It also contained a grappling hook.

"Stand to my left," Luo said. "Five paces away."

Bobby traversed the cliff to Luo's left.

Luo stepped two feet away from the cliff. It was the farthest he could go without losing his balance. He measured two feet of rope beyond the grapple. He swung the rope to his right side, built momentum, and heaved it high over the cement railing on the deck below the castle tower. The grapple clanged over the handrail. Luo yanked on the rope. The grapple made a scraping sound, and then silence. Luo pulled the rope taut.

The grapple didn't budge.

Bobby channeled all his energies into his ears. Prayed he didn't hear footsteps because of the noise the grapple had made. Luo stood motionless, too, looking at Bobby. Luo had told him he'd been a soldier. The certainty with which he'd measured the rope, the confidence with which he'd thrown it, the success he had in sticking it on the first try, all left Bobby wondering exactly what he'd done as a soldier. Bobby had heard of Black Berets, Russia's most elite policemen, the special unit within the FSB. It consisted of the most highly trained operators in the country. Bobby was starting to think Eva's father was one of those Black Berets. Who else could find a dead girl, throw a boomerang with the precision of a bullet coming out of a rifle in a marksman's hands, and feel equally at home on land and ice?

Luo handed Bobby the rope.

Bobby gripped the rope above one of the knots. Placed his left foot flat against the wall, pushed his body out, and followed with his right foot. Put one hand in front of the other and stepped up.

Repeated the process. By the third step he'd developed a cadence. Pull, step, pull, step.

He raced up the remainder of the cliff. Continued up the castle wall to the top. The observation tower loomed in front of him like a giant chess piece. He grabbed the cement handrail and hoisted himself up and over. Rolled onto the cement floor. Sprinted twenty paces toward the first surveillance camera. Pulled the can of paint from his jacket pocket and sprayed the lens with orange paint. Crept along the wall to the second camera and did the same.

An old wooden door that looked like it had been borrowed from some medieval castle led inside the tower. It beckoned to him. Eva was somewhere on the other side of that door.

Bobby lifted the latch and pulled.

The door opened.

A surge of hope enveloped him. He considered going inside but reason asserted itself. He closed the door quietly. He would wait for Luo, as was the plan.

Eva was close.

Soon he would see her face. Soon she would be with him.

CHAPTER 44

LUO COULDN'T BELIEVE HIS EYES. ADAM HAD SCAMPERED UP the cliff as though it were even ground. In all his years training and working with the Black Berets, he'd never seen anything like it.

As soon as Adam jumped over the castle wall, Luo took his turn. In training, he'd timed out as one of the fastest free solo climbers in his class. No harness, no safety rope. He enjoyed the exhilaration of the free solo climb. He'd also stayed in shape and prided himself on having lost no more than a step or two during the twenty-four years that followed. But after watching the kid scale the wall, Luo felt slow and old. In fact, he felt strangely human, as though the boy were a different species.

It took him two minutes to climb the wall. Adam helped pull him over the guardrail. Luo's biceps burned and his knees ached.

A glint shone in Adam's eyes. "The door's open," he said.

Luo had longed to hear those words, but now that he did they filled him with dread. It was a trap, he thought. He and the boy had been blinded by optimism.

Why wasn't a guard stationed at the back full-time? Why hadn't security seen Adam when he climbed the wall, no matter how quickly he moved? Why hadn't they sent someone to investigate? Why was the door to the tower open if the owner was holding a hostage inside? At a minimum, an open door increased the risk of suicide, if nothing else.

But it was too late to change plans now. They were committed.

They raced to the door. Adam grasped the door handle. Luo tapped him on the shoulder. Motioned for him to wait.

Luo lifted his left pant leg. Removed the gun from the holster and affixed the sound suppressor from his pant pocket. The boomerang was his favorite weapon, but he wasn't an idiot. He'd bought the gun at the sporting goods store. Only idiots brought boomerangs to a gunfight.

Luo nudged Adam aside. He opened the door with his gun raised. Glanced inside.

A stairway led downward. A light shone through the window of a door twenty-five to thirty steps below. The stairwell was silent.

They entered the Swallow's Nest.

Luo led the way. When they reached the bottom step, they ducked into opposite corners of the door well to avoid being seen. Luo raised his head slowly until his eyes could see through the window. It was the size of a book.

A hallway awaited them on the other side. Luo glanced in each direction. His line of sight was limited by the size of the window but he didn't see anyone.

He glanced at Adam and put a finger to his lips. Adam nodded. Luo cracked the door open.

A drumbeat sounded in the distance. They weren't real drums. They lacked the percussive echo of the live instrument. No, it was a musical recording. Someone was listening to music in a large interior room, Luo thought, directly across from them. He recalled storming the home of a leader of the Chechen rebels on Lake Kazenoi. It didn't have a tower like the Swallow's Nest, but the bedrooms had remarkable views. Rich people were obsessed with views because they made their fortunes in the city. They thought that by looking at nature they could become one with it, which was absurd.

The bedrooms with the views were on the opposite side of the hallway, facing the lake. The living room, kitchen, and dining rooms had to be on lower levels.

Luo pointed at Adam with his index finger, then patted his own hip. *Stay close to me,* he mouthed.

Adam nodded again.

They slipped into the hallway. Wall sconces in the shape of Siberian tigers illuminated their path. The tigers' eyes glowed orange. The hallway appeared to form a rectangle around the perimeter of the third level.

Luo edged toward the music. Horns had joined the drums to create an electric sound. There was a Polynesian flavor to the beat. It rose to quick peaks and then relaxed for a moment, only to intensify again. Luo glanced behind him to make sure Adam was following. The kid was hugging the wall, knife in his right hand. Luo doubted the kid had ever sunk metal through flesh. But if Eva's life were at stake, he didn't doubt the kid would have the gumption to do it.

They approached the first bedroom. The strip beneath the door was dark. The lights were off. Luo grasped the door handle, turned it slowly, and burst inside.

Rich furnishings made of wood and olive fabric filled the room. The bed looked like a glamorous tent, with four polished mahogany posts. It was perfectly made. A wall of glass faced the lake. Expensive-looking artwork filled the walls. Luo caught a glimpse of the bathroom through an open door. Everything was in place. There was no sign of disruption. No evidence of anyone living there.

They proceeded to the second bedroom. It was similar to the first one, but the furnishings looked sleek and modern, the kind his hockey teammate from Sweden had in his room. Luo closed the door. They continued forward toward the end of the hallway where it turned right to proceed along a perpendicular wall.

The music grew louder. They were approaching the entrance to the interior room. Based on the source of the sound, the entrance to the music room would be around the corner to the right. Luo raised his gun. Adam followed him to the end of the hallway.

The music rose to a fevered pitch. A drumroll. A crash of cymbals. A final smash of the drum—

The music stopped.

"Play it again, play it again," a man said. He spoke fluent Russian, like a Muscovite, but coarse. He sounded young, not too educated. At least not formally. A kid from the streets.

"Yeah," a second man said. He sounded frighteningly similar to the first man. "The theme song is the best part. It's the best part of the show."

"Second best. The girl in the bikini is the best part of the show."

"That's what I meant."

Luo turned the corner. Hugged the inside wall and glanced into the room.

An enormous television covered the far wall. Two rows of plush leather seats faced the television. The height of the seatbacks prevented Luo from seeing the two men he'd heard talking.

The drumroll started again. A giant wave rolled forward on screen. Some English lettering appeared. The title of a movie, Luo thought. A curvaceous Polynesian beauty stepped out of the ocean. A handsome man spun around and looked at the camera. The theme song blared.

Luo glanced past the television room further down the hallway. More bedrooms. One of the doors was open. Why would one door be open while the others were closed?

Luo motioned to Adam that he was headed past the television room toward the open bedroom door. Then he looked inside the room again. The men remained transfixed by the scene on the television.

Luo darted past them to the other side of the door.

A phone rang.

The music stopped.

Voices sounded. They were coming from the front.

Another set of voices sounded. These were more distant, but they were coming from the back. Someone was approaching from the corner they'd just rounded.

"They're bringing her up," one of the men in the television room said. He'd answered the phone and was informing his colleague.

Luo couldn't retreat. He'd be passing the door to the television room. One or both of the men inside might see him. But Adam was still on the other side of the door. Luo glanced at him.

The kid was already backpedalling. He pointed toward the outer wall. Turned his right wrist to simulate opening a door. *I'm going into one of the bedrooms*, he was saying.

Luo nodded. Smart boy.

Adam disappeared around the corner.

Luo hustled into the open bedroom. The floor was neither wood nor carpet. It was made of stiff hay, woven together tightly. There was no bed in the room, either. Just an enormous mat on the floor. Luo had seen pictures of such a floor and sleeping device in a magazine once. It was a travel magazine about the Far East. Evidently, this was the Swallow's Nest's Japanese room. A portrait of a samurai warrior wielding a sword hung on a wall, but the samurai was Russian-looking, not Japanese. There was no sign of any luggage. Eva didn't have luggage, hence it was quite possible she was sleeping in this room—

Footsteps approached. One pair, heels clicking against the wood floor. A former soldier, marching in imaginary formation.

Luo ducked into a spare bathroom. A giant stainless steel soaking tub flanked a black lacquer vanity with cabinets covered with rice paper. He hid behind the door, gun raised to his shoulder, pointing at the ceiling.

A person entered the bedroom. Something clattered. Once, twice, three times. Footsteps started up again and faded.

Luo snuck back in the bedroom.

A tray of food rested on a desk in the corner. A steak, mixed vegetables, mashed potatoes, a bowl of borscht, and a basket of buckwheat bread. A glass of ice and a bottle of Orangina.

A man shouted over the din of the music. "I love this show," he said. He was an ebullient sort with a baritone voice. "Has the girl come out of the water yet?"

A third man, Luo thought. The man who was bringing "her" up. A muffled answer.

"Rewind it, rewind it," the third man said. "I have to see this."

The music stopped. Luo waited for it to restart. When it did, he poked his head out the door.

An elegant but broad-shouldered man in a suit ducked into the television room, his attention fixed on something straight ahead—the television, no doubt—and eyes wide with delight. He disappeared inside.

He left a young woman in the hallway behind him. She too, had turned to face the television. Luo recognized her as the girl from Fukushima. She was tall and lean with broad shoulders and narrow hips. Her dark brown hair fell to her shoulders. It looked recently washed. Good. They had allowed her to bathe. Her slumping shoulders registered defeat. When the third man disappeared into the television room, she glanced down the hallway.

Their eyes met. Luo noted a look of determination in her expression. She was more alert and conscious than her captors thought. She was looking for an escape. Of that Luo was certain.

But he was not certain who this girl was. Once again he didn't recognize her. All he saw was a scared yet resilient girl. Yes, she had an oval face like her mother. And yes, she had his coloring, and her build seemed appropriate for her parents. Yet none of this was conclusive. This girl might be anyone's daughter. Only Adam would know if she was Eva.

She stepped back, as though he was someone to fear, but didn't say anything.

Luo brought his finger to his lips.

Her eyes widened. Only a friend would motion for her to be quiet. She froze. Luo could sense her realization. She understood Luo might be her ally. He might be here to help her. Why else would he be hiding in a bedroom? Why else would he have lifted his finger to his lips?

Luo wished he were on the other side of the entrance to the television room. That way he could simply whisk the girl and Adam down the hallways, up the stairs, and over the wall. But the television room stood between him and the girl. He couldn't take the risk of dashing past it. Any of the three men might see him. If he were in one of the other bedrooms, he could sneak out and grab her right now. The path to the stairs leading to the tower was clear . . .

A shadow appeared behind the girl. A hand reached out to tap her on the shoulder.

Luo recognized the forest-green jacket sleeve.

Adam had come to the same conclusion.

CHAPTER 45

———— ❄ ————

THE PATH TO THE STAIRWELL WAS CLEAR. ALL BOBBY HAD to do was yank Eva out of the doorway and pray that the opening sequence to *Hawaii Five-O* kept the men in the media room occupied. The man who'd escorted Eva past the bedroom where Bobby had hidden had made them crank up the volume. The three men glued to the television screen wouldn't hear anything. The only risk was that one of them would turn around.

Bobby slipped out of the bedroom and skulked down the hallway. Eva stood nine paces away, back to him. He still hadn't seen her face. She was a bit taller than he remembered, but then again, three years had passed. Maybe she'd grown an inch. And she was thinner. That made sense given she'd been in Fukushima. If she were part of a volunteer organization they probably didn't feed her well. And besides, how could anyone not lose weight on a Japanese diet?

Six paces away.

And then he wondered, why had she gone to Fukushima in the first place? What sane person—let alone one who'd grown up around the Ukrainian Zone of Exclusion—would volunteer to go to a radioactive place? The question never bothered him before, but now it consumed him and would not let go.

Three paces.

The sweet smell of honey broke his concentration. Shampoo, he thought, as his eyes fell on her silken hair. Honey shampoo. Very popular with the girls in Russia. It had been Eva's favorite. The owner must have had some here. Perhaps the owner's wife.

The music blared. Bobby couldn't afford to startle Eva. He didn't want to make her jump. Better he wave with his right hand while still out of sight of the entrance to the media room. Try to catch her attention via her peripheral vision.

Bobby started to raise his right hand but dropped it just as quickly. There was no need for him to wave.

The girl turned toward him.

CHAPTER 46

NADIA TRIED CALLING BOBBY THREE MORE TIMES TO NO
avail.

"I'm getting voice mail immediately now," she said. "After
only one ring."

Simmy nodded beside her in the back of the Land Cruiser. "He
turned the phone off. That means he needs silence. That means
they need silence, I should say. I keep forgetting he's not alone."

"Not just silence. Total silence. He could have shut off the
ringer but kept the phone on vibrate. But he didn't. He shut it down
completely. That means they beat us. He's there, at the castle, now."

"*They're* there."

"Right. I keep forgetting, too. They're there." She shook her
head. "I guess I should take some comfort in knowing he's not
alone. But for some reason, I don't."

"Of course you don't," Simmy said. "The fox was born dis-
trustful. It's genetic. There's nothing she can do about it."

The highway from Irkutsk to Listvyanka gave way to a slip-
shod path covered with pebbles. Privacy signs warned tourists to
turn at the roundabout ahead and correct their error in navigation. Sure enough, the owner of the property had actually carved
a turnaround for cars three hundred yards down the path. The
pebble road must have been built to discourage adventurers,

because it soon gave way to freshly paved blacktop complete with yellow dividing lines between lanes.

Streetlights appeared around a bend. A wall reminiscent of a medieval fortress appeared ahead. A small stone cottage stood beside a gate. An iron gate blocked the entry to the compound beneath a stone archway. A dog began barking as they approached the gate. Three men emerged from the cottage. Two carried rifles. One held a leash. The dog at the end of it sat obediently at his feet. It looked like a cross between a sheepdog and a wolf with twice the ferocity of the latter.

The driver pulled up to the gate and lowered the windows. A gust of cold air blew into the cabin and cooled the perspiration on Nadia's forehead. The guards aimed their rifles at the driver and Simmy respectively.

"You've made a mistake," the guard holding the leash said. "This is private property. Please back up, turn your car around, and leave."

Simmy introduced himself. "I'm going to reach into my wallet," he said. "So I can give you a business card. To present to Mr. Golov. Please apologize to him and tell him I'm sorry I didn't call ahead, but I need to speak with him about an urgent matter."

The guard appeared stunned when he heard Simmy's name. He narrowed his eyes, looked closer, and glanced at his colleagues. They, too, appeared shocked.

The guard studied Simmy's business card and frowned. "Like I said, sir. You've made a mistake. This is not the Golov residence."

Not the Golov residence? Nadia glanced at the destination on the map on Simmy's tablet computer. The image of a car had landed on top of the target. It pulsed in red. Nadia recalled Simmy telling her that this region of Lake Baikal was popular with billionaires. Had they missed a turn? Or had the man at the airport purposefully given them the wrong destination? That would mean Bobby was alone. She would never arrive in time to help him.

"Of course it's not," Simmy said. "I understood Mr. Golov to be a guest here this evening."

Good one, Nadia thought. He was making up the story on the fly.

"Please present my card to your employer. Please extend my apologies for this impolite intrusion. And please tell him Simeon Simeonovich would be in his debt if he agreed to a brief visit."

The guard disappeared into the cottage. Nadia could see him through the window placing a phone call. While he was on the phone, Nadia counted eight cameras on the cottage, the walls, the gate, and the overhang. A seeing eye in the form of a black bulb was mounted beside the cottage door. Every conceivable angle was covered. Whomever the guard was calling could see the passengers in Simmy's vehicle.

The guard returned. "We'll need to inspect your vehicle and search the parties in the car. All weapons will have to be left here, to be returned upon your departure."

Nadia, Simmy, the driver, and Simmy's other bodyguard stepped out of the car. Simmy's men surrendered their handguns. One of the men insisted on searching Nadia. The process unnerved her but the man behaved professionally. One of the other guards produced a pole with an illuminated mirror attached to one end. He walked around the perimeter of the car with the mirror beneath the SUV's carriage in search of explosives. The SUV's storage area contained Simmy's overnight bag. Otherwise, it was empty. The heavy bags were in the second SUV, whose headlights had vanished from the side-view mirror as soon as the pebble road turned paved. Nadia had no idea where it had gone, and she knew better than to ask Simmy. If he wanted her to know, he would have told her.

Once the guards were satisfied, they climbed back into the SUV. The lead guard motioned to a colleague to open the gate. The iron grates rose into the air as though a city lay beyond it. The guard gave Simmy a slight bow.

"Mr. Milanovich will see you now, sir."

CHAPTER 47

———— ❄ ————

JOHNNY STUDIED THE MENU AT THE TROPICANA DINER. A MAN knew he was in the right place when they offered a rib-eye steak for $11.95 as a side item for breakfast. The waffle finger was interesting, too. A crispy waffle and three chicken fingers with all the butter and syrup a man could justify. A southern touch to soothe a man's soul in Elizabeth, New Jersey. Johnny had been planning to stick with his egg whites, but the prospect of representing a cop stressed him sufficiently to demand some quality carbohydrates on the side. When his client didn't arrive by 9:00 a.m. sharp, Johnny placed his order for six egg whites and a short stack of golden brown pancakes. Hold the butter, he insisted. The folks who ordered the waffle finger would undoubtedly use it.

Johnny hoped the pancakes might temper his apprehension, too. Nadia still hadn't called him with an update. She was probably in the thick of it now, whatever that meant. He wondered if she was all right. He wondered how Bobby was doing. He hoped the rich man was coming through for them. He wished he were there with them, wherever they were.

Richard Clark sauntered in fifteen minutes late wearing a black nylon warm-up suit, white cross trainers, and a shit-eating grin on his face. A cop on the verge of being arrested should have looked concerned. He should have been on time and reeked of humility. But he wasn't and he didn't. Instead he slid his body-builder-gone-to-pot physique into the booth, rubbed his unshaven face, and grinned like an entitled child armed with a badge and gun. Johnny regretted opting for the short stack instead of the full monty.

"You know," Clark said, "you're a lot older in person than you look on your company website."

"Occupational hazard. Can I see some ID?"

The grin turned into a laugh, then morphed into a look of disdain. "Are you for real?"

"Are you in need of my services?"

Johnny checked Clark's badge and driver's license, not just to verify the man's identity, but to establish the upper hand. And to punish him for being late and to piss him off a bit, too.

Johnny's waitress delivered his pancakes and eggs. She greeted Clark with familiarity—she called him Richie—and a complete lack of enthusiasm. Evidently he tipped like the asshole he was. She poured him a cup of coffee. Clark didn't bother looking at the menu. He ordered his usual, two eggs over easy and the rib-eye steak on the side.

Johnny didn't wait for Clark's food to arrive. He slid the egg whites onto his pancakes, poured syrup over them, and dug in.

"My boss said we know each other," Johnny said. "I can't seem to place you. Refresh my memory."

"Your boss lied. Or you weren't listening. I never said I knew you. I said I knew of you."

Cops knew criminal defense attorneys by reputation. The more successful a lawyer was in defending alleged perpetrators, the more they hated him. Until the day they needed his help, that is.

"What do you know about me?" Johnny said.

"I know you were the lawyer for the James brothers, two of the biggest scumbags ever to walk the sidewalks of Elizabeth."

"Reformed scumbags." The James brothers had been notorious drug dealers but had cleaned up their act. They owned and operated a chain of car washes now. Johnny glanced at Clark. The shit-eating grin still hadn't vanished from his face. "You know, for a guy who's staring at an indictable that might cost him his career and land him in jail for who knows how many years, you don't seem concerned. You want to tell me your story so I can see what I'm missing?"

Clark took a sip of coffee and leaned back, spreading his arms along the top of the booth as though he didn't have a care in the world. "Sure. I'll tell you my story. It's simple. I'm not worried because you're going to be my lawyer."

The certainty in his voice struck Johnny as offensive. Johnny gave Clark his own shit-eating grin. "You sure about that, are you?"

"Absolutely. What you're missing is that my case is just as important to you as it is to me."

"Is that right?"

"Yeah. That's right, counselor. You see, I know the magic word."

Magic word. Clark's arrogance soured the syrup on his breakfast cakes. Johnny sighed. "What's the magic word, Richie?"

Clark broadened his grin. "The magic word is Nadia Tesla."

CHAPTER 48

———————— ❄ ————————

Bobby never thought about the purple streaks in Eva's hair until the girl turned. He'd caught a glimpse of her hair countless times during the trip from Japan. He'd had ample opportunity to consider its color. It had never dawned on him that the absence of purple might be evidence the girl was not Eva. Only when he saw her face did this occur to him. The girl was not wearing purple lipstick either. And he'd never seen Eva without her lips painted her favorite color. Eva was all about purple, and to Bobby the color purple was all about Eva. In his mind, the two were inseparable.

This girl had no trace of purple about her.

And yet, his heart leapt in his chest nonetheless, for the girl he'd faithfully followed for the last three days was Eva.

Other than the absence of purple, she looked exactly the same as he remembered her, except she was totally different. Her high cheekbones seemed more drawn. Dark circles surrounded her eyes. But the creases that sprang to her forehead when she realized there was a man behind her caught Bobby's eye. Only three years had passed since he'd seen her last, since her uncle—the Coach—had told him she'd died. And yet she looked ten years older. Not in a bad way. In a mature way. The latter observation struck fear in Bobby's heart. Maybe she'd think he was too young for her again. She was nineteen. He was about to turn eighteen. Maybe in her eyes he'd gone back to being a kid.

The creases vanished. Her eyes came alive. They shone with intensity. Her lips curled upward. No, they weren't just curling upward. They parted to form a rapturous smile, an uninhibited look of joy the likes of which he'd never seen from her before. She'd been the tough girl with the inscrutable expression. Now she stood before him looking like he were the person in the world she most wanted to see.

He offered her his hand.

She took it. Grabbed it as though it were the hand of her personal Moses. The man who had come to rescue her. The man she knew was coming to rescue her from the moment she'd caught a glimpse of him at Fukushima.

The *Hawaii Five-O* beat gathered itself for its climactic run. The horns blared. The drums pounded. Bobby felt invincible.

He turned and pulled Eva toward the stairs. The name of Moses rang in his ears.

Luo, he thought. He couldn't leave Luo behind. He decelerated. Felt the slack in Eva's arm as she stepped closer to him. Luo would have crossed the entrance to the media room if he thought he could do so undetected. But he didn't, so he couldn't. There was nothing Bobby could do to help him. If Luo was an imposter, he deserved his fate. If he was Eva's father, he would be screaming for Bobby to run—

Bobby raced down the hallway with Eva. He pulled the stairwell door. A dim light shone under the door at the top of the stairs. The peripheral glow from the lights aimed out at the lake, he thought.

Bobby released Eva's hand. He powered up the stairs. He heard her follow behind him. The sound of her footsteps blended with his. Perfect cadence, just like in the Zone when they scavenged for scraps of metal that could be sold on the black market.

They hadn't seen each other in three years, but they were already communicating without speaking.

The music rose to a crescendo. It was muted by the door behind them, but Bobby could still hear it as he approached the top of the stairwell.

He pushed the door open. The handrail stood twenty-five feet in front of him. Beneath it, the cliff. Below the cliff, their skates. Beyond their skates, a runway made of ice, ready for takeoff.

Bobby emerged onto the observation deck. Eva pulled up beside him. The honey scent of her hair, the sound of her breathing, the heat of her shoulder rubbing up against his, electrified him. He found the grapple hanging at the bottom of one of the iron beams.

"There," he said.

Someone slammed the door shut behind them. Two men in suits stepped out from against the walls surrounding the door. They pointed their rifles at Bobby and Eva. Both men wore earphones. One of them took his eyes off Eva and spoke.

"I've got the girl on the observation deck . . . Yes, the observation deck . . . Obviously he's an idiot because she's with me and not in her room . . . And get this. I can't believe it." The man looked at Bobby. "She's not alone. The boy's here. . . . That's right . . . I have no idea how he did it, but he got inside . . . just like you said he would."

CHAPTER 49

---※---

SIMMY'S DRIVER PULLED UP TO A SQUARE PROMENADE AT THE entrance to the Swallow's Nest. Two more armed guards awaited them.

"Milanovich?" Nadia said. "Have you heard of that name?"

"Yes."

"Do you know him?"

"I know of him. Assuming it's the same Milanovich."

"What are the odds there are two Milanoviches with a mansion on Lake Baikal?"

"Low."

"Then obviously it's him. So who is he? Another oligarch? A former Soviet official turned capitalist?"

"No."

"Then who?"

Simmy pressed his lips together. It was a slight gesture, one that would have gone unnoticed by most people. But to a forensic securities analyst used to vetting management during rigorous interviews, and one who'd spent time with Simeon Simeonovich, it was the equivalent of a major revelation during a poker game.

Simmy was concerned.

Nadia had never seen him display one moment of weakness. The sight of it sent a shiver up her spine.

The driver pulled to a stop.

"Simmy?" Nadia said. "Tell me. Who is he?"

Simmy took an audible breath. "He's allegedly the head of a Russian crime syndicate. A global crime syndicate. Many businesses in the countries that once made up the Soviet Union pay roof to him. In some cities, you can't get the electricity turned on without his approval. Drugs, gambling, weapons sales. Among other things. He was number three on your FBI most wanted list until he was mysteriously removed from it two years ago."

Nadia imagined Bobby and the formula in such a man's hands. "That's great news."

Simmy continued speaking as if he hadn't been interrupted. "He may be the most dangerous man alive, except for one person."

The driver stepped out of the car and opened Nadia's door.

"Who's that?" Nadia said.

"The goalie on my soccer team," Simmy said. "The guy can stop anything. He's lethal."

Simmy grinned, winked, and nodded at the open door. His attempt at humor failed to wipe his moment of weakness from Nadia's mind, but it endeared him to her. As did his moment of doubt. He was human after all.

A bored-looking woman in black tights and an obscenely low-cut blouse escorted them into a parlor and left them there. A minute later a man shuffled into the room. He appeared to be in his eighties, with pinched eyes and thick gray hair that swooped back from a widow's peak. Age spots covered his face. The narrow shoulders beneath his baby-blue cardigan sweater contrasted with the belly that bulged below. From the neck down, he looked more like the estranged grandfather of the most dangerous man alive than the man himself. From the neck up, it was his eyes that defined him. Lively and inscrutable, they studied Nadia.

Simmy stood up when he entered the room, which was telling. Nadia wasn't sure if that was proper manners or if his gesture implied deference.

No names were exchanged. No words were spoken. Milanovich sat down in the chair opposite the sofa where Nadia and Simmy were seated. He took a deep breath after arranging himself comfortably.

Milanovich addressed Simmy. "You and I travel in different circles, so we've never met. I know who you are. I read the paper. But do you know who I am?" He spoke in crude Russian.

"Yes," Simmy said.

"Good. That is good. Because I wasn't sure. A man shows up unannounced. It makes him wonder if he has any respect for the person he's visiting."

"I apologize for that—"

Milanovich shook his head and waved his hand. "No, no. No apologies needed. I'm just making sure you understand that by coming here, you've wandered out of your boardroom and into mine. And I am the chairman of the board here."

"Indeed," Simmy said.

"And because I have respect for you—you are a good Russian who cares for his people—I want to give you a chance to leave right now. The door is open. You can walk out with your friend, get in your car, and leave. Because if you don't—if we start having a conversation where information is revealed or exchanged—I'm going to have to protect my business interests. The same way that you would protect yours."

"Let me explain why we're here—"

"Don't bother," Milanovich said. "I know why you're here. I will repeat my offer. Would you like to leave now?"

Simmy glanced at Nadia. She responded the only way a person with any self-respect or integrity could respond. By giving him a blank stare.

Simmy turned back to Milanovich. "We're looking for a girl. We think you may be able to help us find her. I came here hoping you and I might come to a suitable business arrangement in exchange for your help."

"What is it you think you might have that I would want?"

"That depends," Simmy said. "What don't you have that you desperately want?"

Milanovich considered the question for a moment. "Fifteen minutes ago I would have had a different answer. But since then my wildest dream has been answered so I can honestly say—nothing."

Simmy chuckled. "Mr. Milanovich, you know the saying among Russian businessmen. That which does not grow, dies. Please reconsider. There must be something you want. Which is to say, there must be something you need."

"No. I don't want anything, but since you refused my offer to leave, there is something that you're going to need. That something is called luck. And you're going to need a lot of it."

"I don't believe in luck. I believe in preparation. And you should know that I don't stumble in or out of boardrooms. Boardrooms quake when I walk in the door, and they reach for the oxygen tanks when I leave."

If Simmy was intimidated, he'd left any visible signs of weakness in the car. Now he was matching strength with strength, which was the only way to deal with a willful person. The ensuing flow of Russian testosterone, however, was making Nadia queasy.

"You have a lot of nerve," Milanovich said. "To arrive at my home and make a statement like that." He slammed his hand against his armrest. "But that is as it should be. I would have expected nothing else. I'm afraid this is not going to end well for either of you. But we don't have to worry about that now. Let's go to the great room and join the others."

"The others?" Nadia said.

Milanovich frowned as though disgusted the woman had dared speak. "Yes, Nadia, daughter of a thief. The others. The girl *and* the boy." He glanced at Simmy. "They're both here. They're chatting with an old friend of yours as we speak."

Bobby and Genesis II. In the adjacent room. Together.

She'd been dreaming of such a scenario for days. Now, under

the circumstances, it was the worst possible development. Also, Nadia was left with the strange impression that Milanovich had turned his attention to her at the last second, and that the old friend to whom he was referring was hers, not Simmy's.

She only knew three people in Siberia, former friends of her uncle, Bobby's father. They'd known him from his days in the *gulag*, the Russian labor camp, in northern Siberia, thousands of miles away. Sharlam, Fyodor, and Ruchkin. The first two were indigenous Yakut and Evenki tribesmen who'd worked for the camp guards; the third was a bush pilot who'd served time with her uncle. All three of them knew Bobby. Had one of them discovered a formula existed? If so, her money was on Ruchkin. He was a native of Moscow. He was materialistic; the other two weren't.

She followed Milanovich and Simmy into a sprawling room that was part office and part living area. Two sofas flanked a high-backed chair in front of a fireplace made of granite at the far end of the room. Nadia recognized Bobby immediately. She didn't recognize the girl. But she fit the description Bobby had given her. Also, there was something intangible between the two of them. They weren't seated at far ends of the sofa. They were sitting toward the middle. If either one of them stretched their legs, their thighs would touch.

Genesis II was Eva. She was alive.

As soon as Bobby saw Nadia, he stood. A fleeting look of joy washed over his face, replaced with a pair of sealed lips that suggested he wished she were elsewhere. He wished she were safe.

There was a stirring in the high-backed chair beside them.

A man began to stand. He gripped the back of the chair with his hand. The gold ring on his finger faced Nadia. It looked like the number three but it was actually З, the Cyrillic version of the letter Z. Z as in Zaroff. Nadia knew this was the case because she'd seen two such rings on the members of the Zaroff Seven who died in a fire in Chornobyl a month ago.

The man turned to face Nadia.

CHAPTER 50

J OHNNY COULDN'T REMEMBER WHEN AN ALLEGED PERPETRA-
tor had left him speechless, or when a cop had done so, for that
matter. But the sound of Nadia's name rolling off the cop's tongue
left him in a momentary state of shock. He sat dumbfounded for
ten seconds, staring at Clark's grin before he realized the truth.
His appetite vanished immediately. It was replaced by a sense of
utter hopelessness and despair. He wanted so desperately to be
wrong, but he was certain he was right.

"Tell me about the pending charges," Johnny said.

Clark cleared his throat. "They say I tampered with evidence."

Johnny cringed. It was the answer he was hoping not to hear.
The only question left was how they'd put the squeeze on Clark.

"Are you in debt to someone, Richie?" Johnny said.

Johnny's deduction wiped the smile from Clark's face.

"Let me guess. You borrowed money."

Clark remained silent.

"What was it? Gambling?" Johnny studied him. He looked like
a former athlete, probably a high school star, maybe even college.
"Sports gambling."

The cop took a sharp breath through his nose.

Johnny nodded. "You bet on games, it got away from you. Who
put the squeeze on you? What did he look like?"

265

Clark frowned slightly, suggesting Johnny should have known better than to even ask the question.

"It's simple," Johnny said. "You answer my questions, I'm going to represent you. If you don't, I'm walking out of here and whatever leverage you think you have over me you can go ahead and use it. I honestly don't care."

Johnny wasn't sure himself if he was bluffing or not, but he was so angry at the turn of events that he was certain he'd delivered his threat with conviction. They sat staring at each other for a bit longer.

Clark looked both ways, cleared his throat, and leaned in. "There were two of them. In their twenties. Russian."

"Did they tell you to call me? Were they the ones who gave you the magic word?"

"Yeah."

"What was the evidence they told you to get rid of?"

"Five ounces of heroin."

"Where was this heroin found?"

"Under a Lincoln Town Car."

Of course that's where it was found. Johnny had paid the James brothers to plant it there to put Nadia's nemesis away. To put him away for good.

"The owner of the Town Car," Johnny said. "The man who was charged with intent to sell . . ."

"They dropped the charges."

"When?"

"Three days ago."

Johnny ran outside to call Nadia, unable to shake the sensation that he was too late.

Once again he'd tried to help her. Once again he'd come up short. As the call went through he couldn't help but think that in the real world, good intentions didn't pay the rent. In the courtroom, he was formidable. But with this man, even when he thought he was in control, it was a delusion.

With this man, he was perpetually out of his depth.

CHAPTER 51

—————— ❄ ——————

NADIA RECOGNIZED HIM IMMEDIATELY. HE WAS THE AN-
cient weed in the garden, the immortal vine that couldn't
be eradicated with any poison.

There was just one problem. The man she was looking at was
locked up on Rikers Island. Prisoners didn't escape from Rikers.
And the man standing in front of her wasn't a member of the
Zaroff Seven. Not only wasn't he a former Soviet apparatchik
turned oligarch, he'd fled their strict laws for America where a
career criminal could ply his trade more freely and successfully.

"Victor Bodnar," Nadia said. "It looks like you, but it can't
really be you."

"Were you hoping it were someone else?" Victor said.

"Yes."

"Who?"

"Anyone."

"Why?"

"Because I thought there was a strange sense of honor about
you, even though you're a career criminal. I wouldn't have imagined you'd hunt children."

"A thief must go where opportunity takes him. And this so-called
child," he said, glancing at Bobby, "was the one responsible for my
arrest. You didn't expect such an action to go unanswered, did you?"

267

"Yes," Nadia said. "I did. I'm an optimist, and you were behind bars."

"There's much space between the bars of your American jails. If a thin man stands at the proper angle . . ." He turned ninety degrees to the left. "He might disappear, like a pick into a keyhole."

Ice clinked against glass. Milanovich stood at a server along the wall. He poured three inches of amber liquid from a crystal decanter into a glass. He didn't offer anyone else a drink.

Two beefy men in suits occupied opposite corners of the room. Simmy stood beside Nadia. He'd stuffed his hands in his pockets while Victor was speaking. One pocket contained his cell phone, the other a pager with a direct link to the driver of the other SUV.

Nadia eyed the ring on Victor's finger. His left lip curled upward a smidge, the closest thing to a smile Nadia had ever seen from him.

"This old thing?" Victor said. "An obvious thought. The boy Adam killed in New York? We looked into his background. Discovered his father's identity. As I'm sure you did when you proved Adam innocent of the murder charge last month. He was a member of a hunting society called the Zaroff Seven. My colleagues made some inquiries about them. When we learned two more vanished mysteriously during the exact same time you were here, we knew who your antagonists had been."

"And the ring?"

Victor slipped the ring off his finger. "Saw them wearing it in a book on hunting clubs. Old book, like me. Seems they're famous for it, if you know who to ask. And the boss and I have a few connections, don't we Maxim?"

"It's not who you know, Victor," Milanovich said. "It's who you know that owes you."

"A jeweler made us a dozen knockoffs," Victor said. "We had our men wear them in case they were seen. By you. By anyone."

"To make it look like the Zaroff Seven were doing the killing," Simmy said. "Ksenia Melnik. I bet the babushka is dead, too."

A moment of silence confirmed Simmy's theory. Victor glared at Milanovich as though the murders were his doing, and Victor didn't even know about them.

Nadia remembered the babushka and the story of the pet hunters, her rifle, and the root cellar. But mostly she remembered the old woman saving her life.

Victor tossed the ring to Bobby. "Keep it," he said. "As a memento. They should make you an honorary member. After all, you are the prey that got away, aren't you?"

Bobby studied the ring and did what any teenager would have done. He put it in his pocket.

"I knew you would come," Victor said. "I knew you would come for your girl. And I knew you had enough brains, guts, and strength to succeed. I didn't know how you would do it, but I told them to expect you."

Bobby remained stone-faced.

"How did you find Eva?" Nadia glanced at the girl after speaking her name. She didn't seem frightened. Instead she acted like Bobby's female clone. Calm, cool, and calculating.

"The babushka led us to Ksenia Melnik," Victor said. "She knew of the legend of the formula. Said Dr. Arkady loved the boy and the girl like they were his own. He called them *Genesis II* because they would carry the knowledge to change the human race for the better, but they could only achieve that goal as one. Ksenia Melnik knew the girl's death had been staged to protect her from the Zaroff Seven. She knew she was a student at a university in Japan, one of the last places anyone would ever look for her."

That didn't explain how Eva knew to send Bobby an e-mail. How she knew her locket contained half the formula, and how she knew where the second half was. Dr. Arkady must have told her, Nadia thought. He must have deemed her the primary beneficiary of the inheritance he bestowed upon them, if there was one. Given she was older—and her relative maturity would have been much more palpable three years ago—that made sense.

"As fate would have it, there is no formula," Victor said.

He pulled two lockets out of his pocket. The gilding had been scraped off both of them. One contained etchings. It was Bobby's. The other didn't. It had to be Eva's.

"I'm not so sure of that," Milanovich said. "We haven't had a real conversation with her yet. The kind where a girl tells a man all her secrets in exchange for not being fed alive to my pet tiger. And that would be after the necessary biological and genetic tests were conducted on both of these mutants to see if their body chemistry has been altered by this formula. To see if there is money in their blood or bones."

"This is ridiculous," Simmy said. "What are we here, barbarians? Experiments on children for the sake of money? You want money? I'll give you money."

"There are two problems with that proposition," Milanovich said. "First, if there is a formula for a countermeasure to radiation, and the insides of these young people can give it to me, you don't have that much money. And if you do, you wouldn't part with it, so stop playing the hero, Simeonovich. Even your woman doesn't believe your bullshit."

He was right. Nadia could see Simmy generously parting with some amount of money, but he wasn't going to pony up a billion dollars or more.

"We can discuss that," Simmy said. "You invested in a venture with time and labor. I can guarantee you a certain return. I can guarantee your portfolio grows."

Milanovich took a sip of his drink and rubbed his chin. "Now that you put it that way—and you're quoting me back to me—you have a point. Perhaps there is a number. But that still doesn't solve the second problem with your proposition."

"There's a solution for every problem," Simmy said.

"Not this one," Milanovich said.

"Impossible. What is the problem?"

"You'd have to be alive to pay me." Milanovich turned to the nearest bodyguard. "Kill him."

The bodyguard thrust his hand under his jacket. He whipped out a gun and aimed it at Simmy's head.

An object flew in out of nowhere. It connected with the bodyguard's neck. His body crumpled. His severed head fell to the ground.

The same sound echoed behind them. Nadia turned.

The second bodyguard's head rolled off his body. His body fell limp.

A fierce-looking man came flying down the steps. His gun was drawn. He pointed his gun alternately at Milanovich and Victor. What amazed Nadia was that he'd killed two men without firing a shot or making a sound. And he'd killed them in such an unconventional manner that everyone in the room was paralyzed. They were all just trying to comprehend what was happening.

Eva's father, Nadia thought. The man Bobby had met. Was he Eva's father?

Bobby pulled a knife from its sheath around his calf. He stood up and grabbed Eva's hand with his left. Glanced at the man coming down the stairs. Nadia caught a glimmer of the excitement in Bobby's eyes.

The man was Eva's father. He had to be.

Then another bodyguard appeared at the top of the stairwell. Nadia shouted a warning, but it all happened too fast.

The bodyguard shot Eva's father in the back.

CHAPTER 52

L UO REALIZED THE GIRL WAS HIS DAUGHTER. HE KNEW IT BY the gleam in Adam's eyes.

She was a dark angel. A lithe beauty. She had her mother's athletic frame after all. Her father's inscrutable eyes. Even under dire circumstances, with boomerangs and bullets flying, there wasn't a hint of panic about her. How strong she looked. It was his proudest moment, to know he was seeing his offspring in the flesh. It was just as he imagined it would be in his wildest dreams. All that was left was for her to look him in the eyes. She'd glanced at him once as he glided down the staircase, but Bobby had grabbed her hand and yanked her from the sofa before she could realize who he was. Before she could see that it was her long-lost father who'd come to her rescue—

A gunshot. A blow to the back. Someone set his shoulder blade on fire.

Luo tumbled down the stairs. His head bounced off wood. He tried to remember where he was and what was happening, but he couldn't. All he knew was that he was falling and there was nothing he could do about it

A second gunshot. His thigh burned.

A third gunshot. A noise beside his head. Something pierced a surface beside him.

What surface?

His eyes regained focus. A white ceiling. A staircase above him.

He was on the stairs in a criminal's house with his daughter and the boy. A man in an expensive-looking suit was coming down the stairs and shooting—

These Russian mafia types and their clothes . . .

Luo lifted his gun. Stared down the barrel of the bodyguard's weapon and squeezed the trigger.

Two shots rang out.

A force knocked Luo back to the floor. A bullet. A hot iron in his chest. Near the heart. He'd been shot.

Luo lifted his head. The bodyguard lay slumped on the stairs, a hole in his forehead. Luo looked down at his chest. His shirt was soaked. Right near the heart. He could feel his constitution weakening. He'd seen enough chest wounds to know he was bleeding out.

He was dying.

Luo's mind raced. He'd never speak with Eva. She'd never look into his eyes. Their souls would never connect. At least not above ground.

It didn't matter.

He was dead, but she was alive and would survive. The boy would see to that. No matter what the obstacles ahead of them, the boy would protect her. Luo's final vision was of the boy scaling the wall. He'd never seen anything like it.

The boy would be able to protect her.

The boy was no longer human.

The boy was something more.

CHAPTER 53

———— ❄ ————

BOBBY AND EVA ROSE FROM THE FLOOR. THEY'D DROPPED TO their stomachs as soon as they'd heard the gunshot, seen the bodyguard firing at Luo from behind.

The bodyguard's third bullet pierced Luo's chest. Luo collapsed to the floor, his body limp. The bodyguard dropped his gun and fell down the stairs. He remained limp on the floor, a hole in his head just above the eyes.

Bobby jumped to his feet to help Luo. He was Eva's father. He was Bobby's friend. Bobby wanted to save him, whatever the cost. Without Luo, Bobby would have been dead twice already. But a calmer voice prevailed. It was the voice of his father, instructing him to stop indulging in sentiment and focus on his own survival.

Eva was already rising to her feet. Bobby reached out with his hand. As she took it, Bobby saw Nadia and Simeonovich getting up, too. The latter held a gun in his right hand.

"More guards upstairs," Bobby said. "Down is better."

Eva passed Bobby. He didn't wait for a reaction from Nadia. He raced to catch up with her. It dawned on Bobby that he hadn't seen Victor or Milanovich. They were probably still on the ground, he thought. Still hiding.

The bodyguard's corpse lay beside Luo's body on the upward

staircase. Eva rounded the corner to the downward stairwell. Bobby was two steps behind her.

Another guard rounded the flight of stairs from below. He was nine steps away from Eva. The guard looked up.

His eyes met Eva's.

The guard raised his rifle.

Bobby leaped down the staircase. He pushed off his right knee and propelled himself with all his might. His gut resisted the leap. It was too long a distance to cover. His instincts told him he'd land at the man's feet just as he was ready to fire.

His gut was wrong. His instincts were wrong.

The thrust from his thigh catapulted him onto the man in a flash. The guard's rifle got caught between their bodies.

Bobby plunged the knife through the guard's left eye. Rolled off his body and looked up at Eva.

"Come on," he said.

The sound of the blade sliding through wet and soft flesh echoed in his ears. Bile rose up his throat. *What had he done? Killed a man. Why had he done it? To protect Eva.* Bobby willed the bile back down to his stomach. Resisted the urge to glance at his wreckage.

Eva sidestepped the body without taking her eyes off Bobby. She appraised him with a mixture of awe and fear. Awe was good, Bobby thought. He wasn't sure about the other part.

They raced down the stairs. The second floor opened up into a corridor. Bobby spied the entrance to an enormous kitchen on one side, a dining room on the other. Voices shouted from the opposite sides of the walls. Transmitters squawked.

Bobby made a downward motion with his head. Eva followed him another flight down the stairs. They emerged on the first floor from a side entrance. A second staircase—a grand one fit for a king—wound its way up to the second floor. In front of it was a foyer with marble floor. The door outside was thirty feet away but Bobby could spy guards through the windows.

An explosion rocked the castle.

CHAPTER 54

N ADIA SENSED THE MAN BEHIND HER. SHE COULDN'T HEAR, see, or smell him. But she knew he was there. Simmy must have experienced the same sensation because he started to turn.

"Don't turn around," Victor said. Nadia saw the gun pressed to the back of Simmy's head. "You heard what the boy said. Downstairs is better. Run. Both of you."

Victor had ulterior motives. Nadia realized this immediately, but Simmy didn't. How could he? He didn't know Victor as well as she did.

Nadia stepped forward, but Simmy hesitated. The muscles in his gun hand twitched. No doubt he didn't like being given orders. She wondered when he'd last been in a position where he was forced to yield to another man's will.

"Live to play another day," Nadia said.

Simmy pressed his lips tight, as he'd done in the car when he told her about Milanovich. He'd survived and prospered in the new Russia for a reason. A second later he was running across the room beside Nadia. He didn't bother to look over his shoulder.

"Faster," he said. "I gave my men the signal to attack a minute ago."

They found a dead guard in the middle of the stairwell. A knife protruded from his eye. Nadia recognized the knife. It was the one Bobby had pulled from a sheath wrapped around his calf. How had he overpowered a man with a rifle? Where had he found the fortitude to perform such a gruesome task?

Eva, she thought. The girl was most definitely Eva. He'd killed the man for Eva.

As she rounded the stairwell, a deafening noise filled the house. Nadia stopped in her tracks. The castle trembled.

Bomb, Nadia thought.

She wondered if the place where she was standing was about to blow up next. The thought sent a wave of fear down her spine.

A pair of sturdy hands grabbed her shoulders.

She turned.

Simmy tilted his head up a notch and squeezed her. His men were coming, Nadia thought.

No, she realized.

His men were here.

CHAPTER 55

V ICTOR STUCK HIS GUN INSIDE THE WAISTBAND OF HIS PANTS beneath his jacket. He looped around the back of the sofa. He'd seen Milanovich take cover behind it as soon as the heads had started to roll.

"It's me, Sergei," Victor said. "Do you hear me?"

"Victor?"

The boss was partially deaf in his left ear. Victor raised his voice. "Yes, Sergei. It's me. Don't shoot."

Milanovich had pulled out his own pistol as he'd taken cover. He suffered from tremors, the kind that could cause a man to inadvertently squeeze a trigger, especially when he was scared out of his wits. And Victor would have bet a million in Atlantic City that the boss of bosses was more terrified than any of his soldiers could have imagined.

All rich men shared one thing in common, regardless of the source of their wealth: an obsession with eternal life. It was the one thing they absolutely could not buy. Thus the second obsession most of them shared: sexual relationships with much younger women. They could be bought, and provided a temporary nirvana that came closest to approximating what the rich man thought immortality might be like.

"Did you hear me, Sergei?"

"Yes, Victor. I heard you."

Victor took a deep breath for good measure and glanced behind the sofa.

Milanovich sat on the floor cowering behind foam and fabric, neither of which would have stopped a bullet. The gun shook in his hands. It was aimed squarely at Victor's chest.

Victor smiled. "The coast is clear. They're all trying to make their escape. By now the guards are swarming the grounds. They'll be captured or killed immediately."

"They have instructions not to kill the children. We need them for their blood. What if the formula is in their blood? We need them alive to ensure a constant supply. We need them alive."

Victor stifled his repulsion. He was a *Thief In Law*, a member of a loose association of criminals from the countries that once comprised the Soviet Union. A thief could not dictate his opportunities. He had a moral obligation to put thievery above all else. He was not allowed to have a family, yet Victor had discovered he was a father and grandfather a year ago. He'd kept this discovery a secret. He would keep his repulsion for Milanovich's plan a secret as well. If someone had tried to conduct a biological experiment on his grandson, he would have buried him alive in a grave filled with flesh-eating worms.

"Of course they will remain alive," Victor said. "They are *Genesis II*. They are destined to remain alive." Victor reached out with his hand. "Here. Let me help you up."

Milanovich put his gun in his jacket pocket. Victor grabbed his boss's right hand and helped him up.

"Where is Simeonovich?" Milanovich said.

Victor nodded toward the staircase. "Gone with the others."

"He's an amateur. It's easy to tell when an enemy arrives at your front door pretending to be your friend."

"I agree. It's much harder to tell when a friend arrives at your front door and he's actually your enemy."

Victor pulled the gun from his waistband and shot him in the head.

He walked to Milanovich's study behind the great room and pressed a button on a bookshelf. A wall of books opened up to reveal a secret chamber. Victor stepped into the chamber and pressed another button to close the door behind him. He found his protégés waiting for him. One of them was the Gun, the other the Ammunition. Victor could only identify them by the tattoos on their arms. He'd recruited the Timkiv twins out of prison in Ukraine. Computer hackers who looked like California surfer boys with sociopathic tendencies. Perfect companions for an aging thief.

One of the Timkiv twins led the way down the narrow stairs. The other followed behind. Floor lights built into the edges of the steps illuminated their descent. Milanovich had bragged about the secret passageway he'd built as soon as Victor had arrived. He'd spent the equivalent of three million American dollars to build an escape route in the event the Russian FSB or another criminal organization came to assassinate him. The stairs led to a tunnel that would deposit them at an underground garage. A fully fueled Mercedes-Benz truck awaited them. The ground above the garage was heated by the power plant at the Swallow's Nest. The garage would open up with the press of a button. The Timkiv twins would drive him to the airport in Irkutsk. The three of them would be back in New York City in less than twenty-four hours.

Milanovich's death would create a power struggle in his organization. The only way to avoid mass bloodshed would be a division of the empire. Such a negotiation would take a year or more to materialize. It would be preceded by threats, challenges, and skirmishes. During that time frame, Victor would solidify his hold on his businesses in the New York City area. Instead of paying roof to Milanovich or anyone else, his hard-earned cash would go into a savings account for his grandson. No longer would his heir be denied part of his rightful inheritance because of a greedy old man's insatiable appetite for money.

Victor had begun plotting his coup as soon as he was jailed in New Jersey a week ago. His lawyer had acted as conduit, relaying instructions to his men in New York and Kyiv. Victor's mission had been threefold: get the charges against him dismissed, kill Milanovich, and acquire the formula. He'd accomplished two out of his three goals, and they were the most important. The formula was a luxury. He didn't need it to survive, but it would have been the crowning moment of his career if it had happened. His earlier talk of revenge was mere theatre. Victor was a thief. Revenge was an emotion. Based on Victor's experience, emotions weren't going to enrich his grandson.

As for the boy and the girl, Victor was reminded of the time his daughter, Tara, took him to an animal shelter in New York City to find puppies for both of them. When she saw two mutts in a special cage, Tara inquired about them. An attendant told her they were destined for euthanasia. No, we'll take them, Tara said. Initially Victor didn't understand her decision. They'd come for puppies. Why would they want some scraggly looking mixed-breeds? In Victor's experience, the strong ate the weak. Why would she care about two mutts?

Tara had put her arm around her father and whispered three words in his ear.

Let them live.

CHAPTER 56

───────── ❄ ─────────

THE EXPLOSIONS KNOCKED BOBBY AND EVA OFF THEIR FEET. Bobby rose quickly, regained his senses, and looked for Eva. To his surprise, she'd already gotten up. She stood two steps ahead waiting for him. There wasn't a hint of anxiety in her expression. It was as though they were back in the Zone, searching for scraps amidst the radioactive rubble, looking out for each other.

A double glass door opened up onto a veranda. Smoke billowed from the direction of the front entrance. The rat-tat-tat of gunfire filled the air. Two guards were perched beneath the concrete banister shooting at someone in the distance. Men shouted instructions to each other.

Bullets whizzed over Bobby and Eva's heads.

They dropped to the ground.

"Someone's shooting at guards from beyond the entrance," Bobby said. "Nadia and the rich guy. They must not have come alone."

He glanced at the outdoor staircase to the right. It wound its way up to the third and fourth floors of the castle.

"There'll be no guards in the back," he said. "They're all here returning fire. Think you can rappel down a cliff?"

"If you can do it, I can do it," Eva said. "We're the same."

Bobby and Eva waited until the bodyguards raised their rifles and fired at their targets on the ground beyond the castle. Then they raced up the staircase, keeping their heads low. They wound their way around the entire building until they ended up at the top level where Bobby and Luo had arrived. They didn't encounter any guards. They were all preoccupied with the attack on the property as Bobby had suspected.

Cracks of gunfire echoed around the castle. Bobby found the rope and grapple where Luo had hidden them. He removed his climbing gloves from his pocket and gave them to Eva. Told her she'd land on a grassy knoll beneath the foundation.

Eva nodded, climbed over the guardrail, and descended down the side of the cliff. She supported herself effortlessly. After six steps she gained confidence and accelerated her pace. From Bobby's vantage point looking down past the guardrail, Eva appeared to be gliding backward from heaven to earth.

When she reached the bottom, Bobby pulled the rope back up. He heard voices. Men. At least two of them. They weren't coming from the outdoor stairs. They were coming from inside the Swallow's Nest. More guards were coming to fortify the flanks along the front walls, Bobby thought.

Bobby picked up his pace. He swung the rope over the guardrail and rappelled down the side of the cliff with long, bold kicks to the face of the cliff. The rope burned his hands but he barely felt the pain.

Eva was waiting for him at the bottom of the cliff. He slid onto solid ground beside her. She'd already found the knapsacks and pulled the skates out. They sat down on the ground and took their shoes off. Eva wasn't wearing socks.

"Your father bought you a pair just in case," Bobby said. "They're in your skates."

Eva froze. "My father?"

Bobby nodded but continued lacing his skate. "The guy who saved us. The guy with the boomerangs. His name was Luo. He was your father."

Eva stared at Bobby. "I don't know what to say to something like that."

Bobby shrugged. "I hear you. We can talk about it later. The reason I mentioned it is I didn't want to take credit for what your father had done."

"You have a flashlight?"

Bobby glanced at Eva, concerned she was losing a grip on the urgency of the situation. "What?"

"A penlight. A flashlight. Do you have a flashlight?"

"We can't shine a light. You want them to see us? Put your socks on. We have to move."

"I will not put my socks on until you shine a light on my right foot. You can come up close and shield it with your other hand to keep it dim."

Bobby knew better than to argue with her. No one was more stubborn than Eva, except possibly for the man in the mirror. He slid closer to her. She stuck out her right foot. Bobby cupped his left hand around the circumference of the flashlight.

"Shine it at my toes," Eva said. "Just a quick flash so we don't make too much light."

Bobby turned the flashlight on, caught a glimpse of normal-looking toes, and turned the light off. "You've got a callus on the bottom of the big one but otherwise they're fine. Can we go now?"

Eva grabbed her toes and pulled them back. "Now shine it again."

Bobby flashed the light again.

Black insects nestled deep in the groove where the toes met her foot. As if that wasn't bizarre enough, the insects weren't moving. They were dead.

"That's disgusting," Bobby said. "What are they? Some sort of ticks?"

"Look closer."

Bobby put his face up against Eva's foot and shined the light one more time.

The black limbs weren't feet and antennae. They were lines. In fact, Bobby wasn't looking at a row of insects. He was staring at a drawing. The drawing consisted of tiny chemical symbols.

"The formula," Bobby said.

"Tattoo," Eva said. Her teeth shone in the dark. "Dr. Arkady said no one ever looks under the toes."

Eva slipped on her socks and put on her skates. Bobby finished lacing his own. They strapped on their head lights.

"We're going to change the world," Bobby said. "And we might get rich, too."

"As long as we stay together," Eva said.

Bobby looked into her eyes. "I don't think that's going to be a problem. Do you?"

"No. No problem at all."

They skated onto Lake Baikal side by side. A quarter moon hung over the ice. Stars glittered in the sky. Bobby glanced at Eva. She looked at him. Neither of them showed any emotion but they squeezed their hands at the same time. Bobby wondered how life could possibly get any better, but it soon would. They had each other. They had the formula.

He guided Eva left to backtrack along the route he'd taken with Luo. The buhanka was waiting for them. They'd figure out where they were going once they got there.

A spotlight shone directly in their path. Bobby pulled to a stop. Eva slid past him but hung onto his hand and came to a halt. The voices from the Swallow's Nest became animated.

A gunshot sounded. It came from the castle but could have been fired in any direction, Bobby thought. Then he heard the clunk in the ice around them.

Someone was shooting at them.

Lights to the left, castle to the right, the center of the lake was the only escape. Bobby turned toward the center of the lake and pulled Eva with him.

Light shone on the ice ahead. The spotlight had been moved.

Another gunshot.

Bobby and Eva ducked. Bobby changed direction a bit to avoid the spotlight but it moved accordingly.

Bursts of gunfire followed.

Then silence. Bobby thought he heard someone shout his name—

The ice trembled beneath his feet. At first he suspected his nerves were making him shake. But then a cracking noise sounded, like a thousand trees being split in half. The ice began to shake. Eva squeezed his hand harder. Bobby glanced at her, saw the terror in her eyes. The cracking noise rose to a thunderous crescendo. The ice buckled under Bobby's legs.

He fell.

A force pulled Eva's hand from his hand. Adrenaline shot through his body. *Don't let go. Don't let go. Whatever you do, don't let go of her hand—*

Eva's fingers slipped through his grasp.

"Eva," he shouted, hand stretched to the side, grasping at the cold air as he completed his fall.

Bobby landed hard on his hip. He glanced in Eva's direction.

She was gone. The ice where she'd been standing had vanished. It was impossible. She'd just been there three seconds ago, but now she was gone.

Bobby screamed her name. No one answered. Bobby remembered what Luo had told him during the drive. Baikal sat on the deepest continental fissure on Earth. They were almost as active as the ones in the seas of Japan. For that reason, the lake experienced earthquakes. Bobby wondered if the shooting had caused this one.

He crawled to the precipice of the ice. A six-foot-wide fissure had formed in the lake. Ice shimmered beyond the chasm. Bobby hung his head over the ice and looked into the hole. He screamed her name again. Still, no one answered. At first the hole looked black, but then an image formed under the glint of the moonlight.

At first it looked like a multi-spoke wheel, but then some of the lines disappeared. The image became clearer.

It was a Ferris wheel in black and white.

Bobby thought he was dreaming. He batted his eyes twice rapidly to clear his head and looked again. The Ferris wheel was still there. The image reminded Bobby of something else Luo had said. That fishermen swore they saw trains, castles, and ships at the bottom of the lake. Just as he was seeing an amusement park now.

Cars sat suspended in midair atop iron cross beams. A ladder appeared. It was attached to one of the beams. It looked exactly like the ladder he and Eva had used to climb to the top of the Ferris wheel in Pripyat. Roofing, they'd called it. They'd climbed together to the rooftops of the Cultural Center, the hotel, and the abandoned apartment buildings, too.

And as his eyes followed the ladder toward the highest car, Bobby saw her one last time, resting at the top, looking down at the wasteland where they used to scavenge.

The ice moved.

Bobby raised his head. The two big blocks of ice were sliding toward each other. The hole into which Eva had fallen was closing.

Bobby lay helpless. He looked down into the narrowing chasm and screamed Eva's name over and over.

The fissure disappeared. The lake became one again.

Eva was gone.

Only then was Bobby aware of voices, people shouting at him from the Swallow's Nest. He rose to his skates. His first three strides were uneasy. Part of him feared the earth would open up again and swallow him. The other part of him wished it would do just that. His instincts guided him away from the Swallow's Nest and the shore. Instead he headed toward the middle of the lake where four miles of ice awaited him.

He vaguely remembered the promise of biological experiments. They would hunt him. Even if Eva was dead they would hunt him forever just to assure themselves his blood didn't contain further clues about the formula. He would miss Nadia and his hockey career, but he could never go back to America. He could never return to civilization.

Exactly where he would go and what he would do he did not know and did not care. His sorrow had extinguished all his ambition, and in his moment of despair Bobby knew to do only one thing.

Skate.

CHAPTER 57

─────────────※─────────────

A s Bobby rose to his feet, Nadia screamed his name. When he didn't acknowledge her, she continued shouting it repeatedly.

Simmy's men overpowered Milanovich's bodyguards. Afterwards, one of them found a grapple secured to the bottom of the guardrail. Nadia and Simmy rushed up the stairs. They arrived on the deck of the Swallow's Nest to find Bobby and Eva skating away from shore. Then the ground began to shake beneath them.

Nadia held onto the guardrail with both hands and prayed the castle would not collapse. Her concern for her own safety proved fleeting. A thunderous cracking sound filled the air. The ice parted and Eva disappeared. Nadia stood helpless beside Simmy. She tried to imagine Bobby's anguish.

The ice moved. The chasm disappeared and the lake became one. As Bobby rose to his feet, the spotlight from the Swallow's Nest caught the blade of his skate. It cast a ray of light that shimmied up his clothes and face, and for a split second, Bobby appeared to glow in the dark.

And then, in a flash, he skated away into the darkness and he was gone.

"We have to do something," Nadia said.

Simmy put his arm around her. "What would you have us do? I'm sure there are some skates around here. Which one of us is going to find him, let alone catch up to him?"

A premonition gripped Nadia. She would not see Bobby again. Ever. She tried to banish the thought, but it wouldn't go away. He'd probably heard Milanovich's promise to conduct biological experiments. Bobby was no fool. He would assume he'd be hunted for the rest of his life, regardless of whether Eva was dead or alive. Bobby would rather disappear from civilization or die. Toss in his anguish from Eva's death, and he was probably ambivalent between the two alternatives at this point.

"He has the other man's mobile phone, does he not?" Simmy said.

"I think so," Nadia said.

"Then he will call."

"Yes. He will call."

She could hear the lie in her own voice. He wouldn't call. Not for a long time, if ever. Not until the Milanoviches of the world had forgotten about him. Not until the world had given up on a formula that mesmerized even the richest of men and left bodies in its wake. A formula that seemed so real and valuable to Nadia up until five minutes ago. Now, faced with the reality that she might never see Bobby again, she couldn't have cared less about it. For in the end life was about people, and the vanishing of a loved one rendered all material pursuits immediately irrelevant, faster than they'd become a compulsion in the first place.

Where would he go? What would he eat? Who would give him shelter? Nadia knew these questions would consume her, but for now she took comfort in what she knew with certainty. That Bobby was no ordinary boy. He was Adam Tesla, a boy from Ukraine, a country of survivors used to fighting adversity on a daily basis. He was smart, clever, and resilient.

No, he was not ordinary. He was extraordinary.

"Of course he will call," Simmy said, "That which does not grow dies. A man can only grow if he is part of a community. Part of civilization. Bobby does not want to die. Therefore, by definition, he will return to you. He will probably find cell phone service on the other side of the lake across from Listvyanka. I predict he will call you tomorrow."

"Yes," Nadia said. "Tomorrow. Of course. He will call me tomorrow."

And as she heard the deceit in her own voice again, Nadia was reminded of the most accomplished liar she had ever known. Victor Bodnar had let them go for some reason. She hadn't thought about the potential reasons until this very moment. None came to mind except the obvious one.

He believed Simmy and she were worth more alive than dead. Whether he considered them as individuals or as a couple was an entirely different question, and one Nadia still hadn't resolved in her own mind, though she was leaning toward the latter now.

More important to her was that Victor had let Adam go, too. He was out there on the ice, skating at warp speed toward a destination unknown. And as despair set in once again, it was her thought of Victor and Adam in the same breath that gave Nadia comfort. For Victor brought to mind another old thief, one she'd met in Chornobyl, and reminded her that wherever Bobby went, whatever his path in life, he would always be his father's son.

He would always be the fox.

EPILOGUE

One month later

T HE PLANE CRASHED IN THE REPUBLIC OF BURYATIA IN Eastern Siberia. It was an AN-2 plane, built for light transport and agricultural use. According to media reports, Evenki reindeer herders came to the rescue of the pilot and seven passengers on board. They pulled the passengers from the wreckage before the fire in the cabin spread to the fuel tank and the plane exploded. They provided water, food, and warm clothing until authorities were notified of the accident by satellite phone and airlifted the passengers to safety by helicopter.

In fact, the plane exploded before the Evenki men ever got close to it. They'd spotted the crash from the ridge of a mountain five hundred meters away. The descent by horseback required a circuitous route—the path straight down was too steep. While the horses galloped around the trail, a young man accompanying the herdsmen slid off his mare and ran straight down the mountain. The herdsmen circled to level ground just in time to see the young man race the final hundred meters to the plane. They would later argue among themselves about the young man's speed. All agreed he was the fastest human they had ever seen.

Some said he was faster than any horse they'd ever ridden, while others insisted that was exaggeration.

The young man pulled eight people from the wreckage. Some of the Evenki swore he carried them two at a time, one under each arm, though that too sounded like an overstatement to others. The plane exploded thirty seconds later.

Afterwards, the young man insisted on going back to the village before the authorities arrived. He said he didn't want any credit for his actions. He said he would not be alive if it were not for the Evenki who'd given him food and shelter when he wandered into the village a week ago. The Evenki were most grateful for his humility, especially when the passengers insisted on expressing their thanks with a monetary reward.

When the herdsmen returned to their village, they tried to learn more about this young man. His dark complexion suggested he was from Siberia, but he spoke elegant Russian as though he were from St. Petersburg. He had half-ears, the likes of which no one in the village had ever seen. It was as though he came from a cruel culture where fathers punished their male children by the saw, not the hide.

To add to their confusion, the young man had arrived without any belongings. The woman who cared for him upon his arrival said she searched through his pockets while he was sleeping. She found what looked like a foreign passport with his picture inside. She didn't recognize the language because the letters were in Roman. The herdsmen feared he might be a foreign spy, but his bravery during the plane crash won their admiration. And his athletic skills would make him a superior herdsman or hunter who could contribute mightily to the village's economy.

The young man called himself Luo. He asked if he could stay awhile. The village leaders said yes. The young man who called himself Luo expressed an interest in learning how to throw a boomerang. The latter was a Chukchi device, but one of the older

Evenki herdsmen had some experience with the weapon. Young Luo became his constant companion. He practiced with the boomerang daily.

The village elders gradually made inquiries in surrounding villages about their strange visitor. Their investigation led them to three and only three conclusions.

He came from nowhere.

No one had ever heard of him or seen him before.

No one knew who he was.

ACKNOWLEDGMENTS

I am grateful to the countless journalists and writers who published works about the Fukushima Daiichi nuclear disaster and Lake Baikal. Among them was William Sargent's "Fukushima: Nuclear Disaster on the Ring of Fire." The credit for the historical content of this novel goes to these writers, however, all mistakes are entirely my own.

Thanks also to the many people who continue to support my work, including Lou Paglia, Jon Brolin, Irka Kachorowsky, John Walton, Sumire Hasimoto, Roman Voronka, George Saj, Annie Buhay and the ladies of UWLA Branch 115, Bob Simeone, Kim and Jeff Palmer, and Mary Jane and James Cronin. Charlotte Herscher's editorial insight is exceeded only by her thoughtfulness. I'm indebted to the entire Thomas & Mercer team, especially Alison Dasho, for their enthusiastic, congenial, and inclusive publication process. My literary agent, Erica Silverman, remains fierce and fabulous. And my wife, Robin, was a source of light during the entire excruciating enterprise.

ABOUT THE AUTHOR

OREST STELMACH WAS BORN IN Connecticut to Ukrainian immigrants and didn't speak English when he was a child. He's earned a living washing dishes, stocking department store shelves, teaching English in Japan, and managing international investments. In addition to English, he speaks Japanese, Spanish, and Ukrainian.